"It was so beautiful, Bruce,"

Katie Lee said, breaking the silence between them. "These precious moments with you make me forget my sorrows . . . my pain. Thank you, darling. Thank you."

"It could be forever, you know," Bruce said, tracing her breast with a forefinger and smiling as he saw her quiver with pleasure. "It would take only two words."

Katie Lee looked away from him. "But one must be ready to say 'I do,' Bruce. And I'm not."

Bruce sighed heavily and ran his hand down the curve of her stomach to the juncture of her thighs. "Darling, tonight has proven to you what we could share every night if we were married," he said thickly. "I shall leave you with that reminder and not propose again. You will now have to be the one who speaks of marriage. Not I."

He placed a forefinger to Katie Lee's chin and turned her face around to him. "And you will, my darling," he said softly. "You will."

Dear Reader:

We appreciate the feedback you've been giving us on Harlequin Historicals. It's nice to hear that so many of you share our enthusiasm.

During the long winter months, everyone looks forward to spring; and coming in April and May we'll have a wonderful surprise for you. In an unprecedented publishing venture, acclaimed Western romance writer Dorothy Garlock, writing here as Dorothy Glenn, joins forces with popular Kristin James to produce companion historical romances. *The Gentleman* and *The Hell Raiser* tell the stories of two Montana brothers who were separated as children, raised in entirely different lifestyles and reunited as adults—only to clash bitterly and fall in love with each other's woman! Each book stands alone—together they're sensational. To celebrate the occasion, the heroes will be featured on the covers. Look for both books this spring from Harlequin Historicals.

As always, we look forward to your comments and suggestions. After all, these books are for you; so keep those letters coming. Meanwhile, enjoy!

The Editors
Harlequin Historicals
P.O. Box 7372
Grand Central Station
New York, NY 10017

Passion's Embrace

Cassie Edwards

Harlequin Books

TORONTO • NEW YORK • LONDON
AMSTERDAM • PARIS • SYDNEY • HAMBURG
STOCKHOLM • ATHENS • TOKYO • MILAN

Harlequin Historical first edition March 1990

ISBN 0-373-28642-2

Books by Cassie Edwards

Harlequin Historicals

Passion in the Wind #5
A Gentle Passion #17
Passion's Embrace #42

CASSIE EDWARDS

is the author of over twenty romances and has traveled the U.S. doing research for her books. When she's not on the road, Cassie spends seven days a week writing in her office in the Illinois home she shares with her husband, Charlie.

For Ava Janson,
a friend and an avid reader of romance

Chapter One

The state of Washington
May 1889

Light blue wood smoke rose sluggishly from the chimneys on the two story whitewashed plaster house surrounded by a high picket fence. The shutters and doors were painted a bright green, the roof was of split shakes. Land had been cleared from the dense green forest, and wild bluegrass now grew waist high on each side of a dirt road that led to the Holden Inn, an overnight stop for stagecoaches traveling from Portland, Oregon to Seattle, Washington.

The aromas of black-eyed peas, okra, mustard-baked ham and corn bread wafted through the open windows of the inn. Katie Lee Holden, stately, tall, her shiny hair worn long and free to her waist, stood at the dining-room window, watching the road. She was anxious for the stagecoach to arrive. Every day all sorts of people stayed overnight at her parents' inn. She never tired of their conversation as food was served to them at the large oak dining table.

At eighteen, Katie Lee wanted so much more than life at a stagecoach inn. On occasion she had been tempted to leave and head for Seattle, but she knew that her father would follow and bring her back. In the Holden family he was the law, and he never let Katie Lee or her mother forget it. He had even said that he would choose a husband for Katie Lee when a likely prospect showed up at the inn.

Thus far none had suited her father's taste, and Katie Lee did not think anyone ever would. Her father wanted her to himself. Besides his wife, she was all the family he had.

"Katie Lee, you haven't set the table yet," Madge Holden scolded as she lumbered into the dining room, carrying a platter of homemade bread and slabs of freshly churned butter. "You know the stagecoach will be arriving any minute now." She set the platter of bread and butter on the table and went to Katie Lee. Placing a pudgy hand gently on Katie Lee's arm, she urged her daughter to turn around and face her. "Honey, quit your daydreamin'. It don't get you nowhere. Your papa sees to that."

Katie Lee turned her wistful blue eyes to her mother and took in her flour-smudged apron and cotton dress, her fleshy rose-colored cheeks and the perspiration-dampened tendrils of gray hair that framed her face. "I know," she murmured. "Will he ever realize that I am no longer a child? That I cannot remain here forever helping you serve the stage-coach passengers? I have the right to live a life of my own. Why can't Papa see that?''

With callused fingers, Madge smoothed Katie Lee's golden hair, studying the vulnerable and innocent face, its bright and sensually shaped lips in a sullen pout. "Daughter, your father has his own ideas of what is best for you," she said, her voice soft and comforting. "Give him time. Be patient. One day he will see that you are no longer his little girl."

Madge's gaze swept once more over Katie Lee as she admired her daughter. Even in her plain and simple calico dress and clean white apron, there was no hiding how beautiful Katie Lee was. Her long eyelashes set off a stunning set of blue eyes in a delicate oval face. Tall, her sylphlike figure was very, very slender and graceful.

But it was her breasts that troubled Madge. They were developed far beyond what a mother would deem appropriate for a daughter's bust line. Men always watched Katie Lee with a lust in their hungry devilish eyes. Even now her breasts were straining beneath the confines of her dress.

Never knowing what to say, Madge swung away from Katie Lee and nodded toward the table. "Hon, this ain't the time for talk," she said. She cleared her throat nervously when she glanced at Katie Lee and saw the same downcast look that she always got when her daughter knew that she was being evaded. "Before long you'll hear the stagecoach comin' up the road, which means there will be several mouths to feed. It's my reputation to have things ready."

"Yes, I know, even if the stagecoach is delayed." Katie Lee sighed, going to the china cabinet to gather a stack of dishes in her arms. "Many a meal has been spoiled because you are so dependable. By the time people sit down, the vegetables are limp and the meat is like leather. It wouldn't hurt if you were late for once. I am sure no one would die of hunger. For once I wish you would see my problems as more important than a stagecoach full of strangers coming here to eat our food and sleep in our beds." She sighed again, placing the dishes on the table one by one. "Just once, Mama. Just once."

After the plates were set out, Katie Lee began placing the silverware, and her mother lumbered quietly from the room. Katie Lee looked around, seeing everything that was familiar to her—a plain room, but comfortable enough for the strangers who tracked over the bare oak floors.

The bedrooms upstairs were sparsely furnished, she knew, yet nice bedspreads, bedding and wash-stands made them presentable. The downstairs had a pleasant sitting room with many overstuffed chairs and a sofa placed in front of the fireplace, a dining room and a kitchen that smelled of mouth-watering stews, breads and pies.

Katie Lee looked pensively toward the window. When her mother wasn't cooking, she was tending her flower garden. Her father was a farmer as well as an innkeeper. He kept on hand a good many tools, some of which had been left with him by passing emigrants. When he wasn't working, he collected geology specimens as a hobby. And Katie Lee passed the time looking at birds—watching them, studying them, learning their calls.

"But I want more out of life than birds," she said, slamming linen napkins down beside the plates.

"Now, now, Katie Lee, what seems to be troubling *you*?"

Her father's voice, loud and authoritative, made Katie Lee tense. But when he came and placed his thick hands on her waist and turned her to face him, she forced a smile, for in spite of his unremitting possessiveness she did love him dearly.

"Oh, I guess it's only spring fever, Papa," Katie Lee said, knowing that she was lying. She hated herself for not being honest with him as she was with her mother, but she knew that in his strong arms she would find no sympathy—only love.

She gazed up into fading blue eyes, then took in his thick gray mustache and thinning hair. His face was lined, and beneath his blue plaid cotton shirt his shoulders were rounded. His coarse, dark trousers were hanging more limply around his waist than they used to, his suspenders having been taken up a notch or two to allow for his height, which seemed to be lessening.

Seeing him age hurt Katie Lee. Suddenly she felt guilty for wanting to leave. If she left, and something happened to her father or mother while she was gone, she would never be able to live with herself.

A strange melancholia gripped her. She lunged into her father's arms and laid her cheek against his massive chest. "I do love you, Papa," she murmured. "Truly I do."

Geoffrey Holden returned his daughter's hug for a moment. "Daughter, what *is* this all about?" he said, chuckling. "If I didn't know better, I'd think this was the last hug we'd ever share. You got plans I don't know about?"

Laughing softly, Katie Lee drew away from him. "No, nothing," she said, lifting the skirt of her dress as she spun around to place freshly filled salt and pepper shakers on the table. "As I said, Papa, it's only spring fever."

"I most certainly hope that's all it is," Geoffrey said, watching Katie Lee for a moment longer, then left the room, smiling to himself as he heard her begin to sing softly to herself. Things *were* all right. She was singing. And when she sang, didn't she sound like an angel?

"But I'll be damned if you'll marry just *any* drifter," he whispered, going to stand before the fireplace to fill his pipe with tobacco. "In time the right one will come along."

He lighted his pipe and sat slouched on the sofa, watching flames engulf a log on the grate. "What will I do then?" he whispered, frowning. "I don't want to lose you, *ever.*"

* * *

His magnificent strawberry roan trailed the dust-covered stagecoach, which rocked and swayed along a dirt road, its wheels occasionally dipping into a rut and jostling the passengers. On each side of the road the forest was deep and dark. Ahead lay a sun-splashed hillside bright with wildflowers.

Bruce Cabot sat within the crowded confines of the stagecoach, a handsome Ivy Leaguer fresh out of Yale. Today he had dressed the part of the business-man he hoped to become after arriving in Seattle. He sported a silk hat, a bobtail cutaway opened to dis-close a white waistcoat, trousers of a peachy hue creased carefully over toothpick-pointed patent leather shoes, and a baby-blue tie fastened with a scroll and key pin. He leaned his weight on the ma-lacca cane that he held in his hands, clad in a pair of immaculate doeskin gloves.

Bruce was muscled, tall and lean, with sandy-red hair cut just above the collar and combed to perfec-tion. He had golden-brown eyes, thick eyebrows, high cheekbones, a straight nose and wide, sensual lips.

Just visible beneath his coat was a revolver, thrust into a shoulder holster. A traveler never knew when thieves or Indians might decide to raid a stagecoach, he'd thought before leaving.

Weary from the long ride from Portland, Bruce attempted to stretch his long legs inside the crowded coach, but grimaced and drew back his foot quickly when the bulldog that sat on the floor opposite him emitted a low, threatening growl.

Bruce glared at Leonard Conty, the dog's owner. "Why in hell would you travel with that mangy mongrel?" he inquired in a refined, deep voice. "Riding in a stagecoach is uncomfortable enough without being forced to compete for space with a drooling, stinking bulldog!"

He wanted also to comment on Doc Porter, Leonard Conty's bodyguard, who sat at the other man's right, and on his brother, a burly man with a reputation for toughness, who was squeezed in next to Bruce. Bruce found these men even more unpleasant traveling companions than the bulldog, but he didn't voice his disgruntlement. He was quite outnumbered, and holstered pistols at the waists of Conty's two companions bespoke their intentions.

Again Bruce looked at Leonard Conty with distaste. He was the owner of two theaters, one in Seattle and one in Portland. In truth they were so-called box houses, saloons with a theater attached. Bruce had gone to the Conty Theater in Portland and had discovered that the curtained box seats in the low balconies were used for more than viewing the performers on the stage. Prostitutes made their living behind the garish red draperies.

In Bruce's opinion, Conty's box houses should be condemned as a public nuisance.

Bruce's gaze swept yet again over Leonard, seeing how his appearance revealed that he was a rich man.

A large man, he wore a brown derby, a gray rain cape and white gloves. He stood just under six feet, his heavy build giving him a stocky appearance. His face was round, his nose short and stubby, and his gray eyes squinted. Their expression was pitiless. Beneath his cape he wore a conservative gray suit with a gaudy tie, Bruce had noticed.

Leonard Conty's politeness thus far on the trip had not hidden the fact that he could be cold and furious when crossed. Bruce had read many newspaper accounts of this man....

Leonard's squinty eyes glinted with amusement as he looked at Bruce. "My dog very rarely leaves my side," he said smoothly. "And he knows when he's being insulted." His gloves shone immaculately white in the light from the stagecoach window as he began to stroke his dog's head. "Why, lad, he's perhaps more human than most people I've met." He cleared his throat pompously. "What did you say your name was?"

A half smile played on Bruce's lips. "I didn't," he replied, tapping his cane on the floor of the coach. "Rarely have I had a chance even to speak. I've had to sit and listen to your ramblings since we left Portland. You're a mite hung up on yourself, wouldn't you say?"

Leonard Conty chuckled low. He held his gloved hands before him and stretched his fingers leisurely. "Son, I'm a man of means and confidence," he bragged. "In my business I have reason to be. I'm quite successful. And you?'' His gaze traveled over Bruce, seeing his youth as a potential threat; Leonard had just passed his fiftieth birthday and felt time slipping by too quickly. ''What is your name, and why are you traveling to Seattle?''

''Though I feel none of that is any of your concern, I see no reason not to reply,'' Bruce said, eyeing the dog disgustedly as it resumed its panting and began drooling again. ''Bruce Cabot is the name, and I'm on my way to Seattle to join my brother, Alex. We are soon to be in partnership of Cabot Sawmill. Alex got the business established while I was attending Yale. I proudly join him now.''

''Cabot, did you say?'' Leonard asked, his gaze slowly moving over Bruce. ''I think I know both your father and brother. Your father owns Cabot Sawmill in Portland, doesn't he? And I know of your brother in Seattle. He's competing with the likes of Henry Yesler, the man from Ohio who built the first sawmill in Seattle.''

''Yes, Father began the business in Portland several years ago,'' Bruce said proudly. ''And as for Henry Yesler, it is rumored that he spends more of his time making money on real estate than lumber these days. There truly is no competition. Logging camps are roaring everywhere, and men are getting sixty to eighty dollars a month. An estimated ten thousand loggers are camped within a radius of fifty miles of Seattle. Why, there is a limitless quantity of timber crowding the mountains.''

"Yes, much is being said about the world of green groves where ambitious schemes flourish in construction, real estate and salesmanship," Leonard replied, folding his hands on his lap. "Washington has become a state where the strength of people equals the riches of its natural resources."

"The states of Washington and Oregon have the richest forests in the world," Bruce said, looking out the window, admiring the towering ponderosa pines. The thought of Seattle was exciting. The city was prosperous and booming. It was the pulsing heart of the timber empire of the Pacific Northwest. Foreign sails crowded her harbor. Great ships moored at the docks to load the logs that had been hauled to tidewater. His father had already made his fortune from lumber, and had generously shared it with his two sons.

It was now Bruce and Alex's turn to prove that they could become even more successful.

"The white pine have all their bark cut off them in Wisconsin and surrounding states," Bruce continued, entranced with his dreams. "They've wasted their substance back there, as the saying goes. Now they have to come to Seattle, and we will have the lumber to give them."

"And there's China with her teeming millions," Leonard teased. "And then there are the Japanese, livin' in paper houses."

Bruce looked quickly at Leonard, hearing the sarcasm in his voice. There was no trade from China, nor from Japan. But that would come! Surely in the future that would come!

"Yes, there are China and Japan," Bruce said firmly, watching Leonard's reaction. "The boundaries for sales of lumber from Cabot Sawmill will be endless."

Smiling to himself, Bruce leaned closer to the window, and while the clip-clop of the horses' hooves and the rattle of the wheels filled one small coach, he let his mind drift to what lay ahead.

Seattle! Amid a somber forest of firs a city had arisen as if by a stroke of a sorcerer's wand. The first settlers had carved the streets and squares from the primeval forest that lined the glassy waters of Puget Sound. Now it was a city prepared to handle the commerce of the world. A town constructed of wood, a town that clung to the sides of the steep hills, it was already a lumber center.

Bruce Cabot was anxious to be a part of it all. In Seattle he would be living his dream of running a sawmill with Alex.

"In two more days I'll be there," he whispered to himself, his eyes shining. "Two more days..."

Katie Lee measured freshly ground coffee into the pot and set it upon the stove, then her heart nervously skipped a beat when she heard the sound of approaching horses. Her eyes shining, she jerked off her apron and flew to the window. Looking toward the road, she was now able to see the stagecoach, though the sun had set and dusk was quickly falling. She silently prayed that some of the passengers would be women, so that she could discuss the latest fashions with them.

Drawing aside the sheer white curtain, Katie Lee watched the team of horses pulling the swaying stagecoach behind them pass through the opened gate. Her gaze fell on the lone, beautiful strawberry roan.

"The stage has arrived," her mother announced from behind her. "Let's get the food on the table. Remember, we don't want no complaints. We are here to please."

Katie Lee turned pleading eyes to her mother. "Mama, *please*?" she said softly. "I want to see who the passengers are. I am always anxious to make acquaintance with the ladies. It is so nice to have them to talk with. Let me go out for at least a moment, then I can return very quickly and help you place the food on the table. Anyhow, the guests have to wash up before eating. We have time."

Madge's gaze wavered, then she nodded. "Just for a moment," she said, understanding a daughter who had nothing but chores. "Just for a moment. Do you hear, Katie Lee?"

Katie Lee ran to her mother and embraced her. "Thank you," she murmured, then turned away and went through the dining and sitting rooms to the front porch.

The cool evening breeze whipped her hair from her shoulders and her skirt around her legs as she stood square-shouldered, anxiously watching the stage-coach door that was closest to her. Disappointment quickly assailed her when a burly man armed with heavy, thick pistols moved from the carriage, and then a squat bulldog, its tongue hanging from the corner of its mouth as it panted and drooled. Next a fancy gentleman with a gray rain cape stepped from the coach and gave her a flirtatious grin, which she ignored.

Hope of lady passengers being on this stagecoach dwindled as she craned her neck and saw that only two other gentlemen still remained.

Sighing deeply, Katie Lee began to turn to go back inside the inn, but stopped and stared openly as the most handsome man she had ever seen stepped from the carriage. He was immaculately dressed, and his clothes did not hide the fact that he was well muscled. He was tall and lean with golden-brown eyes that were crowned by thick eyebrows. For a man, his full lips were unusually sensual. As did most rich gentlemen today, he had on a silk top hat.

His eyes locked and held hers, Katie Lee melted inside, and her heart beat an erratic tattoo.

She stood stricken. Love at first sight was something one heard about, but was it possible that it could happen to her? And this stranger seemed as dumbstruck as she. He hadn't moved since he had touched the ground outside the coach. Only his eyes moved slowly up and down her figure, sparking her nerves and heating her skin.

"Katie Lee!"

Katie Lee jumped as if she'd been shot when she heard her mother calling for her. She smiled awkwardly at the new guest, then spun around and hurriedly started to walk away. But she stopped short when a refined masculine voice spoke from behind her.

"Miss? Where might I wash up?" Bruce asked, his heart beating wildly within his chest, not wanting to let the lady out of his sight until he knew who she was. He had seen her reaction, but surely she couldn't have been as captivated by him as he had been with her.

As Katie Lee turned to face him, Bruce's loins flamed with desire, something which was quite new to him. Until now he had made the acquaintance of a number of young ladies, but most encounters had been brief. And most had not captured his heart as this lady had. She looked so innocent . . . so vulnerable, and she had such a lonesome sadness in the depths of her blue eyes.

Had he ever seen such a pure, perfect profile, such delicate chiseling? Though tall and sylphlike, she had an exquisite bust that heaved with excitement. Most surely it was caused by his presence, for no one else was in sight except for the stagecoach driver, who was beginning to tend to the horses. Everyone else had ventured inside the inn.

"Sir?" Katie Lee inquired, her voice soft and lilting. "Did you address me, sir?"

Bruce drew himself from his reverie and walked toward her. He laughed softly. "Please don't call me sir," he said, removing his hat from his head in a gesture of politeness to reveal sandy-red waves blowing gently in the breeze. "My name is Bruce. Bruce Cabot. And what, may I ask, is yours?"

Katie Lee fluttered her eyelashes nervously as Bruce came to a stop directly before her. He was much taller than she, and she was forced to look up at him. "Katie Lee. Katie Lee Holden," she said, smiling sweetly.

Bruce looked toward the inn, then down into Katie Lee's eyes. "Are you a guest here, or are you acquainted with the proprietor?" he asked, already knowing the answer. He had heard someone shouting Katie Lee's name in commanding tones.

"I'm—I'm the proprietor's daughter, sir," Katie Lee stammered, then laughed softly. "I mean, Bruce. My father owns this inn. It is managed by both my mother and father. I help as much as possible."

Casting a nervous glance toward the house, she started to inch away from Bruce. "I really must go," she murmured. "My mother needs me."

Bruce glanced toward the pump that sat close to the back door of the inn. "Is that where I can wash up, Katie Lee?" he asked, giving her another warm smile.

Katie Lee's pulse raced, and feelings of sweet rapture spread through her. His voice was a caress as he spoke her name.

Knowing that her mother would scold her later, Katie Lee nonetheless lifted the skirt of her dress and began walking toward the pump. "This way," she urged. "I shall show you and then I must return to the kitchen."

A porcelain basin and a bar of soap lay on a tree stump close to the pump, along with a folded, clean towel. Katie Lee stood back and watched as the wooden pump creaked; water started to gush from it as Bruce worked the handle. Grabbing the basin, she held it beneath the water and let it fill up, then placed it upon the stump.

"Now isn't this a pretty sight?"

Bruce stiffened at the sound of Leonard Conty's voice, knowing how Leonard would size up this pretty, innocent woman. He was most surely in search of someone to show off in his theaters.

Leonard Conty shouldered his way past Bruce and stood over Katie Lee, appraising her with his squinty gaze. "Do I get the same personal attention that you are giving this lad?" he teased. "If I hadn't come here when I did, would you have gone so far as to wash the man's hands for him? Will you wash mine?"

Katie Lee's face flamed. She gave Bruce a quick glance, then gathered her skirt into her arms and rushed away, her head bowed. She wanted to die of embarrassment. Had it been so obvious that she had so quickly become enamored of Bruce Cabot? She would have to be careful around her parents, especially her father. He would not understand the needs that were building within her.

Rushing inside the inn and into the dining room, Katie Lee evaded her mother's watchful eye.

Outside Bruce took a bold step toward Leonard, a fist doubled at his side. "I want you to listen to me real good, Conty," he growled. "You leave this innocent thing alone. Don't get any ideas about her entertaining men in your box houses. There are many other women who suit the role. But not this one, Conty. Not this one."

Leonard laughed sardonically, then bent over and began to splash water onto his perspiring face.

Chapter Two

Candles flickered on the long oak dining table. Katie Lee hurriedly removed the soiled dishes as her mother brought in an apple pie from the kitchen, began cutting slices and arranging them on small saucers.

The table cleared, Katie Lee made a turn around the table with a coffeepot, refilling the empty cups. Even though her father was sitting at the head of the table, watching the men's every move, Katie Lee was quite aware that two sets of eyes were fixed on her. She blushed as she looked from Bruce Cabot to Leonard Conty and saw again how admiringly they looked at her. They were making no effort whatsoever to hide their feelings.

Katie Lee looked quickly away from the men. Of the two, Bruce was the one who fascinated her. She was in awe of him and his powerful effect on her. As for Leonard Conty, she had concluded that his interest in her must be the same as that he would show for most women. Surely he was a womanizer. She found it easy to ignore his eyes.

But not Bruce's.

As his gaze continued to follow Katie Lee, she felt a dizzy spinning inside her head, so was quite relieved when she finally had the opportunity to leave the dining room and escape into the privacy of the kitchen.

Replacing the coffeepot on the stove, Katie Lee went to the kitchen table and leaned heavily against it, bowing her head and closing her eyes, trying to still her heart's crazy thumping.

It was impossible for her to ignore Bruce Cabot's attraction to her. What they had discovered between them had to be special.

But by tomorrow morning Bruce Cabot would be gone from Katie Lee's life, just as quickly as he had come into it. It was not wise to let herself get caught up in thinking about him.

Jerking herself upright, Katie Lee looked desperately around the kitchen and saw the huge piles of dirty pots, pans and dishes on stove and table. "If I get busy I can forget such foolishness," she whispered, desperate to forget about Bruce. It was obvious that he would not be her father's chosen mate for her; in her father's eyes there had been nothing but a controlled contempt for the way Bruce had so openly watched her.

"I must get busy," she whispered. "I must."

Taking a heated teakettle from the stove, Katie Lee poured water into a porcelain basin. Groaning, she lifted a large wooden bucket and added enough cold water to the hot so that she could stand to immerse her hands in it. She blew a loose strand of hair back from her eyes and began washing dishes with a bar of soap and a dishrag. To force her mind from Bruce, she started to sing, her voice soft and lilting as the melody drifted out of the kitchen and into the dining room.

"Mr. Cabot, what may I ask is the reason for your journey to Seattle?" Geoffrey Holden looked over at Bruce as he sliced his fork into his piece of pie. "I don't believe I've ever had the pleasure of seeing you at my inn before."

Bruce returned the look, trying to concentrate on what the older man had said, but most of his attention was on the sound of the sweet, soft voice coming from the kitchen. Though he had been quickly taken by Katie Lee's loveliness and sweet innocence, her singing was touching his heart as nothing ever had before.

Never had a woman affected him in such a way. Perhaps none ever would again. He resolved to meet her privately.

He'd planned to travel to Seattle to sign all of the legal papers with his brother that would make them co-owners of Cabot Sawmill. Then he could come back to speak with Katie Lee's father. Out here in the wilderness there was no time for true courting.

Nervously clearing his throat, Bruce ran a long, lean finger between his collar and the column of his throat. "Sir? Were you addressing me?" he asked, his voice drawn. "I believe my mind was...elsewhere."

Geoffrey slipped a bite of pie between his lips and glowered. His eyes narrowed as he looked from Bruce to Leonard Conty. "I didn't expect you to hear my question all that clearly," he growled, angrily chewing the pie, the knuckles of his right hand white as he clutched his fork. "Neither of you have paid any attention to anything tonight but my daughter. Now I ain't sayin' I ain't used to that sort of behavior from men toward my daughter, because she is something special. But I am saying that you two sons of bitches had better keep your distance from her. Now do I make myself clear?"

Ignoring Katie Lee's father, Leonard Conty looked in the direction of the singing. His mind was on something far more important than a beautiful woman or a pretty voice. Money! His loins grew hot at the thought of the money Katie Lee Holden could make for him. He had been wanting a class act for his theater in Seattle. He had told Bruce Cabot earlier that he had the carriage trade at his theaters now, but in truth, rarely did anyone who traveled by fancy carriage ever venture into Conty's Theater. Most knew the box house for what it was and stayed as far away as possible. It was common knowledge that women, drink and faro were the most interesting features of his theaters.

But with the likes of Katie Lee Holden on the stage, everyone would come to his theater. Everyone!

Geoffrey wiped his lips with his linen napkin, pushed back his chair and rose, glaring from one man to the other. He looked at Bruce again, knowing for damn sure what was on that young man's mind. His eyes narrowed as he stopped momentarily to assess the worth of Leonard Conty, who was watching the door that led into the kitchen.

Then he moved his gaze to Leonard's brother and the bodyguard. The light of the candles glinted off the handles of the two men's pistols, thrust into holsters at their waists. The stagecoach wouldn't come early enough in the morning to satisfy Geoffrey Holden.

Slamming down the napkin onto the table, Geoffrey put his full weight against the palms of his hands as he leaned down to look more directly into the eyes of the men, most of whom were finishing off their pie. "Now listen good to what I have to say," he said in a low, threatening growl. "Most of the time there are ladies aboard the stagecoach to even things up a mite around here. But tonight it ain't that way. It's just my wife and daughter against the four of you. Let's make sure no one gets out of line. Do you hear? It ain't as though I can stand around and watch over my daughter all night. I've my chores to see to. While I'm gone, I would suggest you all go to your rooms and forget any notion you might have of making further acquaintance with my Katie Lee."

Geoffrey slowly stretched himself to his full height. He picked up a toothpick from a crystal goblet in the center of the table and thrust it into the corner of his mouth. He smiled sardonically from one man to the next, not letting the pistols intimidate him.

"I believe I've made myself clear enough, haven't I?" he drawled. "A daughter is a man's pride and joy. He don't take kindly to any tampering."

He chuckled, spun around on his heel and sauntered from the room.

Leonard Conty blinked and looked at Bruce. "What was he rambling about?" he asked, idly scratching his brow. "I only caught the last of it. Something about tampering."

Bruce set his jaw firmly as he glowered at Leonard. "He said to get your mind out of the gutter," he snapped angrily. "Or something to that effect." He glanced toward the kitchen. Katie Lee's singing was still tugging at his heartstrings. "And, by damn, Conty, you had better pay heed to the warning. Stay away from her."

"I don't know where you get off, thinking you can tell me what I can and cannot do," Leonard said, rising so quickly from his chair that it fell with a bang onto the floor. He reached down and righted the chair, giving Bruce a steady stare, his eyes gray and pitiless. "You just watch me. No college kid is going to tell me what to do. I've got plans for the little lady in there singing the pretty tunes. Big plans. And I wouldn't get in the way if I were you."

He patted his bulldog, who had been sleeping at his feet, arousing him enough to make him stretch his legs and begin panting all over again. Leonard saw a scrap of meat that had not been brushed from the tablecloth and set it down before the dog's nose, smiling as his pet thrust out his long, wet tongue and devoured the morsel in one swallow.

Giving Bruce a slow smile, Leonard headed determinedly toward the kitchen. Cold panic seized Bruce. He scrambled to his feet. Ignoring Leonard's bodyguard and brother, who were watching all of this with quiet amusement in their eyes, he hurried after Leonard.

"You son of a bitch, you don't care for anything but your wallet, do you?" Bruce said, his voice a low growl as he hurried to position himself in front of Leonard, blocking his way. "I know what your plans are before you even spell them out. It's not so much the lady that you are interested in but the money she'll bring in. Conty, your reputation precedes you."

Leonard's smile faded. His face grew beet red with anger, and he placed a stocky hand firmly on Bruce's shoulder. "Lad, you don't know half that you should about me," he said dryly. "If I were you, I wouldn't tamper with the unknown."

With a firm brush, Bruce removed Leonard's hand. "Conty, your threats aren't worth a grain of salt when used against me," he said, chuckling. He glanced over his shoulder at the two armed men, then glared at Leonard. "Though I am fresh out of college, don't be misled into thinking that I don't know how to handle a gun." He smoothed his coat aside, revealing the pistol thrust into his shoulder holster. "My father taught me all sorts of skills needed to protect myself when I was barely old enough to take even my first steps." He buttoned his coat and wove his fingers through his thick, wavy hair. "Seems things haven't changed all that much, have they? With the likes of you running loose..."

Katie Lee had heard Bruce and Conty's angry voices. While her mother had stepped out the back door to empty the dishwater, Katie Lee had the opportunity to leave the kitchen for a moment. Wiping her hands on her apron, she went to see what was causing the commotion.

Running bodily into Leonard Conty, whose back was to the kitchen door, Katie Lee faltered and felt the color rush to her cheeks. She steadied herself and stepped around Leonard, wishing now that she had not come to investigate. She was caught midway between two men whose eyes were lit with fire as they stared at each other.

Katie Lee looked slowly up at Bruce. In truth, he had been her reason for leaving the kitchen.

Bruce was stunned, rendered speechless by Katie Lee's appearance. She was the epitome of innocence as she gazed up at him and then at Leonard. Damn. She had most surely heard them arguing.

Or had she?

No. He thought not. She was too shy to want to join in a conversation that concerned her virtue.

"Gentlemen, please excuse me," Katie Lee said softly, still feeling trapped by the curiosity that had drawn her from her duties. She started to inch backward toward the door, smiling sheepishly from one man to the other. "I did not mean to interfere." She tried to laugh. "Do please pardon me."

Her pulse racing, Katie Lee ducked her head, turned quickly and rushed back into the kitchen. She went to the table and leaned against it, shaking her head, wishing that she had thought twice before coming face-to-face with Bruce Cabot again. All the man had to do was look at her, and she felt foolish, awkward. Surely he thought her no less than daft!

Bruce and Leonard stared blankly for a moment, then both stepped forward at once and found themselves trying to pass through the kitchen door at the same time. They almost became lodged together in the small space.

Frustrated, Bruce jerked himself free. Knowing that short of shooting him, he had no true way to stop Leonard from doing what he had in mind, he stepped aside, bowed mockingly at Leonard and let him pass.

Leonard returned the bow and moved on into the kitchen, stopping close behind Katie Lee, smiling at her as she slowly turned to face him. Again she felt trapped—the table at her back, Leonard Conty in front, bearing down on her.

"Yes?" she murmured, aware of Bruce standing behind Leonard. Out of the corner of her eye she saw her mother come back into the kitchen through the rear door. She wondered where her father was.

"Ma'am, may I have a moment of your time?" Leonard asked, nervously fidgeting with the cuff of his left sleeve.

"I don't know why on earth for," Katie Lee said weakly, tilting her chin stubbornly as she looked up at him.

"Miss Holden, I heard you singing a while ago," Leonard said, now clasping his hands tightly together behind him. He was recalling her father's threats. But surely a woman her age made decisions of her own. If he made the offer colorful enough, she most surely would leave this drab setting. "Your voice has a most entertaining quality. Did anyone ever tell you that before?"

Katie Lee's hand went to her throat, and she emitted a soft gasp. Again a blush flooded her face. "Good Lord, no," she said in hardly more than a whisper. "I only sing when I am happy...or—"

"When you are troubled?"

Katie Lee heard the tightness in Bruce's voice as he interrupted her. She stiffened when he stepped up to Leonard Conty's side and frowned down at her. "You sing when you are troubled, also, don't you?" he said dryly. "I apologize if this man and I are the cause of making you feel uneasy, ma'am. I am sure Mr. Conty wishes to apologize to you also."

Leonard ignored Bruce. He reached for and took one of her hands in his, smoothing his thumb over the back of it. "I would like to make you an offer that I hope you can't refuse," he said thickly. "Miss Holden, it would please me greatly if you would come to Seattle soon and become a part of my theater group. I have never heard such a beautiful voice before in my life. Everyone in Seattle would come to hear you, once the news spread of your nightly performance." He squeezed her hand affectionately. "I would pay you well, my dear. *Very* well."

Katie Lee was stupefied by the offer. Her face grew ashen in color and her throat went dry. Did this man truly consider her talented? Was he actually willing to pay her for singing? Only famous people got paid to sing on the stage.

"Unhand my daughter this minute or, by damn, expect to head out for Seattle tonight by foot!" Geoffrey Holden thundered.

Katie Lee looked over Conty's shoulder, squarely into the eyes of her father. Never had she seen him so angry! And he was carrying a loaded shotgun to prove his point.

She wished that the floor would open and swallow her up.

"I only pretended to go outside to do my chores," Geoffrey said, his face twisting into a knowing smile. "I suspected that once my back was turned, one of you men would go sniffing after the skirts of my daughter. No, as a matter of fact, I expected both of you to pester her." He chuckled. "Seems I was right."

He aimed the shotgun at Leonard, who seemed to be the most annoying. "As I said, unhand my daughter," he grumbled, his eyes dancing when Leonard dropped Katie Lee's hand as though it were a hot coal. "Get along with you both. I don't need neither of you gettin' crazy notions about my daughter. It just ain't in the cards for either of you to have her."

Katie Lee had taken just about all that she could of her father's humiliation. She dashed past him, tears burning her eyes.

Suddenly she stopped, deciding to defy her father for the first time. "Papa!" she cried. "How could you do this to me? I am no longer a child. Don't you think I am capable of making my own decisions?"

Seeing the stunned expression on her father's face, Katie Lee quickly regretted having spoken so openly to him in front of strangers. Even though he had deserved the tongue-lashing, she wished now that her own reaction had been less humiliating. A parent deserved respect.

"Oh, damn!" she whispered beneath her breath, then rushed from the room, only too conscious that she was leaving a strained, awkward silence behind her.

Chapter Three

The moon was high and bright. With the wick of her lamp turned low so that she could not be seen at her upstairs bedroom window, Katie Lee looked toward the dark edge of the forest. Only moments ago she had seen Bruce wander in that direction and walk inside the barn.

Her breath caught in her throat as she watched him reappear with the strawberry roan. She stepped closer to the window, peering through the darkness, observing Bruce as he led the horse close to the corral fence, then stopped and began to brush its mane.

"Why, that lovely thing must be his horse," she whispered to herself.

As Katie Lee continued to observe him, noticing how attentive he was to the animal, she could not help but become enamored of the man anew. He was a tall, fine-boned figure of a man, with narrow hips and muscular thighs. His features were strong and masculine, his golden-brown eyes haunting.

Katie Lee's attraction to him had been immediate, but it would take forever to forget him!

Freshly bathed, she was dressed in a full-skirted cotton dress that was gathered at the waist and had a bodice cut much lower than she wore while serving the travelers at the dining table. She had drawn her hair back from her face and secured it with combs. But the change of clothes failed to cheer her. Disheartened, Katie Lee swung away from the window.

"I must force myself not to think about him," she said, plopping onto her bed.

Squeezing her eyes tightly shut, she managed to turn her thoughts to Leonard Conty—she would never forget his offer to sing at his theater. What a thrill it surely must be to hear applause and to know that it was directed at yourself!

Despite the excitement, Katie Lee's thoughts drifted back to Bruce. Surely the greatest thrill of her life would be his kiss. Though eighteen and a woman in every way, Katie Lee had never been kissed by a man. Her father had guarded her with his life. Even tonight he had made his point quite clear to the other men present that she was not to be touched.

Checking the clock on her nightstand, Katie Lee saw that the time was nearing ten o'clock; she smiled devilishly. Her father was an early riser, which meant that he also went to bed early. By now he would be fast asleep, so she was free to move about as she wished.

And wasn't Bruce Cabot just as restless as she? He should be weary from the journey and fast asleep, yet he was idling the time away with his horse. And hadn't she caught him glancing toward her window more than once?

Without wasting another minute, Katie Lee bounced from the bed. She grabbed a shawl and wrapped it around her shoulders, then tiptoed from her room past all of the closed bedroom doors along both sides of the corridor. She crept down the oak stairs and waited to break into a run until she was safely outside.

Breathless, Katie Lee stepped into the shadows of the inn and pressed herself against its wall. The darkness enveloped her as though it were a second skin. She took several deep breaths as her eyes adjusted to the darkness. Then the world melted away as she got a good look at Bruce's face. He turned himself so that the moon silvered his handsome features with its light. His jaw was relaxed, his expression calm.

She lowered her gaze. She was close enough to see his long, lean fingers as he continued to brush the beautiful mane of his horse.

A strange longing seized Katie Lee's heart; she wanted to be the one who was the recipient of his gentle touch and adoring eyes. She felt quite wicked at having come out into the night to become better acquainted with a stranger, and even more wicked when her thoughts turned to forbidden fantasies.

Surely it was because her father had kept her too much to himself. . . .

Bracing herself, Katie Lee stepped boldly into view and began walking toward Bruce. Her knees grew weak when, startled at her sudden presence, he quickly looked her way, dropping the brush.

"Ma'am?" Bruce said, stepping away from his horse. His heart began to race. How vulnerable and sweet she was beneath the soft rays of the moon.

His gaze swept over her. Her golden hair spilled seductively over her shoulders, her features were flawless, and no shawl draped loosely from arm to arm could hide her feminine curves.

Looking at Katie Lee was dangerous; everything within Bruce wanted her to be in his arms. He already knew that her lips would taste like honey and that her breasts would be as soft as the petals of a rose.

The closer she drew to him, the better he saw the whiteness of her breasts that lay partially exposed above the low-cut bodice of her dress. A sweet perfumed fragrance wafted through the air, and he guessed that it was not only her hair that smelled so wonderful, but also her lily-white skin.

"Good evening," Katie Lee murmured, blushing beneath Bruce's scrutiny.

Bruce nervously clasped his hands behind him, stopping as Katie Lee moved to stand only a breath away. "You couldn't sleep?" he asked, his mouth suddenly dry. "Or do you always wander around at this time of night?'' He lowered his eyes. ''Or is this the only time you can get away from your father?''

Katie Lee was not accustomed to talking freely with any man, especially not during these ungodly hours of the night. And she most certainly had never discussed her father with anyone except her mother. Somehow that seemed disrespectful.

She avoided responding, and instead walked on past him, feeling a need to get out of the range of his eyes. Having always loved horses, she went to the strawberry roan and began stroking its magnificent mane.

''I had wondered whose horse was traveling along with the stagecoach,'' she said softly. ''It is yours, isn't it?''

Bruce moved to her side, where he stooped, picked up the brush and began brushing his horse again. ''Yes, he's mine,'' he said. ''A gift of sorts from my father.''

Katie Lee gave Bruce a glance. ''Oh?'' she said, tilting her head to one side.

Bruce chuckled. He laid the brush aside and let the horse nuzzle the palm of his hand. ''A gift for sticking to my studies and graduating from Yale,'' he said, squaring his shoulders proudly. ''It took a lot of willpower at times. I knew that my brother was having all of the fun, since he chose to go a different way in life. He didn't want anything to do with studying. He is a man of the outdoors.''

"Your brother? Is he in Seattle? Is that why you are traveling there?" Katie Lee asked, amazed to find it so easy to talk with this man . . . this stranger.

"Yes, Alex is in Seattle," Bruce said, clamping his fingers around the corral's fence as he looked into the darkness of the forest. "We will soon be in joint ownership of Cabot Sawmill. That is, as soon as I get there and sign the necessary legal papers. Alex went ahead of me and saw to all of the details. I haven't seen the sawmill yet, but I know that it is grand. Anything my brother decides to do, he does right."

Katie Lee moved to Bruce's side. Drawing the shawl more snugly around her shoulders, she sighed. "You must be so excited," she said, a longing in her voice. "How grand it would be to be able to do something with one's life. I . . ."

She stopped short, realizing that she had almost revealed too much of herself to Bruce. Yes, she was lonely, but she need not bore him with the details.

"You were saying?" Bruce urged, having heard her voice trail off. He had also heard the loneliness in her voice. He could see it in her eyes as she peered off into the distance. Damn her father. He was stifling her in every way.

"I was speaking out of turn," Katie Lee said in barely a whisper, her hair fluttering in the cool breeze. She dared not look at him, for she knew that he would be able to read of her deepest desires in her eyes, and she understood the dangers in that. Though she had never been with a man before, she knew that these feelings that were plaguing her had to be the sort that troubled a woman when she felt passion for a man.

Without thinking of the consequences, Bruce turned suddenly to Katie Lee and took her hands, easing her around so that they could look into one another's eyes. The feel of her soft, tiny hands within his own was sheer magic. The way she looked up at him, as though she idolized him, made his pulse quicken. He saw no fear in her eyes. He saw so much, much more than he had wished for. She had dared everything to come out here this evening, and he knew why. It was to experience these shared moments.

"Katie Lee, I did not mean to pry," Bruce said thickly. "I am just glad that you have come. From that moment we first met, I have wanted to be alone with you. I have wanted to know you better."

"I have never spoken with a man so openly before," Katie Lee said, her eyes wide as she looked up at him. "Perhaps I shouldn't have. Should my father find out, we would both be in trouble."

She tried to remove her hands from Bruce's grip. "I truly had better return to my room," she said, fearing the torrents of feelings that were washing through her. The longer she remained with Bruce, the stronger they grew. It was as though she had no control over her emotions. What if he kissed her? How would she react to that?

And, Lord, he was lowering his lips closer... closer....

"Please, I really must return to my room," she said, desperation rising inside her. His nearness... his touch... the desire inside her was frightening.

She struggled to get her wrists free, but was rendered helpless within his strong grip. As he pressed his hard body against hers, dizziness overwhelmed her, frightening her even more.

"It is not appropriate that I am here," she whispered, inhaling the intoxicating male scent of him. He was now so close that she could feel his breath on her lips. "I shouldn't have come. I don't know what I was thinking of."

"Don't be afraid," Bruce said, brushing his mouth against her lips. "There is nothing wrong with having feelings for a man. That is why you defied your father by coming out here tonight, isn't it? Let me kiss you. Kiss me...."

Bruce suddenly released her wrists, but Katie Lee was not aware of it. All that she was conscious of was the press of his body against hers as he wrapped his arms around her waist and claimed her lips in a passionate kiss. A strange curling heat invaded the juncture of her thighs, and her knees felt weak.

Unable to push him away, she placed her arms around his neck and returned his kiss with abandon. It seemed so natural, so right to be with him, to kiss him.

Such an incredible sweetness soared through her.

At the feel of her body against his, the sensation of her breasts crushed against his chest, Bruce became lost in her. Though she was not the first woman he had desired, for him she could be the last. He ached with wanting. His hands itched to touch her breasts, to claim them as his own. He hungered to teach her all of the secrets of life that until now had surely been kept from her.

The nervous neigh of a horse and the ensuing snap of a twig from somewhere close by drew Bruce and Katie Lee apart. Katie Lee felt giddy from the kiss, yet fear gripped her heart as she quickly looked around.

Bruce's spine stiffened; he realized how foolish it had been to come out here into the dark without his pistol. Anyone could be lurking in the shadows. Even Indians...

Spinning on his heel, his eyes narrowed as he looked cautiously around him, then a laugh erupted from deep inside him when he saw the shine of an animal's eyes only a few yards away. Then an opossum, several tiny babies clinging to its backside, scampered away beneath the bright light of the moon.

"My word, but that animal gave me such a fright," Katie Lee exclaimed softly, exhaling a nervous sigh of relief. "I thought that it might be..."

Bruce turned to her and took her hands. "Your father?" he asked thickly. "Katie Lee, you shouldn't be so afraid of him. You are old enough to do as you wish . . . Have there truly been no other men? . . ."

Katie Lee's face turned hot with a blush, and she lowered her eyes. "No, no other men," she confessed, feeling like a wallflower for having to admit such truths to this man, who surely had been with many women. Anyone as handsome and as worldly, a college graduate at that, must have been given all opportunities to choose between women. Katie Lee could not help but wonder how she compared with the others. Did he really see her as a country bumpkin? Yet he had no cause to think otherwise.

"Until this moment there has been no special lady in my life," Bruce said, squeezing her hands affectionately, drawing her closer. "Tell me that you feel something special for me. Katie Lee, tomorrow I must leave for Seattle. We have only tonight. Let's not keep our feelings from one another. Never have I felt this way. Never!"

Bruce's talking so openly of his feelings for her frightened Katie Lee anew, and she was sorely reminded of the impossibilities of this situation. It was apparent that her father did not approve of Bruce, though there was no apparent reason why. Nevertheless, a future with him was not possible.

Katie Lee had considered running away in the past. This time there was more of a reason.

But by doing so she would alienate her father, and he and her mother were all that she had in the world.

Family was too important to let the ties be severed so easily, so quickly.

Especially over a man who perhaps was not being sincere. After all, most men wanted women for only one reason. And once they had conquered this part of her, it was well-known that they usually looked elsewhere for more varied entertainment.

Katie Lee was not quite ready to be called a conquest, even if she wanted Bruce as badly as she did.

"None of this that we are doing is proper," Katie Lee said, jerking her hands away. Her heart was beating loudly as she edged away from Bruce, seeing a wounded expression in his eyes. "I should not have come here. I should not have spoken so openly to you, nor let you kiss me. You are a stranger—and, yes, you will be gone tomorrow. I will never see you again. I know it!"

Lifting the hem of her dress, Katie Lee spun around and began running toward the inn, ignoring Bruce's quiet pleadings that were growing fainter, the faster she ran. When she reached the back door, she rushed inside and up the stairs, half stumbling into her room.

Sobbing, she went to her bedroom window and looked down at Bruce, torn with her feelings for him. She wanted to trust him. She wanted to love him. But she was free to do neither.

Bruce felt empty as he looked up at Katie Lee's window. He understood devotion to family—he had spent a lifetime loving and working to make his mother and father happy. But he had never encountered a woman whose family forbade her to fall in love.

When it came to women, nothing got in his way. Katie Lee was a challenge, for damn sure, and even though he did not have time for challenges, he would make time for her....

"Seems you lost in love, lad."

The voice was familiar. Bruce cringed, realizing that Leonard Conty had probably been standing in the shadows for some time. He was reminded that Katie Lee's father was not his only competition.

Turning on his heel, Bruce clenched his fists at his sides. "Just how long have you been hanging around?" he growled, watching Leonard move out of the shadows, his bulldog on a leash beside him. "And don't tell me that you're here only to walk your dog. You were snooping. Is Peeping Tom your middle name?"

Conty chuckled, and his gray eyes appeared sinister in the dark. "Never mind why I am here," he said dryly. "It's what I saw while I was here that I find amusing." He laughed beneath his breath. "She kissed you, then left you hot and bothered, huh? I guess you can't win 'em all, Cabot. Now it's *my* turn."

Bruce took two quick steps toward Conty and grabbed the man's thick shoulders. "If you so much as go near her tonight, I'll kill you," he threatened.

"Leave her be. She's too frail to be tampered with. I realize now that I stepped out of line with her. Tomorrow I'm going to do what I should've done tonight. I'm going to ask her to marry me. That should stop all that nonsense you're trying to put into her head. An entertainer at your box house, indeed. You'd try to turn her into a whore, and you know it."

"The young and innocent ones turn into the best whores," Conty said, smoothing Bruce's hands from his shoulders. His dog bared his teeth. "Now you should know that, Cabot. Surely a young lad like you has been in plenty of whorehouses."

Bruce ignored the threat of the dog but not Conty's insulting comments about the young and innocent. The man was referring to Katie Lee. Half-crazed with anger, he doubled a fist and hit Conty on the chin, laughing to himself when the other man fell to the ground with a loud thud. Even the dog shrank away.

"Now I would advise you to keep any further filthy comments to yourself while we are discussing Miss Holden," Bruce said, kneading his sore fist. He gave Conty another angry stare, then turned and grabbed his horse's reins and led him back into the stable.

"Yes, that's what I'll do," he whispered to himself. "I'll ask Katie Lee to marry me. Tomorrow! I'll ask her to go to Seattle with me. Surely her father won't hold her against her will."

Patting his horse, Bruce smiled. Though he had only just met this lovely lady, there was no doubt that she could never be replaced in his heart.

Chapter Four

The air was filled with the pleasant aromas of sausage, eggs and coffee. Fresh butter lay on a platter in the center of the table alongside a varied assortment of jellies and jams. Her hair drawn back into one long braid down her back, wearing an apron over her modest cotton dress, Katie Lee served biscuits to the morning guests.

Carrying a small wicker basket piled high with the steaming biscuits, Katie Lee tried to evade Bruce's solemn stare and Leonard Conty's watchful eye as both took biscuits and placed them on their plates. She was filled with remembrances of Bruce's kiss and the way his arms had held her so close, stirring wondrous feelings throughout her that she had not wanted to end. Even now thinking of the passion they'd shared beneath the moonlight made her knees weak . . . her breathing short.

Surely Bruce could see her uneasiness and knew why.

As for Leonard Conty, he had yet to pursue her further, though he still watched her every move. Instinctively she knew that Conty would not give up easily. He was the sort who always got what he wanted. The diamond rings on his fingers attested to that.

Relieved that her chore of serving breakfast was ended, Katie Lee took the empty wicker basket into the kitchen, slipped off her apron and began walking toward the back door. Her mother's gentle voice stopped her.

"Katie Lee, you've got to get out of this mood," Madge said, placing a pudgy hand on Katie Lee's arm. "Don't let a drifter who you'll never see again bother you like this. Honey, one day the right man will come along. You'll know it when it happens. Your father will recognize it also, and give you and this man his blessing. Though I know that you see life slipping away, being eighteen and all, you've got time. Give yourself time."

Madge lowered her eyes and cleared her throat nervously, then looked back up at Katie Lee, her blue eyes filling with tears. "If I hadn't been so anxious to have a man I could call my own, perhaps I'd have had more out of life than bein' a cook and maid for passing travelers," she said sadly. "I got married at age sixteen, Katie Lee, and before havin' you I had already had two miscarriages. Katie Lee, you are all I have left in life that means anything to me. Please don't be in such a hurry to take off with a man and forget you have a mother.''

Katie Lee's heart ached. She lunged into her mother's arms, then hugged her tightly. "Oh, Mama, I'm not going anywhere," she murmured. "I'll be here for a long time. But I am finding it hard to control my restlessness. I see so many people who have so much excitement in their lives. I feel that I never shall have anything exciting in mine."

"This man...this Bruce," Madge said softly, easing from Katie Lee's arms to look her daughter directly in the eye. "After last night I thought you just might decide to leave with him."

Katie Lee paled. Her eyes wavered. "Mama, what about last night?" she asked, her voice faint.

"Hon, I couldn't sleep," Madge said, opening the back door. She looked toward the corral. "I came down to the kitchen and poured me some milk. I saw the door standing ajar, so I went to close it, and when I did, I...I saw you in that man's arms."

Gasping, Katie Lee felt guilt tie her stomach into a knot. "Oh, Mama, you didn't!" she cried. "You surely also saw me..."

Madge spun around and faced Katie Lee, placing a hand to her cheek. "Hon, yes, I also saw you kiss the man," she said, her voice trembling. "And I understand. You are a woman with womanly needs. It is only natural that you would want to be kissed...to be embraced."

Dropping her hand, Madge lumbered to the kitchen table and spread flour across its surface, then began rolling out the pie dough. "But I am glad that you knew enough to stop with a kiss," she said blandly, evading Katie Lee's quizzical stare. "Hon, when you came rushing back through the kitchen, you just barely missed stepping on me. I was standing in the shadows."

Madge paused and shoved back a strand of hair from her brow. "You see, I, too, once had such passions," she confessed softly. "That is why *you* are here, Daughter."

Katie Lee felt her face flood with color. She looked awkwardly away from her mother and swallowed hard. Her mother had never spoken so openly with her about sins of the flesh. Katie Lee had never envisioned her mother in a passionate embrace. Madge had always been "Mama"—nothing more. And now to know that her mother had experienced such passions . . . such desires, was so very unsettling.

"So what do we have here?" Geoffrey inquired as he walked into the room. His presence caused a sudden silence. Both Katie Lee's and Madge's faces wore strained expressions. "A hen party?"

He went to Madge and hugged her affectionately around the waist. "Are you tellin' our daughter about the birds and bees?" he teased. "Don't leave nothin' out, darlin'. There's a couple of men out there in the dining room who would steal her away in a minute if given half the chance."

"Papa, please," Katie Lee said, sighing heavily. "Don't you have enough to worry about without always worrying about me? I thought when I celebrated my eighteenth birthday I would be looked to as an adult, and adults should be able to worry about themselves." She ran her hands nervously over the gathers at the front of her dress. "I would gladly take the responsibility of my own worries and concerns." She cleared her throat. "Papa, if you would just let me."

Geoffrey laughed softly and kissed his wife on the cheek. He went to Katie Lee, framed her face between his hands and placed a kiss on the tip of her nose. "Daughter, we'll talk about all of this later," he said, drawing away from her. "Right now I'm going to go and make sure the stagecoach is ready to depart. I can't get this group of passengers out of here fast enough. I hope the next one brings all women. These damn men are gettin' a bit out of line where you are concerned."

Taking long strides, he went to the door, then gave Katie Lee another quick glance before leaving.

Katie Lee shook her head in disgust. She too went to the door and watched her father disappear into the barn and come out again, leading Bruce's strawberry roan behind him. "He is most anxious to see the stagecoach on its way, Mama," she murmured. "He's not even waiting for Bruce to see to his own horse. What is there about Bruce that he doesn't like?"

Madge wiped her hands on her apron and went to stand beside Katie Lee. "Hon, there ain't nothin' in particular about the young man that your father doesn't like," she said softly. "It's just that he's a man—a man he didn't get the chance to point out to you before the man sought you out first. Your father is determined to do the pointing, Katie Lee. It ain't going to be any other way unless you . . . you—"

"Unless I leave on my own and choose the man I want to marry—away from my father's watchful, accusing eye?" Katie Lee asked, interrupting. She kneaded her temples with trembling fingers. "Mama, perhaps that's what I may eventually have to do."

Madge looked quickly at Katie Lee, fear flashing in her eyes. Though Katie Lee had only a short while ago promised that she would not leave, she had just hinted broadly that she might do that very thing.

Katie Lee's face was pink with color when she stepped outside to watch the horses being attached to the stagecoach. She clasped her hands firmly behind her as Bruce and Leonard Conty walked from the inn. Bruce was carrying his walking stick and gloves, his hat hiding his beautiful sandy-red hair, and Conty was leading his bulldog, its tongue hanging from the corner of its mouth as it panted and drooled.

Katie Lee shifted her feet when both men started walking toward her. Her blush deepened when both stopped before her, their eyes revealing an intenseness that unnerved her. Though she had not expected them to leave without confronting her again, she could not help but be disturbed by their forwardness. Her father might come from the house at any moment!

Both Bruce and Conty spoke at the same time, their voices blending as they said her name in unison.

"Katie Lee..."

Bruce glowered at Conty, and the other man returned the steady, intense stare. But Bruce was the more gentlemanly of the two and waited his turn.

"Miss Holden," Conty said, resuming his planned speech. He cleared his throat nervously and ran a finger inside his suddenly tight collar. "My offer stands. If you are ever in Seattle, please look me up. Come to my theater. I will put you on the stage. You will become the darling of Seattle." He then slipped his hand inside his vest pocket and withdrew a business card. "Take my card. Consider very carefully what I offer. Honey, follow me and you'll wear diamonds."

Katie Lee's hand shook as she accepted the business card. She was feeling more and more important by the minute, as though she could amount to something in life.

Yet how foolish she was to even let herself think for a moment that she could be an entertainer. She was nothing but a shy country bumpkin. The thought of the stage terrified her!

And there were her mother and father. They would be terribly humiliated if their daughter left home to become a singer.

No. This was just something that one dreamed about.

Curling her fingers around the business card so that her father would not see it, she smiled up at Leonard Conty. "Thank you," she murmured. "I am honored that you think so highly of my singing, but, sir, it is best that you search for a singer elsewhere. I could never perform on a stage. Why, it has never even been a dream of mine to do so. I would much rather continue singing for my own pleasure."

Conty tipped his hat, smiling devilishly down at her. "Ma'am, many a star never had such dreams, either," he said, chuckling. He placed a thick hand against Katie Lee's cheek. "Just think about it. The idea will grow on you. I'm not an impatient man. I will wait for you until hell freezes over, if I must."

Katie Lee stepped away from his sweaty hand, her eyes wide. She was glad when he jerked slightly on his dog's leash and moved to board the stagecoach, followed by his brother and bodyguard.

This left her alone with Bruce. She looked timidly up at him and could not help but give him her most winsome smile. Her lashes fluttered nervously as she again became enmeshed in passion's web; his eyes were branding her as his.

Then her world melted away when he took her hand, causing her to drop the business card. He entwined his fingers through hers; a fever heated her flesh at his mere touch.

"Katie Lee, I didn't sleep at all last night after our brief moments together," Bruce said thickly, his heart thudding wildly against his ribs. "Tell me that you were able to sleep, and I won't believe you. You feel the same as I. It is something that we cannot turn our backs on. Katie Lee, if I go on to Seattle without you, I fear that I may never see you again. Come with me. Marry me. It is senseless to wait a proper time for courting. And how can I court you? Many miles will separate us once I set foot on the coach." He squeezed her hands more tightly, and his eyes became two points of fire. "Just this once think of your needs, Katie Lee. Not your family's."

Katie Lee felt her heart pound so loudly that she was sure everyone could hear it. Everything within her wanted to say yes to Bruce, but there were many reasons why she could not. Her family was only one of them. If she got married, she would be placing herself in the same shoes as her mother—she would never have a chance to experience anything in life other than being a wife and mother. If Katie Lee ever did have an opportunity to get away from this stage-coach stop, surely it would be best for her to explore life just a little bit before settling down? she thought, trying to justify her attitude.

She bit her lip in anguish. Surely there could never be another man who would make her feel as Bruce did. Just to look at him, just to be touched by him made her head reel with a strange sort of pleasure.

But with so many factors against saying yes to him, she had no choice but to refuse.

"Bruce, I can't," she murmured, easing her hand from his and placing it behind her so that he could not recapture it. "I barely know you. We have shared only... only a kiss. That is not enough to base a future on. I cannot go to Seattle and marry you." She swallowed hard, her pulse racing. "But I am so pleased that you asked me. Last night was very special. I wouldn't have wanted to believe that you kissed me like that just because you saw me as another conquest. I am glad that you kissed me because you feel a fondness for me. I shall always cherish remembrances of last night."

Bruce's eyes wavered, the rejection tearing his heart in two. "I will try to understand your reason for not accepting my proposal," he said, then laughed softly. "I guess I am too impetuous at times. How did I ever believe that you would just up and leave for Seattle to be my wife? Certainly you don't know me." He leaned closer to her, their lips only a hairbreadth apart. "But, my dear, I promise that you will. These many miles will not keep me from courting you, if that is what is required. And your father had just better get used to the idea. I am not a man who gives up all that easily."

His mouth grazed her lips, but he was rudely interrupted when a firm hand grabbed him by the shoulder and yanked him away from Katie Lee.

"Lad, I think it's time you board the stagecoach," Geoffrey growled, his pipe thrust into one corner of his mouth. He released his grip on Bruce and nodded toward the open door. "Go on and board the coach, before I do something I may regret the rest of my life."

Bruce tightened his free hand into a fist at his side, squinting as he looked at Katie Lee's father. "I'm leaving now," he said, his voice tight with anger. "But I'll be back—to see your daughter. You may as well prepare yourself for *losing* her once my courting is finished. I do plan to marry your daughter. You can't keep her to yourself much longer. Enjoy her, sir. Enjoy her."

Before Geoffrey had the chance to hit him, Bruce walked briskly to the stagecoach and climbed inside. He had not wanted to have a fistfight with Geoffrey in front of Katie Lee, but had the older man started swinging, Bruce would not have held back. Then he would have lost Katie Lee for certain. The true fight—the fight to win her hand—lay ahead.

Bruce ignored Leonard Conty's aggravating stare and the menacing dog, and leaned closer to the window to gaze at Katie Lee. He grimaced when he saw her stoop to pick up Conty's business card. His insides grew cold as he watched her studying what was written on it, as though debating whether to take up

Conty on his offer. Would she choose such a career over marriage? The very thought made him ill, for he knew damn well what that sort of career would entail.

Katie Lee looked at the card, intrigued. Her eyes rose slowly, and she met Bruce's gaze. Her insides grew warm as she recalled *his* offer. Surely it would be heaven to awaken every morning in his embrace.

Two men. Two offers.

"Katie Lee, we've much to do," Madge called from the door. "We've fresh linen to place on the beds. We've laundry water to get warm. We must prepare for the arrival of the next stagecoach. Do you hear? Now, Katie Lee. Now."

A keen sadness consumed Katie Lee as the stagecoach made a wide turn, and the horses began to guide it toward the opened gate. When Bruce waved at her, tears grew hot in her eyes. She scarcely knew him, but with all of her heart she knew that she loved him. She missed him already.

"Katie Lee, are you coming?" Madge shouted again. "I've pies to make. You must do the other chores! Come on now. Time is wastin'."

Blinking away a tear, Katie Lee raised her hand and waved eagerly to Bruce, but it was too late. The stagecoach was already traveling briskly along the road and on into the forest.

Chapter Five

Being attentive to her mother in the kitchen, Katie Lee placed a hot loaf of bread on the windowsill to cool while her mother kneaded more bread dough. Several pies had already cooled on a counter beneath the window.

She peered into the forest, uneasy. It had been several days since Chief Black Raven of the Snoqualmies Indian tribe, along with several of his braves, had made his unnerving visit. She shuddered at the thought of how the intrusive Indians, instead of knocking, would make questioning grunts at the door until someone opened it to let them in. They would always sit around for a while, visiting among themselves and eating anything Katie Lee's mother would offer them, her mother being afraid not to do so.

The chief was friendly, in a restrained fashion. He spoke some English and was decidedly intelligent. There was no denying that he resented Geoffrey Holden, whom he saw as an intruder on the land of his people, but had less resentment for Madge and Katie Lee, who, as women, only followed Geoffrey's lead.

Over the years he had apparently grown to tolerate Geoffrey and those like him, for the Indians had found out that there was no way to stop all the white intruders settling on the land. The Indians had lost the brief wars with the white men in the Oregon and Washington territories. And for the most part the Indians lived on reservations.

"But Chief Black Raven travels way beyond the boundaries of the reservation," Katie Lee muttered to herself.

"What's that you're mumbling about?" Madge asked, resting her hands for a moment. She wiped a bead of perspiration from her brow, leaving behind a smudge of flour. "Are you daydreamin' about that man again? Katie Lee, you'll never learn. Daydreamin' is such a waste of time."

Katie Lee spun around, her face flushed—not only from the heat of the kitchen. She, too, wiped the dampness from her forehead. In these parts the weather was unusually hot for the month of May. There had not been enough rain to keep all of the creeks flowing freely. The threat of fires would become a worry if it didn't rain soon.

"I wasn't thinking about Bruce at all," she said, telling a partial lie. "I'm concerned over Chief Black Raven's sudden absence from our front door. It's not like him, Mama. He knows the time of day you bake bread. Chief Black Raven loves it, so why hasn't he come these past several days? Do you think Papa insulted him the last time he was here?''

Madge looked toward the opened back door, an uneasy feeling racing up and down her spine, having been worrying herself about why the Indian chief hadn't been seen. Katie Lee was right—it wasn't like him.

She grew cold inside when she recalled how not long ago, after the chief and several of his braves had helped themselves to all of the food that Madge had cooked, Geoffrey had ordered the chief from the house, telling him that soon all the Snoqualmie Indians would be gone and the land would be full of white men. Then the Holden family would not have to be bothered by "flea-bitten Indians."

Madge had seen hatred in the chief's eyes and she understood why. Even she had hated her husband at that moment. Surely the Indian chief would rebel.

Wiping her hands on her apron, Madge went to the door and closed it. Breathing harshly, she looked at the open window, seeing it as the only way to get some air into the hot, sweltering kitchen, yet something told her to close it also.

"Katie Lee, shut the window," she said, her voice strained.

Katie Lee's eyes widened, and she swallowed hard. "Mama?" she asked.

"Remove the bread and close the window," Madge said flatly, her widened eyes revealing her fear.

"Mama, don't you think you are overreacting a bit?" Katie Lee suggested, turning to look out the window into the dark forest. "Surely Chief Black Raven is not that angry with Papa."

She turned and went to her mother, easing her away from the door. Slowly Katie Lee opened it to prove to her mother that she was not afraid. "It's too hot to close the kitchen up," she said reassuringly. "I'm sorry I even brought up Chief Black Raven's name."

She smiled awkwardly toward the bread sitting on the windowsill. "Just you watch," she murmured. "The chief will smell the bread and make an appearance. It's probably just taken some time for him to forget what Papa said."

Madge resumed kneading her bread and baking it in her Dutch oven, a loaf at a time. "Were you the Indian, would you forget insults so easily?" she asked softly, her eyes no less troubled as she looked at Katie Lee.

Her mother's words chilled her heart like a rush of cold winter air. Katie Lee turned back to the window, her pulse racing.

Being cramped in the confines of the small stagecoach with three men and a rank bulldog disgusted Bruce, and he leaned closer to the window, trying to get a breath of fresh air, his mind drifting to more pleasant thoughts...to Katie Lee. It was hard to get his mind off her, but for now he must. He had much ahead of him that required his full attention.

Looking into the depths of the forest, he envisioned men there, busily sawing the trees and loading them onto wagons pulled by oxen. Before long he would be in Seattle, a true witness to such activities. At the thought, he felt his blood run hot in his veins.

Suddenly Bruce's breathing quickened. Amid the shadows he could see Indians winding their way through the trees on horseback. Their grotesque war paint looked anything but peaceful.

"What are you gaping at?" Leonard Conty asked, wiping his face with a sparkling white handkerchief.

Bruce kneaded his chin contemplatively, looking at Conty, into the forest, then back to the other man. "Indians," he said dryly. "I saw several Indians traveling on horseback through the forest. Why the hell aren't they traveling on the road?"

"Perhaps they don't want to associate with us civil breed of men by sharing a civil way to travel," Leonard Conty said, laughing boisterously. "And who cares? As long as they are in the forest and we are in the stagecoach, going in the opposite direction, who cares why they are going anywhere?" His face paled, and he looked past Bruce and out the window. "They *are* going in the opposite direction, aren't they?"

Bruce shook his head, disgusted with the short, stocky man who thought only of himself and his needs. Leonard Conty would be the sort to stand and watch an Indian massacre, if he was assured that *he* would never be slain!

"Yes, they are going the opposite way," Bruce finally answered, then also grew pale.

"God!" he gasped, scooting to the edge of the seat. "Katie Lee! Those Indians are traveling in the direction of Katie Lee's house!"

Desperation seized him, and without further thought he stuck his head from the window and began to yell at the stagecoach driver. "Driver! Stop the coach!" he shouted. When the vehicle kept on rambling down the road, Bruce doubled a fist and shouted again. "Stop this stagecoach this minute! I'm about to puke up my insides! If you want the coach stinking for your next passengers, just continue on your way, damn you!"

The stagecoach jerked and teetered, then came to a halt. Bruce made a quick exit and ran around to speak with the driver. "I saw Indians," he said, breathless with anxiety. He pointed toward the forest. "In there. They were traveling in the forest. And damn it, their bodies were decorated hideously with war paint. They can't have anything good on their minds. We must all saddle up horses and follow after them. What if they plan to massacre an innocent family? By God, we must go and make sure the Holdens are all right."

The driver pushed back his hat and glared down at Bruce. At his side the barrel of the guard's rifle caught the rays of the sun. "Is that why you stopped me?" he growled. "Not because you were ill? But because you saw a few mangy Injuns? Get back inside the coach so we can continue on our way. I don't like anyone manipulating me. I'm in charge here."

Bruce shifted his feet nervously, refusing to budge. "You may be in charge now," he said in a low grumble. "But you may not be later. Once the Indians slaughter an innocent family, they will be back to finish us off. I'm sure they saw us. Now what do you have to say about being in charge? An arrow can sure enough change your status in life pretty quick. Is that the way you want to die?"

The driver lifted his reins, as though ready to slap them against the horse's manes. "Sonny, either you get back inside the coach now, or you'll have a long walk ahead of you," he drawled.

"You can't mean that!" Bruce gasped. "You are ignoring the threat of Indians? I saw them. No Indian decks out in war paint for the fun of it. We must try to defend those who are being threatened."

"Sonny, there have been no Indian fracases in these parts in years," the driver said, trying to hold on to his patience. "Believe me when I tell you there ain't going to be any now. If I were you, I wouldn't let a little war paint scare me." He nodded his head. "Get aboard now or, by God, you'll walk."

"I'll get aboard, but if I didn't, I sure as hell wouldn't walk to Seattle," Bruce argued. "I think you're forgetting whose horse that is tailing along behind."

Bruce stomped back to the stagecoach door and pulled himself up inside, disgruntled. Conty's throaty laugh grated on his nerves as the stagecoach resumed its trip.

Ignoring Conty, Bruce turned to look out the window again. Suddenly in his mind's eye he saw Katie Lee cowering away from an Indian, his hatchet raised. . . .

Bruce lunged his head back out the window. "Stop this damn thing!" he shouted. "I'm getting off."

He could not continue with this journey until he saw that Katie Lee and her family were all right. If he was wrong and the Indians had just passed by, he would catch up with the stagecoach at the next stop. The knowledge that Katie Lee was safe would enable him to live with Leonard Conty's sarcastic taunts for the rest of the journey.

But that didn't matter. Katie Lee was all that mattered at this moment.

As the stagecoach drew to a halt, Bruce jumped down and untied his horse. Riding bareback, letting the wind take his fancy hat, he headed back in the direction of Holden Inn.

The dishes washed and cleared away, Katie Lee took off her apron; the rest of the day was hers. Her mother was lounging in front of the fireplace with her father, both taking a respite from their chores.

Once outside, the spring air soft and gentle on her face, Katie Lee headed toward the edges of the forest to listen to the birdcalls. She would jot down her impressions later when she was in bed for the night.

Stopping in midstep, ice filled Katie Lee's veins. She was hearing all sorts of birdcalls, but none was familiar to her. Her back stiff, her shoulders tense, she leaned an ear toward the forest and listened more carefully, quickly becoming aware that these were not true birdcalls at all.

"Indians," she whispered, feeling herself grow pale.

Her knees suddenly weak, she turned and moved slowly back toward the house, knowing that if she broke into a run the Indians would know that she was aware of their presence. She was afraid that her earlier fears were well-founded. Never before had she observed Indians lingering in the forest around her house, performing birdcalls for the fun of it. Chief Black Raven had been angered to extremes by her father and planned to retaliate.

Raising her eyes toward the sky, Katie Lee began praying softly, wanting so badly to be wrong.

"Please let it not be Indians," she whispered over and over again, sighing with relief when she reached the door and stepped into the kitchen.

Scarcely breathing, she went to the window and peered out, looking toward the forest. She jumped with alarm when she saw a sudden movement behind a tree and recognized the copper skin of an Indian.

With a jerk she turned her eyes elsewhere and went numb when she saw Chief Black Raven partly hidden behind a corner of the barn, the barrel of a gun pointing out between the end of the logs.

As though frozen in time, Katie Lee stared at the face pressed against the musket stock. Grotesque designs covered the face and body of the chief.

Her gaze shifted, and she found herself looking into the muzzle of the chief's weapon.

"Daughter, move away from that window!" Geoffrey ordered, keeping his voice lowered to a bare whisper so that the Indians would not hear him. He had heard the birdcalls, too, and knew that they were false.

She felt firm hands on her waist and cried softly as she was hurled from the window by her mother, while her father slammed the door shut and barred it. All of this happened in the twinkling of an eye, and Katie Lee was amazed at the explosive power and speed of her normally gentle mother.

"Katie Lee, you must get to safety!" Madge cried, half dragging her daughter across the kitchen. "I must get you to the root cellar. Oh, Lord, don't let anyone harm my baby...."

Katie Lee became aware of yelling, the banging of muskets and the crashing of glass as she made her exit, and pulled herself free. Turning, she saw her father reach to close and bolt the kitchen window; outside she could see a dozen Indians charging on the house, waving hatchets and muskets.

A volley of musket balls shattered the window. Katie Lee watched, horrified, as her father's body convulsed and fell to the floor.

"No!" she screamed, running to him as blood streamed from his wounds. His moans lasted for only a moment, then he lay quiet, his eyes staring blankly at the ceiling.

"Oh, God, Geoffrey!" Madge cried, stopping dead in her tracks.

But the loud reports of the muskets and the splintering of wood made her regain her senses.

Taking Katie Lee by the arm, mother and daughter moved hurriedly into the parlor.

Kicking away the oval braided rug that lay in front of the fireplace, Madge thrust Katie Lee to her knees. "Open the trapdoor!" she cried. "You don't have much time."

"What do you mean, *I* don't have much time?" Katie Lee sobbed, wiping hot tears from her eyes. "What about you, Mama? I can't leave you up here to die."

Determined, Madge fell to her knees and opened the trapdoor herself. The strong smell of onions, potato and cabbage stung her nostrils. Taking Katie Lee by the wrist she forced her to the steps and pushed her down. "We can't both be saved, Katie

Lee," she said solemnly. "Who would close the trapdoor? Who would cover it with the rug? One of us must stay up here, and it will be me. I have had my life. Yours has only just begun. Perhaps it is time for you to chase your dreams."

Katie Lee looked up at her mother. Her mother leaned down and embraced her. "Anyhow, Katie Lee, I have no quarrel with the chief," she tried to reassure her daughter. "We have always gotten along famously. His quarrel is with your father, and...and your father is dead."

They clung, sobbing, but when musket balls crashed through the parlor window and embedded themselves in the wall opposite the fireplace, making clean, round holes, Madge gave Katie Lee a final shove and dropped the trapdoor back into place.

She studied the closed trapdoor, glad that Geoffrey had been clever enough to disguise it so well. No one could tell one crack in the wooden floor from the next. The concealment had been planned purposely, in case there ever was an Indian attack. Even if the Indians chose to carry away the rug that usually lay on the parlor floor, they would still be unaware of the door that could lead them to other valuable treasures—namely a daughter!

Trembling and sobbing, Katie Lee huddled in the dark with the stored vegetables and canned goods. "Oh, Mama...Papa..." she whispered, still hearing gunfire.

She grew quiet when she heard a different sort of gunfire. It was the sharp explosions of her father's six-shooter. Her mother was firing it, defending herself, clearly never having thought to have a peaceful reconciliation with Chief Black Raven.

Panicked, Katie Lee started up the steps to help her mother, but stopped, numb, when she heard her mother cry out, then the ensuing thump as she fell to the floor, suddenly quiet.

"No!" Katie Lee cried to herself, placing her hands over her ears to keep out the continued heavy, sickening explosions of muskets outside the house. The stench of gun smoke began to penetrate the cracks in the floor, threatening to choke her. She crumpled to the steps, desperately wanting to go to her mother, but knowing that to do so would mean her own death.

The gunfire ceased. Voices grew close, and then the floorboards overhead squeaked ominously. Katie Lee watched the planks above her, praying that the trapdoor would not be found. She also prayed that her mother was truly dead, for the Indians often scalped and tortured their victims.

Katie Lee even wished that she were dead. She did not know if she could bear to live, now that she had lost her mother and father.

Guilt chilled her blood as she let herself recall how often she had thought of breaking her ties with her parents. Lord, it had been done so quickly, so unmercifully. Now she would do anything to take back all of her wicked thoughts of freedom, of independence. All she wanted in life at this moment was to see her mother's and father's smiling faces again.

Chief Black Raven's voice could be heard plainly above those of the other Indians. Katie Lee cringed when she heard her name mentioned. Cowering, she listened as Chief Black Raven spoke. What was he saying?

Then her heart froze when she saw light filter through the cracks of the trapdoor. The rug had been removed. She waited, scarcely breathing, for the door to fly open.

But it appeared that her father's skills had been more than adequate. The trapdoor had not been noticed.

Thus far her life had been spared.

Breathing hard, her pulse racing, Katie Lee huddled in the hole, listening to the fading sound of footsteps overhead, and then to the galloping of horses. Silence fell at last but Katie Lee was still too afraid to leave her hiding place. She cried softly as she searched for the courage to endure.

Once again she grew tense when she heard another horse approach, then quick, heavy footsteps overhead. The person gasped, apparently upon discovering the dead bodies, Katie Lee guessed.

"Oh, God!" the voice exclaimed.

"Katie Lee!" it cried. "Oh, God, Katie Lee..."

Katie Lee's breath caught in her throat. The voice! It . . . it was Bruce's!

Sobbing, she began banging on the heavy trap-door.

Chapter Six

Bruce took a step back, startled by the pounding. He grabbed his pistol from his shoulder holster and looked quizzically at the floor, trying to discover where the sound was coming from. Then a small, weak voice from somewhere below him thrilled his heart. Somehow Katie Lee had survived the killing.

Slipping the pistol back into its holster, he fell to his knees and with his fingers searched the cracks in the floorboards. His pulse raced.

"Bruce, help me lift the trapdoor," Katie Lee sobbed. "Fear and remorse have taken my strength away. Oh, Bruce, how is it that you even came back?"

"God, Katie Lee, I saw Indians traveling through the forest," he said, his voice thick with emotion. "If it hadn't been for the stubborn stagecoach driver, perhaps I would have been here sooner. The Indians are the ones who did this, aren't they?"

"Yes, it was Indians," Katie Lee cried. "Bruce, it was...so...horrible. Thank God, they are gone."

Sweat beaded her brow as she pushed at the trap-door with all her might. Finally she managed to budge it at least enough to show Bruce exactly where it was.

"I see it," Bruce said, sliding his fingers along the edges of the door. "When your father planned this secret hiding place he did it well."

He yanked up the door and settled it against the floor. When he saw Katie Lee cowering in the tiny hole, her face streaked with tears, her eyes filled with remorse, he swallowed hard.

They looked at one another for a moment, then Bruce reached for Katie Lee's hands and began to help her up the creaky, wooden steps into the parlor.

Suddenly he remembered that her mother lay only a few footsteps away. It would be best for Katie Lee not to see her. He started to block her view, but discovered that he was too late.

Katie Lee's gaze left Bruce long enough for her to glance across the room. When she saw her mother lying lifeless in a pool of blood, her stomach revolted and she felt a crazy spinning in her head. Before she could say anything to Bruce, darkness engulfed her and she crumpled into his arms, just as he drew her completely up from the cellar.

"Katie Lee, Katie Lee," Bruce whispered, holding her limp body, her face resting against his chest. He held her there for a moment longer, gazing down at her. "Darling, I'm so sorry about all of this. I . . . am . . . so sorry."

He knew that he should not waste any more time than was necessary. Wanting to get her out of this place of death and blood, his eyes wavered as he carried her past her mother's body, and he was sure that her father lay just as dead in another room.

Everything was eerily quiet, yet through the stench of the spent gunpowder he could still smell the sweet aromas of freshly baked bread and pies, reminding Bruce of Katie Lee's mother. Then the scent of pipe tobacco reminded him of Geoffrey Holden.

It was damned tragic. The Holden family had been so content, just living their simple life.

An aroma as delicate as lily of the valley drew Bruce's gaze back to Katie Lee as he carried her across the living-room floor. Her cheek still resting on his chest, her face was peaceful in her unconscious state.

Katie Lee's hair was drawn back from her face in a long braid. He studied the long, thick lashes that veiled her closed eyes and the full, sensual lips that reminded him of their passionate kiss in the moonlight.

If only she could be as peaceful when she awakened. If only she would not be plagued with remembrances. If only one blink of the eye could erase these past hours!

But it was all too real. Katie Lee had been orphaned in a matter of moments, and it was now up to him to protect her.

"Darling, I will give you such a wonderful life. You will soon forget a good measure of the pain of this terrible day," he whispered, holding Katie Lee more securely in his arms as he stepped outside. "We will be married. I will make you the happiest bride in America!"

Now was not the time to be thinking about anything but getting Katie Lee away from there. But he had one dreaded chore to complete before leaving. He must bury her parents. A proper burial would enable Katie Lee to have at least a measure of peace when she left them behind.

Stopping just outside the inn, Bruce glanced from side to side, then to the dark forest. There was no one in sight. There were no sounds. Even the birds had ceased to sing, the gunfire having apparently chased them all away. Smoke still rose from the chimneys, making everything appear normal. When the next stagecoach arrived, no one would be any the wiser—until they stepped inside and looked around. . . .

Hurrying to the edge of the yard, where a gigantic oak spread its shade over the green grass, Bruce placed Katie Lee on the ground. Her eyes were still closed, in what he could only call a merciful escape from the present. Hating to leave her for even a moment, Bruce knew nonetheless that he had no choice but to see to her parents' burial. It was the only right thing to do.

Giving Katie Lee a last searching look, he ran to the barn and grabbed a shovel. Rushing back outside, he chose a piece of land that was bordered by Mrs. Holden's flower garden and began to dig. Sweat poured from his brow, and his shoulder muscles flexed as he dug more deeply into the soil.

Finally he had the graves prepared.

Dreading the chore that lay ahead, Bruce peered toward the inn, then back at Katie Lee.

Wanting to put the burial behind him, he removed his coat and laid it neatly beside the open grave, then groaned disconsolately as he began walking toward the inn. Never before had he faced death so crudely.

The sun streaming through a gap in the leaves overhead settled in a golden sheen on Katie Lee's face. Slowly she began to awaken, a fresh sob in her throat when she suddenly remembered the sight of her mother lying on the floor. She covered her face with her hands, trying to block out the image of her mother as she had lain there so deathly still, blood staining her dress, her eyes staring.

"Mama," she cried softly, choking on another sob. "Oh, Papa."

A soft breeze spurred her to remove her hands and open her eyes. She was no longer in the house. She was outside!

Wiping away the tears, she sat up and looked toward her mother's flower garden. There she saw two freshly dug graves, and Bruce bowing over two bodies that lay beside them and had been wrapped in blankets. His soft prayer made Katie Lee's heart ache. Seeing him so attentive, so caring, suddenly made her heart swell. He was a very special man.

She pushed herself up, feeling her knees still weak and began to walk toward Bruce and the wrapped bodies. Again tears welled up in her eyes as she looked from one rolled blanket to the other.

How could she bear to see her parents lowered into the ground? Yet she had no choice.

She must learn to accept that giving up the ones you loved was part of life.

Bruce rose to his full height, then jumped with alarm when Katie Lee moved to his side and draped an arm around his waist. She hugged him to herself, still looking down at the bodies. "You are so kind," she murmured, swallowing back another urge to cry. "Father was so wrong about you. If he had only given you a chance, oh, how he could have idolized you."

Bruce slipped an arm around her waist. "I couldn't find any blankets in the house," he said with difficulty. "I guess the Indians took them all, as well as the horses from the barn. They must have overlooked these that I found in the loft. Though soiled, they will have to do. I hope you don't mind."

"No, I don't mind," she said, her voice strained. "I would have hated having to lower them into the ground without...without anything wrapped around them. Thank you, Bruce, for caring."

"Katie Lee, we must not wait around here much longer," Bruce said, their eyes meeting as she looked up at him. "You never know—the Indians just may return. When they get to thinking about having left you behind, they could come looking."

"Yes, you're right," she said softly. "Chief Black Raven is a very intelligent man. This is why my father's insults cut him so deeply that he would do such a thing."

"Chief Black Raven?"

"Please," Katie Lee said, ducking her head, trying not to reveal fresh tears in her eyes, "let's not talk about him just yet. It's much too painful."

Bruce edged away, took her hands and turned her to face him. "I'm going to place your parents' bodies in their graves now," he said heavily. "Are you going to be all right?"

"Yes," Katie Lee whispered, slowly raising her eyes to gaze once more into his. "But I would like to take one last look."

A visible shudder gripped him. "Hon, I don't think that would be wise," he said hoarsely. "Just remember your parents as you knew them. You will have much more pleasant remembrances. Let me get them buried, and then I will give you a few moments of privacy beside the graves." He squeezed her hands affectionately. "That *is* best, Katie Lee. Trust me."

"Perhaps you are right," she murmured, swallowing hard. "Whatever you say."

Bruce kissed her softly, then bent and lifted first one body into his arms and lowered it into a grave, then the other. Katie Lee could tell who had gone into which grave from the size of each bundle. She began to tremble, and the pit of her stomach felt strangely empty as Bruce began shoveling dirt into the shallow graves.

When there were two mounds of dirt on the ground, Katie Lee went to her mother's flower garden, picked two huge bouquets of snapdragons and took them to the graves, placing one on each.

"I'll be waiting by my horse," Bruce said, his voice drawn. He bowed his head as he turned away, his heart almost breaking when he heard Katie Lee begin to weep behind him. Never would he let anything as terrible happen to her again.

Sitting on top of the strawberry roan, Katie Lee clung to Bruce's waist as the cloudless sky slowly changed from a light orange to a deep red and finally to gray. Every bone in her body ached from the ride; her legs felt numb from straddling the horse. The skirt of her dress, hiked way above her knees, whipped in the wind.

"How much longer are we going to ride today?" she asked loudly, so that her words would carry over the clip-clop of the horse's hooves. "Bruce, I'm so weary. Please stop. Let us rest the night and then go on tomorrow."

"I had hoped to catch up with the stagecoach at the next stop," he said, glancing back at her. "But I see now that it's impossible. As soon as I see a place that can afford us some privacy, we'll stop. My only concern is Chief Black Raven."

"I am sure he is many miles away," Katie Lee said, trying to reassure him. "You see, he is not loved all that much in Seattle and tries to keep as far away as possible. And soon he will wish that he had stayed away from our inn. As soon as we reach Seattle, I plan to go straight to the authorities. Hopefully Chief Black Raven will never get the chance to kill another person."

The soft splash of a waterfall drew Bruce's attention.

"I think we've found the spot," he announced, wheeling his horse to the right and entering the forest. "We'll go to the river and follow it farther into the forest. Perhaps we may even take the chance of lighting a fire, if you truly believe Chief Black Raven is no threat. The thought of a fish dinner makes my mouth water. How about you, Katie Lee?"

Katie Lee did not want to even think of food, fearing that if she took one bite she might retch, yet there was no denying how empty her stomach was. She would have to try to eat. She had to keep her strength to survive, and survive she would, if only to live long enough to point an accusing finger at Chief Black Raven!

"A fish dinner sounds wonderful," she said, squaring her shoulders.

Chapter Seven

Deep in the forest, among the ferns, wild rose-bushes and Oregon grape, Katie Lee sat beside Bruce, eating fish. Bruce held another fish stuck onto a stick over a low-burning fire.

"This isn't exactly what I had in mind when I had thought of wanting to take you out to dinner," Bruce said, chuckling as he glanced over at her. He gave her a lingering look, noting how ravenously she ate the fish. "But I see that it really doesn't matter." His eyes grew dark, his feelings intense. "Katie Lee I'm so glad to see you eating. I had feared that you wouldn't after... after, well, you know...."

Katie Lee tossed the stripped fish bones into the weeds and wiped her mouth clean with the back of her hand. "I must keep my strength, and to do so I must eat," she said determinedly.

She lowered her eyes, not wanting Bruce to see the tears. "Somehow I will get past this terrible day," she murmured.

Bruce took the cooked fish from the stick and quickly bit into the tasty flesh, watching silently as Katie Lee began unbraiding her hair. As the moonlight streamed through the break in the trees overhead, her now-loosened hair tumbled over her shoulders. As she stared into the fire, he could see the silver shine of unshed tears in the depths of her eyes and a haunted look that spoke of her trauma.

"Do you want to talk about it now, Katie Lee?" he asked, throwing the fish bones into the tall grasses behind him. He scooted closer to her, so wanting to take her into his arms to tell her that he loved her, would always love her, but knowing that this was not the proper time.

"Maybe you would feel better if you talked to me about it," he said gently. "If you keep it inside, you may never get over it."

Katie Lee ran her fingers through the soft tendrils of her hair, ridding them of their tangles. "Yes, perhaps I should talk about it," she said softly, then looked toward the glow of the moonlight on the river. "And then, even though it is quite chilly tonight, I would like to wash off."

She swallowed hard. "I feel I must get the stink of...of death and gunpowder from my skin," she added quickly.

"I understand," he said, nodding. "Perhaps then you will be able to sleep. Rest as well as food is important for you to keep up your strength."

"Yes, I know," Katie Lee said, then smiled over at Bruce as he took one of her hands and squeezed it reassuringly.

"Bruce, what happened today was my papa's fault," she said, her voice breaking. She looked at Bruce, then into the dancing flames of the fire. "Until recently Chief Black Raven and my papa were on friendly enough terms. My father had grown used to having to tolerate the chief and his braves coming into our inn at all hours of the day, eating up food and just downright getting in the way of our daily chores."

She cleared her throat nervously, as though it was hard to continue, then resumed speaking.

"One late afternoon, just prior to the arrival of a stagecoach, when Mama was busy preparing dinner, Chief Black Raven and many of his braves came into the inn and helped themselves to everything Mama was cooking, leaving hardly a thing for the travelers."

She supported her head with her free hand before continuing to speak, this time in a monotone.

"Papa and I knew how Mama placed such importance on having everything ready exactly when the stagecoaches arrived, and that it would unsettle her nerves terribly if anything happened to delay the meal," she said dully. "When Papa saw the empty pots and pans in the kitchen after the Indians emptied them, he flew into a rage. He shouted at the chief. He warned him and his braves against coming into the inn again, eating up food and making a damn nuisance of themselves.''

She looked over at Bruce, her eyes wide. "Bruce, he said so much more to the chief that he shouldn't have. He bragged about the white man taking over the Indians' land! When Papa went into a rage over anything, his insults could inflame the Lord," she said. "I am not at all surprised that the chief had been offended by it. But never had I thought that he would come and kill Papa for it."

She choked back a sob. "And Mama," she added in a near whisper.

She jerked her hand from Bruce's and rose shakily to her feet, holding her head in her hands and sobbing. "How could he?" she cried.

Bruce rose quickly to his feet and embraced Katie Lee, holding her tightly. He felt a warm glow inside when she stretched her arms around him, apparently welcoming his attentions. "Cry it all out," he crooned, burrowing his face into the depths of her hair. "Just you wait and see. You'll feel much better."

The more that she cried, letting her tears pour from her like a soft summer rain, the more Katie Lee felt the emptiness fade away, felt the burdens of guilt and sorrow become lighter. She clung to Bruce, loving the feel of his muscled body against hers. That he had returned to check for her safety was a miracle. That he cared was a blessing. She had thought that she would never see him again! Only in her wildest fantasies had she thought that she would ever be totally alone with him.

A shudder coursed through her. Never did she want to think of this day as the fulfillment of a fantasy. It was a nightmare!

Bruce felt her shudder and eased her away to look down into her eyes. "Are you cold?" he asked softly.

"I'm fine," she murmured. "Do not worry yourself so about me."

Katie Lee's hair tumbled down her back as she looked up at him, mesmerized anew by his handsomeness, yet knowing this was not the time to think such thoughts of a man. At this moment in time, her thoughts should primarily be of herself, of what the future held for her. Bruce had asked her to marry him before tragedy had struck. At that time the thought had thrilled her, for she did feel that she had fallen in love with him at first sight.

But now everything had changed. She had decisions to make, and she was not sure if marriage was the answer.

Even if she did love Bruce with all of her heart, hadn't her mother once loved her father as much? Katie Lee could not help but think of how miserable her mother's life had become. Marriage had not been a bed of roses for her. Perhaps it was not a bed of roses for any woman, no matter what promises a man might make.

"I think I shall go to the river now," she said uneasily, inching away from Bruce, sensing that he could read too much in her eyes. She did not want him to ever think that she was ungrateful for rescuing her. She was grateful, and she loved him from the bottom of her heart. And though she feared all of her tomorrows, she did not want to have to fully depend on him. In the back of her mind she was toying with Leonard Conty's proposal. The stage offered unquestionable independence.

She flushed scarlet then, suddenly guilty. If her parents were alive, they would abhor the idea of her singing before an audience. Perhaps she should still consider their feelings. . . .

Shaking her head in an attempt to clear her muddled thoughts, Katie Lee turned and began walking toward the river. She had no change of clothes. She didn't even have a washcloth or towel! Bruce had encouraged her to leave the graves as quickly as possible, without so much as a look behind her.

"Katie Lee, wait up," Bruce said, grabbing his pistol.

Katie Lee paled at the thought of Bruce being witness to her sponge bath. She stopped dead in her tracks and spun around. "You said that you would keep watch," she said thinly. "But do you have to come along? It would be most indecent, Bruce. It would be improper."

Bruce chuckled beneath his breath. "Hon, I will keep my back to you the entire time," he said, smiling down at her.

His insides grew warm when she smiled sweetly back at him, relief evident in her blue eyes. "I promise," he added. "Now get along with you. We'd best hit the sack soon. We've a lot of riding to do tomorrow if we're going to catch up with that damn stagecoach, and we'll have to start with the sunrise."

"A stagecoach will be much more comfortable than riding bareback with you," Katie Lee said, laughing as she rubbed her behind. "I'm not sure if I shall ever be able to sit down again."

Both laughing now, they headed for the river together. Then Bruce's laughter faded when he thought further about traveling in the stagecoach. Leonard Conty would still be aboard. The lout would have the opportunity to approach Katie Lee again with the invitation to sing in his box house!

Bruce turned his eyes once more to Katie Lee. His gaze swept over her, the moonlight illuminating her as she stepped to the water's edge and stretched her arms over her head, yawning. Though she was dressed in a modest dress with a high collar and long sleeves, she would not be dressed so genteelly if she sang in Leonard Conty's establishment. She would be forced to wear skimpy, gaudy satin garments that would show more than half her breasts! Her delicate pink face would be painted with bright rouges and lipsticks! Her eyelashes would be plastered with mascara!

If Leonard Conty had his way, Katie Lee would become his whore!

Yes, the threat of Leonard Conty would become real enough again, but not if Bruce prevented Conty from having the same attraction to Katie Lee as he had before.

There was nothing standing in the way of her accepting Bruce's proposal of marriage now. She was free to do as she wished, and he would see to it that sometime before they reached the next stagecoach stop, she would agree to be his wife.

But now did not seem the proper time to ask her. In the morning. He would ask her in the morning....

Katie Lee swung around and looked up at Bruce, blushing. She clasped her hands behind her back and smiled sheepishly. "Well?" she inquired. "Are you going to turn your back so I can bathe? We're at the riverbank, or didn't you notice?"

Bruce laughed and reached out to run his hand over her soft, fine hair. "Your beauty muddles my mind," he said, his heart aching. "God, you're so beautiful. How am I expected to have the ability to concentrate?"

Katie Lee stepped away from him and once again placed her back to him. Her smile faded. She did not want to become intimate with Bruce now that she knew that her plans would not include him. "Bruce, I truly would like to proceed with my sponge bath, so that I can retire for the night," she murmured. "I am so tired . . . so very bone weary."

Feeling stunned by what seemed to be her decision to openly avoid him, Bruce was rendered momentarily speechless. It was as though she had slapped him in the face. His cheeks stung from her rejection. Surely he had done nothing to make her dislike him. Earlier there had been so much in her kiss and in the way she had clung to him. There had been so much in her eyes that could not be denied.

"Go ahead," he said dully, turning his back on her. He walked a good distance from the riverbank and leaned against the trunk of a tree, the pistol a deadweight as he kept it secure in his hand. "You're safe to do as you wish. My eyes are elsewhere, Katie Lee. Enjoy your bath."

Feeling guilty for having mistreated Bruce, Katie Lee turned and looked at him. Her fingers trembled as she began to unfasten her dress. Her knees weakened as she lowered it over her shoulders, exposing her flesh to the silver beams of the moon. At this moment she wanted nothing more than to have Bruce hold her . . . teach her the mysteries of rapture. Surely if he kissed and held her, caressed her trembling flesh, she could forget for the moment all the sadness of life. Even now her breasts throbbed for his mouth, his hands. She lowered her petticoat to rest on her hips. Her nipples were erect, as though beckoning to this man who stood only a heartbeat away. A man she would refuse to marry!

Sighing heavily with the knowledge that such lust was wrong, Katie Lee spun around and fell to her knees at the water's edge. The water reflected her face and tumbling hair in the light of the moon. At this moment she was seeing so much about herself that she did not recognize—a young girl who was now a woman, with womanly desires. She moaned and sank her hands deep into the water. The sting of the cold water a moment later made her flinch.

Her face refreshed, she began smoothing water over her strangely swollen breasts. Anger and frustration at such unchecked desires brought tears to her eyes. With quick, jerky movements, she tore her clothes off and forced herself to step bodily into the river, hoping the frigid water might return a measure of sanity to her thoughts. She cried out as she ducked into the water, then grew quiet when Bruce turned with a start.

Their eyes met and held; the upper lobes of her breasts were quite visible to Bruce just beneath the surface where the moon caressed them. Her breath was stolen away when he took a step toward the river, then stopped and went back to the tree, his willpower stronger than hers.

She sighed with relief and closed her eyes momentarily, striving for control over her raging emotions. Then freezing in the chill water, she stepped out and quickly dressed before returning to Bruce and taking his hand.

"I'm finished," she murmured, melting when he returned her steady gaze. "Would you like for me to stand guard while you bathe? I wouldn't mind."

Bruce laughed awkwardly. "No, I feel just fine the way I am," he said, lying. A cold bath was exactly what he needed. His loins were on fire. And the damnedest thing about all of this was that when he had begun to walk toward the river with plans to join her in the water, she had not tried to stop him. He had missed perhaps the one chance he would get to make love to her before they reached Seattle.

Chapter Eight

Snuggled into Bruce's arms beside the glowing embers of the fire, Katie Lee was finding it hard to control the wild beating of her heart. Lying with her head resting on Bruce's chest, his muscular arms protectively around her, she could hear the wild thuds of his heart against her cheek.

If she could only go to sleep! It was not right to be feeling desire for a man, when only a short while ago she had prayed over her parents' graves. She had her longed-for freedom now. But could she ever be happy with its savage origins?

Slowly, she escaped into sleep. Her body relaxed in Bruce's arms, and dreams began to transport her into another world where Bruce laughed and joked with her as they spun around a ballroom floor. How beautiful she felt in her long and flowing satin gown with its revealing bodice. She could feel Bruce's eyes appraise her partially exposed breasts, causing her to blush terribly from the attention.

Spinning...spinning...spinning, they went around the dance floor, her golden hair lifting from her shoulders, her eyes filled with laughter.

Breathless, she let Bruce lead her from the dance floor out onto the terrace, and then down a flight of stairs to a garden of exotic fragrances. In the darkness he drew her into his arms and touched her lips wonderingly with his mouth, causing sweet currents of desire to flood through her.

When his hand went to her breast, his fingertips caressing the exposed flesh, her breath was stolen away by the inflaming passion within her.

And then he led her farther away from the music and laughter of the crowd, into the shadows of tall, graceful pines. Murmuring her name and how much he loved her, he unbuttoned her dress and smoothed it and her undergarments away, leaving her satiny nude before him. Trembling, she closed her eyes and let him have his way with her, his lips setting fires along her flesh as he kissed first her lips, then her breasts, then lower...

Suddenly her dream changed. She no longer felt the pleasure of Bruce's lips on her body. Gunfire exploded around her. Her nostrils burned with the stench of gunpowder. Her gaze was frozen on her father as he crumpled to the floor, then on her mother who lay in a pool of blood....

Screams awakened her with a start, and she soon realized they were her own. She looked wildly up into dark, troubled eyes as Bruce held her at arm's length and stared down at her.

"Katie Lee, you must've been having a nightmare," Bruce said, drawing her into his arms, holding her tightly. He began stroking his fingers through her hair, his heart aching as she continued to sob against his chest.

"You're going to be all right," he crooned. "You might have these terrible dreams for some time. I'm sorry, Katie Lee. So very, very sorry."

Katie Lee clung to him, gradually recalling the sweet part of her dream. Her fright eased; her tears slowed. Dancing with Bruce had seemed so real. His kisses and embraces even now sent a spark of pleasure through her, flooding her senses with a warm sweetness.

Looking up into his eyes, eyes that were filled with concern, Katie Lee dared to move her face closer to his, and then let her tongue brush his lips lightly.

She smiled up at him when she heard his harsh intake of breath, understanding that she was surprising him with her boldness. It was something she could not explain even to herself. She ached for Bruce in ways she had never ached before. And she needed something at this moment to help her to put all sadness behind her. In her dream she had discovered exactly what that something was. It was Bruce and his love for her. She would not let guilt stand in the way of what she was offering him tonight.

She loved him. Oh, how she loved him. . . .

"Katie Lee?" Bruce whispered against her lips. "You know how I want you...how I've wanted you since the moment I first saw you. If you don't stop, I won't be responsible—"

Katie Lee placed a forefinger to his lips, silencing his words. "Bruce, love me," she murmured, her pulse racing wildly. "Please...love...me."

Bruce's mouth went dry and his heart raced. "Katie Lee, do you know what you are asking?" he inquired hoarsely.

She blinked her eyes nervously. "Bruce, if you don't kiss me now and hold me, I may change my mind," she said, her fingers trembling as she began tracing the masculine planes of his face. "Never have I so boldly asked...."

Bruce took her hand from his face and kissed the tips of her fingers, then drew each one individually between his lips to suck on them. Katie Lee forgot what she was trying to say as a strange heat invaded the juncture of her thighs. She was suddenly stunned by the intensity of her feelings.

Their lips met in a passionate kiss, and his hands moved between their bodies to curve over her breasts, kneading them through the cotton of her dress.

Her soft cry of passion fired his insides into a raging inferno. He placed his hands at Katie Lee's waist and laid her on the ground. Continuing to kiss her, he began unfastening her dress and slowly lowered it to her waist.

Soon not only the dress but also her undergarments were bunched over her hips, exposing her satiny white, heaving breasts.

Moving to straddle her, Bruce looked down at her with passion-filled eyes, then bent his lips to one of her breasts and flicked his tongue around its nipple, causing it to stiffen into a taut tip. This time her cry was one of unleashed pleasure.

Katie Lee writhed on the grass, not feeling the coldness of the night, aware only of the heat flowing through her veins. Bruce reverently breathed her name as he bent closer to her, his mouth once more finding her lips in a fiery kiss, one hand kneading a breast while the other swept lower to continue smoothing her clothes down her hips.

Katie Lee's mind was spinning. She had guessed that being with Bruce in this way would be rapturous, but never had she expected anything so sweetly wonderful as these feelings that he was arousing inside her. He knew the right places to touch. He knew how to touch. When he found the juncture of her thighs and began to caress the core of her womanhood, a moan of pleasure erupted from the depths of her being. She was now mindless, feeling only his love, his beautiful, sensuous love.

Bruce drew momentarily away from her, his eyes dark as he looked down at her. He cupped each of her breasts, his thumb and forefinger circling the nipples. ''Darling, are you sure you want this?'' he asked, his brow furrowing. "You must be sure, so that you won't hate me once it is over."

Katie Lee smiled up at Bruce, touched by his concern. "You are so gallant," she murmured, melting as his hands continued to set her aglow inside. "What other man would demand to know that it was all right to make love to a woman who has already shown that she is willing?"

She threw her arms around his neck and drew his lips to her own. "Please don't stop being the gentleman that you are," she said, kissing him softly. "And, darling, I am more sure about what I am doing at this moment than perhaps any other moment in my life. Please make love to me, Bruce. I want you so badly."

He placed his arms around her and drew her close, kissing her with an exquisite tenderness. Then he rose to stand over her and began unbuttoning his shirt, all the while looking down at her, his heart racing out of control.

The moonlight streamed through a break in the trees overhead, and the tantalizing curves and valleys of Katie Lee's exquisite body gleamed under the silver rays. Never had Bruce seen such a woman. Her body was slim and sinuous, with long, tapering calves and silken thighs. Her waist was narrow and supple, her hips were perfectly rounded, her breasts full and ripe.

Below the gentle curve of her stomach lay the patch of golden hair at the juncture of her thighs, where a promise of heaven lay waiting for him....

Katie Lee's breathing quickened as she watched Bruce remove his clothes. He tossed aside his shirt, revealing wide shoulders that tapered to narrow hips, a hard, flat stomach and a sleekly muscled chest with curling hair. Then he lowered his breeches.

Katie Lee clenched her fingers into tight fists at her sides; desire shot through her at her first sight of a man fully unclothed. Bruce's manhood was swollen with need; it was much larger than Katie Lee had imagined a man would be. Though she wanted him now more than ever, her body tensed with fright.

Seeing fear fill Katie Lee's eyes at the sight of him made Bruce wary. He was suddenly afraid himself, for he was about to make love to a virgin. But all of this would be put right, once they reached Seattle and he made her his wife. He would not only be the first man to make love with her... but the last.

Moving to his knees and straddling her once more, Bruce wrapped his arms around her and eased his body fully over hers. Feeling the warm silk of her flesh against the entire length of his body made his blood quicken and his loins throb unmercifully.

But he must take his time. He must not rush things....

"I love you, Katie Lee," Bruce whispered, aware that he had never said this to a woman before.

With his mouth he forced her lips apart, then kissed her, growing more and more passionate. Eager to pleasure her, he caressed her breast while once again stroking the core of her womanhood, readying her for his first thrust. His whole body throbbed with need. His head was reeling, his pulse racing....

And Katie Lee was filled with wondrous desire, acutely aware of his body, of the strength of his manhood as it lay warm and velvet soft against her thigh. Strange how it pulsed against her flesh. Her lips quivered with the passion of his kiss, her breast throbbed where his fingers continued to knead and fondle.

But she was most alive under the ministrations of his other hand. She could not help but arch her hips, drawing his hand closer to her, the friction of his fingers creating a sensation too wonderful to be real.

She clung to his neck, returning his kiss with abandon, then tensed when she felt him shift his body; now his manhood was probing where his fingers had just been.

Catching her breath, opening her eyes wide and easing her lips from his mouth, Katie Lee started to question Bruce, but was stopped by another heated kiss as he slowly began to insert his hardness inside her. He locked his arms around her waist and held her tightly to himself and his lips kept her mouth sealed as he thrust once. Now he was deep inside her, the momentary pain searing in its fiery assault.

And then the pain began to change to a wondrous curling heat that spread within her. She clung to Bruce, lifting her hips to meet his every eager stroke, her heart pounding from the ecstasy.

Bruce moved his lips from her mouth to rain kisses along the soft planes of her face. "Darling, darling..." he whispered, breathless with the building pleasure. "How I love you. I shall always love you."

Katie Lee's lips parted in a leisurely, pleasurable sigh, and she closed her eyes, reeling with intense pleasure. "As I also love you," she whispered, twining her fingers through his hair. She wrapped her legs around him, drawing him still closer.

They rocked together feverishly, one body, one soul.

"I can't hold back any longer," Bruce finally whispered, his breath warm on Katie Lee's ear. "Darling, let yourself go. Enjoy it with me. Experience the pleasure that we have brought to one another."

Perspiration suddenly dampened Katie Lee's brow as her breathing grew short and raspy. She had never known such sweet rapture, such glorious moments.

She felt her fingernails dig into Bruce's back as she took a deep breath, then let her body explode with passion. Sparks of bliss overpowered her, making her become momentarily light-headed. What ensued was wonderfully fulfilling; she was left with a peaceful lethargy that could be compared to nothing else she had ever felt before. Surely she could never have the same euphoric experience again. Love like this could happen but once in a lifetime.

When Bruce began to groan and cling to her with all of his might, his body trembling violently, she believed that he was enjoying the moment as much as she, and was glad.

She clung to him, letting him take from her all the pleasure he wanted, then caressed his perspiration-laced back as he grew quiet.

"It was beautifully sweet, Bruce," Katie Lee whispered, blushing at the thought of what she had just shared with him.

"I hope I didn't hurt you too much," Bruce said softly. "The first time is sometimes very hard on a woman." He smoothed back a strand of her golden hair from her eyes.

"The pain was forgotten in an instant," Katie Lee confessed, lowering her eyes, suddenly shy again. "After that I was filled with only ecstasy."

Bruce embraced her again, reveling in the touch of her breasts against his chest. "I'm so glad," he murmured. He paused for a moment, then looked into her eyes. "Darling, there is something I would like to talk to you about. There is a question I need to ask you again. It is about . . ."

Katie Lee tensed. She knew what the question would be. He wanted her to marry him.

Quickly placing a hand over his mouth, she looked innocently up at him.

"Please, let's not talk tonight about anything else," she murmured. "I am suddenly so tired, Bruce. And if you plan to arise quite early, I do need to get some sleep. Please understand."

Bruce looked down at her questioningly and took her hand away from his mouth. She surely knew what was on his mind. It should be, after they had committed so much to each other already.

Perhaps her virginity was not a matter that could be talked about so openly. Most likely she didn't want to discuss what they had shared, nor the fact that she was no longer pure.

"If you don't want to talk anymore tonight, we won't talk," Bruce said, moving away from her. A cold breeze made him shiver. He looked down at Katie Lee, realizing how cold she must be. Scooping up her clothes, he handed them to her, then reached for his own and dressed.

Shivering, Katie Lee hurried into her clothes. She was glad when Bruce went to the camp fire and placed more wood on the dying embers. She watched the shadows of the flames dance on his handsome face, loving him so much that she was not sure she could deny his proposal of marriage.

But she knew too much about marriage, had seen how it was with her own mother. A wife had no freedom whatsoever.

Chapter Nine

The horse's neighing awakened Katie Lee. She looked slowly around her, having momentarily forgotten where she was and how she had gotten there. The full moon illuminated the twisted limbs of the trees overhead, transforming them into grotesque shapes.

Then she became acutely aware of the hard ground beneath her and of her aching body. She looked to her side, now recalling that she'd fallen asleep in Bruce's arms.

"Bruce?" she gasped, seeing him gone. She rose on one elbow, searching the forest around her. The freshly stoked camp fire burned bright, its flames warming her face.

"So Sleeping Beauty has awakened?" Bruce said, stepping out of the darkest depths of the forest.

Startled, yet very relieved, Katie Lee turned and saw him. "For a moment I thought I was totally alone," she said, quickly noticing how he held his hands hidden behind him. She gave him a slow smile, expecting flowers. "What have you got? Or is it not for me?"

As she looked up, moved to passion at the mere sight of him, her thoughts drifted back to only a few hours ago, when he had taught her the meaning of rapture. It had given her the peace that she had needed to get her through the night.

As he looked down at her now, his eyes reflected a gentle happiness. "I've brought you your breakfast," Bruce said, nodding toward the fire. "Come and sit beside the fire with me. Let's get your bones warmed and your stomach comfortable before we get back on that horse. It's going to be hard enough on you, as it is. We have a ways to go before getting to the next stagecoach stop."

Katie Lee arched an eyebrow. "Breakfast?" she inquired, rising to her feet. She combed her fingers through her hair in an attempt to work out the tangles. "Fish?"

"No, it's not fish," Bruce said, laughing softly. She joined him at his side and they walked on to the fire. Placing his hands in front of him, he revealed two great bunches of grapes. "But something else quite pleasing to the tongue."

Katie Lee's mouth watered. She took a bunch, smiling a silent thank-you to Bruce, then plucked a grape from the stem and popped it into her mouth.

"Katie Lee, when we reach the next stop, you will be boarding the stagecoach," Bruce said, nervously fingering the grapes instead of eating them. "And so will I. We won't have privacy to talk again until we reach Seattle. I would like to take advantage of our privacy now to speak of some things with you.''

Katie Lee tensed; her throat constricted and she almost choked on the sweet grapes. She coughed and swallowed hard, fighting to regain her composure.

Looking over at Bruce, she saw his eyes on her. Bashfully she lowered her lashes. If only she could say yes to what he was going to ask of her, surely her life would be much simpler.

But until now a simple life was all she had had! There had to be more to life than cooking, scrubbing floors and sewing.

''What things, Bruce?'' she asked reluctantly. How she hated to disappoint and hurt him. She did so love him.

''I would like to speak of both our futures,'' Bruce said, puzzled by her sudden quiet. Only moments before she had sparkled with life. ''Katie Lee,'' he continued, not letting anything dissuade him, ''you know that I am soon to fulfill one of my dreams— that of being in part ownership of Cabot Sawmill in Seattle.''

He cleared his throat nervously and laid the grapes aside. He turned to her then and intertwined his fingers with hers, glad that she was finally looking up at him.

''The other dream of mine is to make you my wife,'' he said huskily. ''I want to take care of you. I want to cherish you. You will never want for another thing. I will build you a beautiful house in Seattle. We will have social affairs that will be the talk of the town!''

Katie Lee was breathless. What woman could ask for more than what Bruce was offering? It all sounded divinely perfect!

Yet that one vital link was missing—her chance to see how it felt to be free of anyone's bonds.

Bruce saw her hesitation. For some reason she was torn, and it made no sense whatsoever. She had proven her love for him. He had done the same for her. Why would she find it so hard to accept what he was offering?

He scooted closer and enveloped her within his arms, drawing her to him. He kissed her gently, then pleaded as he looked down at her. "Marry me, Katie Lee," he whispered, his voice breaking with emotion. "As soon as we reach Seattle, marry me."

She looked up at Bruce, mesmerized by his nearness, fighting to keep her senses.

How could she make him understand? She wanted to prove to herself that she was a strong woman, a woman who did not have to depend on a man to survive in this world.

Bruce felt her tense in his arms and became fearful of her continued hesitation. He looked at her questioningly.

"Katie Lee, why don't you answer me?" he asked thickly. "You said that you love me. You know that I love you. What more is needed to help you make a decision? I am offering you the world, darling. The world!"

Katie Lee's face grew hot. She swallowed hard, then nodded. "I know what you are offering," she murmured. "And I *do* love you. But..."

She stopped trying to find the words. She did not want to hurt him.

"But what?" Bruce prodded, frowning down at her. "My God, you're all alone in the world now, except for me. How can you even hesitate to agree?"

Katie Lee pulled at Bruce's fingers, freeing herself from his grasp. She rose to her feet, turning her back to him as she stared pensively down into the flames of the camp fire. "Yes, I am alone, and yes, I love you," she said, her voice drawn. "But I don't want to agree to marriage at this time."

She turned slowly as he rose to face her. She grimaced when she saw a strange fire burning in his eyes. He was more angry than hurt. Perhaps that was best.

"How can you say that?" Bruce demanded, nervously raking his fingers through his hair. "God, Katie Lee, I don't understand. What is it you want out of life?"

Katie Lee lowered her eyes and fidgeted with the gathers of her dress. "Perhaps I don't even know myself," she murmured, "but I must be given the chance to find out. I would like to see if I am capable of making my own way in the world. My mama...she was never given that chance. She got married and...and that was all she ever had.''

She slowly raised her eyes. "And Mama was never all that content, Bruce," she added, her voice breaking.

Bruce grabbed her by the arms. "You are not your mama," he growled. "And by damn, I am certainly not like your father. I have sworn that you would be treated well. Though married, you will be given a chance to have a life of your own. You will be able to make friends. You can visit with them daily."

Katie Lee shook her head. "Bruce, it wouldn't be the same," she said softly. "I would like to see if I can make my way in the world alone."

She reached a hand to his cheek. "And once I've proven this to myself, then I would like to consider marrying you," she added, smiling up at him.

Frustrated, Bruce pulled away from her. "Well, thank you, but no thank you," he growled, kicking dirt onto the fire to snuff out the flames. "It's time to go. The world is waiting for you, Katie Lee. Let's see if you can go and conquer it."

Stunned by the depth of his anger, Katie Lee took a step back. She watched him make sure the fire was out, then go to the horse and grab its reins. When he looked at her, his eyes were filled with a dark fury. She felt herself grow weak at the knees; there was a strange emptiness at the pit of her stomach. Forcing herself to be strong, she lifted the hem of her skirt and moved toward the horse.

Bruce's hand was cold and firm when he reached out to help Katie Lee mount the horse. His jaw was tight, his lips were drawn in a stern line as he stared at her for a moment, then turned his back to her and swung himself onto the horse.

Clinging to Bruce, Katie Lee lurched clumsily as they sped through the forest and out onto the dirt road.

Her hair flew in the wind, her skirt was hiked high above her knees and her eyes stung from unshed tears....

The sky was streaked in a purplish-red haze as the sun began to creep up over the horizon. Katie Lee felt drained of all emotion; the ride thus far had been void of talk or reassurance. It was all she could do to keep her grip and hold back tears of sorrow and frustration.

Then Bruce finally broke the silence. "I see smoke from a chimney through the trees ahead," he said dryly. "I think we're just about there. I hope the stagecoach hasn't left. If we timed this right, everyone should be sitting down at the breakfast table."

Bruce's thoughts turned to Leonard Conty. His insides grew cold; the chances were great that Conty would once again offer Katie Lee a job. In her state of mind she would most surely accept. If she did, she certainly would learn the ways of the world—all of them!

Yes, she could be proving that she could make her own way, but in the meantime, if she agreed to work for Leonard Conty, Bruce decided that he would have to give her a bit of advice, whether she wanted it or not. If he didn't and anything happened to her, he would blame himself.

The two-story inn came into view as the road wound through a vast cover of trees. Sadness overwhelmed Katie Lee as she looked at a structure that was not much different from the one her father had been so proud of having built. If she closed her eyes she could envision her mother busy in the kitchen, the whole house filled with aromas that made one's stomach growl. Her father would be welcoming a stagecoach, a pipe hanging from the corner of his mouth.

A sob rose from deep within her as she forced these memories from her mind. She coughed and swallowed hard, blinking back tears. The past was past. To survive she must stay alert, watch everything, be wary of everyone....

Bruce guided his horse into the driveway that led to the inn, then reined in his mount beside a hitching rail. He sighed with relief when he saw that out by the barn the horses were being attached to the stagecoach. He looked toward the house as he dismounted and helped Katie Lee to the ground. The sound of his horse had attracted several people to the windows—and among them was Leonard Conty.

"Damn it," Bruce said beneath his breath, glancing down at Katie Lee, who seemed to be too busy straightening the skirt of her dress to notice the theater owner.

Katie Lee glanced quickly up at Bruce, having heard him whisper something. "Were you speaking to me?" she asked softly. "Are you finally deciding not to be mad at me?"

Bruce felt himself waver. Katie Lee's face was so innocent, her eyes appeared so trusting as she looked up at him. He could not help but smile down at her. "No," he said, taking her hands and squeezing them affectionately. "I'm no longer angry. How could I stay angry with you? God, Katie Lee I love you too much."

The sound of the inn's front door being opened drew Katie Lee and Bruce apart. They turned and faced several people who were looking at them with deep concern in their eyes.

Katie Lee recognized the woman. She had come with a group of ladies to work on a quilt with her mother not many months before and had stayed the night, since there were so many miles between their residences. She was Karen Seymour, wife of the innkeeper here.

Travis Seymour, Karen's husband, then stepped forward.

"Katie Lee? Katie Lee Holden?" he said, moving to stand before her, worry in the depths of his dark eyes. "Why are you here? There was some discussion at the supper table last night about a passenger—a Bruce Cabot—leaving the stagecoach because he had seen Indians. No one had taken him seriously. Heaven forbid, Katie Lee, don't tell me that his fears were founded.''

Bruce intervened. ''Sir, I am Bruce Cabot,'' he said firmly, shaking the other man's hand. He gave Katie Lee a quick glance as he dropped his hand to his side, then looked back at the innkeeper. ''Sir, the news is not good at all. There was a massacre. Katie Lee is the only survivor.''

''No!'' Travis Seymour gasped, paling. ''Don't tell me it was the Indians! They have been pests at times, but never have I felt threatened by them.''

''Perhaps because you have not threatened them,'' Bruce said, wrapping an arm around Katie Lee's waist, drawing her to his side. He looked down at her. ''You're very lucky to be seeing this young lady standing here. She was hiding when the Indians went into the inn. They left without her.''

Karen Seymour went to Katie Lee and drew her away from Bruce. ''You dear child,'' she said softly. ''Come on into the house. You poor dear!''

Karen's short, stocky build reminded Katie Lee of her mother. A knot formed in her throat. She swallowed hard and blinked back the tears that were threatening to spill from her eyes.

As she walked away from the men who had encircled Bruce to hear his tale of the massacre, Katie Lee was aware of one passenger who had not joined the others. He was standing at the window, watching her with a half smile. Leonard Conty.

A chill coursed through her veins. There was so much about that man that she did not like, but she could not put her finger on any particular reason. Then his smile widened as he gave her a mock salute, and she trembled when her gaze met and held his.

Chapter Ten

Katie Lee was led into the inn, where the fragrant aroma of baking bread reminded her of home. Battling to control her emotions, she was silent when Karen Seymour moved from her side and turned her to peer into her face. The older woman, her gray hair drawn back from her full face, looked Katie Lee up and down with wide-set green eyes.

"I'm not going to ask you to explain about what happened back there at your home," Karen said. "There is no need in putting you through the experience again." She brushed a few leaves from the skirt of Katie Lee's soiled dress. "What I'd like to do is see you get into something more presentable, and then we can talk about your future."

She gave Katie Lee a wavering look. "Dear, you come on upstairs with me to my room. I think I have a dress you can change into." She smiled softly. "You see, I haven't always been this heavy. Only a few years ago I was as thin and pretty as you. Cooking puts on the pounds. The food is there, always tempting a soul with its smells. And, Lord, do I love the fresh butter I churn each day.''

She patted Katie Lee's arm. ''You've got to stay away from the kitchen as much as possible,'' she said, laughing. ''Or, honey, you'll get as round as I am, and I bet you can guess that I'm not all that proud of my figure.''

Katie Lee tensed. Surely she wasn't wrong to want to delay marriage—and a thickening waist. If only Bruce would understand and be patient.

Glancing toward the dining room, Katie Lee saw steaming platters of eggs, sausage and bacon on the table that everyone had abandoned upon her and Bruce's arrival. To her embarrassment, her stomach growled hungrily.

''My child, you're hungry, aren't you?'' Karen said, placing a hand on Katie Lee's arm. ''I tell you what. Let's go to my room and let you choose a dress from my trunk, and while I'm pressing it with a hot iron, you can eat some breakfast. By then your young man should have satisfied everyone's curiosity.''

Karen gave Katie Lee a curious stare. ''What is his name again?'' she asked.

Katie Lee fought the blush that she felt warming her cheeks. ''His name is Bruce Cabot. He is a very brave man,'' she blurted. ''I had only met him that once, when he came with the stagecoach and stayed the night at our inn. If he hadn't suspected danger when he saw Chief Black Raven...''

Karen blanched. She placed a hand to her throat. "Chief Black Raven?" she gasped. "Is he the one who...who—?"

Katie Lee did not want to hear Karen say the word "murder," so she interrupted her. "Yes, he is the one," she said, lowering her eyes, at least glad that her mention of Bruce had been forgotten.

"Why, he has come into our home quite often," Karen said, placing a hand to Katie Lee's elbow as she guided her up the staircase. "Many a time I have given him food. He especially likes—"

"Bread," Katie Lee said quickly. "Yes, bread was his favorite in my mother's kitchen, also."

Reaching the second-floor landing, Karen turned Katie Lee to face her. "We'll not speak of the savage again," she said blandly. "Nor of what he did. Let's go and choose a dress for you. It would delight me to see you wear what I once fit into."

Katie Lee welcomed the warm friendship Karen was offering. She smiled and nodded as she followed Karen Seymour into a bedroom where a huge trunk sat at the foot of a high oak four-poster.

Karen bent to open it, and Katie Lee knelt beside her, suddenly breathless at the sight of the assortment of colorful lace-trimmed dresses she saw there. Most had low necklines and fully gathered waists.

Karen Seymour pulled one of the dresses from the trunk and rose to her feet. Holding it out before her, she went to the pier glass that stood beside the window and eyed herself and the dress, clearly dreaming of when she had been able to fit into it. "I loved this dress," she murmured. "Back in Boston when I attended balls, this was my favorite. But after I got married, I..."

Her voice faded, and Katie Lee realized that this woman, too, had been a victim of marriage. Watching her now, Katie Lee felt her own resolve strengthen. More than ever she was determined to seek her own destiny.

Karen swung around and hurried to Katie Lee. She forced the dress into her hands. "This would look lovely on you," she said, her eyes brimming with tears. "I'm sure it would fit you, but maybe you should try it on to make sure."

Katie Lee held the dress up before her, then next to her body, sizing it up. "I do believe it will do just fine," she said, but her gaze wavered as she looked toward Karen. "Surely you don't want to part with it. It is *so* beautiful."

"Dear, in a sense I won't be parting with it," Karen said, patting Katie Lee on the cheek. "You'll be here...living with us. I'll still be able to see the dress whenever I like. Later on today you can even go through the rest of the clothes. I believe we can fill up a wardrobe quite fast for you. You'll be the prettiest thing alive when you meet the stagecoaches each day. All the gents will plumb fall head over heels in love with you." She pinched Katie Lee's cheek. "And one of these days one of those gents will sweep you right off your feet and ask you to marry him. I'll have to look him over as if I were your real mother, Katie Lee, giving approval.''

Katie Lee was stunned by what Karen Seymour was saying. Without even talking it over with her, Karen was taking it for granted that Katie Lee was going to live with her, since she was now orphaned.

Katie Lee blinked nervously and shook her head. Slowly she eased the dress away from her body, now afraid to accept it, fearing that a commitment of sorts would go with it. ''Mrs. Seymour, perhaps it would be best if I don't take the dress, though it *is* beautiful and I appreciate your kindness,'' she said, trying to push the dress into Karen's arms. She cleared her throat nervously. ''You see, Mrs. Seymour, I don't plan to stay.''

The older woman blanched. She dropped her arms to her sides, refusing to take the dress. ''What do you mean?'' she asked dryly. ''My dear child, where are you going? Do you have relatives in Seattle? Is that what you are tryin' to tell me?''

Feeling awkward, Katie Lee laid the dress across the bed and went to the window to peer down at the stagecoach that was being readied. Bruce's strawberry roan was reined to the hitching rail. The front porch was quiet, the men having returned to the house to resume eating their breakfast. She placed a hand to her stomach as the thought of food made it growl again.

With an abrupt movement, she turned on a heel to face Karen. ''No, Mrs. Seymour, I have no relatives in Seattle," she said, seeing the shock in Karen's green eyes. "I plan to go there, alone, to seek my own way in the world. Seattle is a large city. Surely there are places of employment for women."

Katie Lee did not dare mention Conty Theater. Most likely it would have the same effect on this genteel lady as it would have had on Madge and Geoffrey Holden.

Katie Lee would not let herself even consider the possible ill effects of singing for a living. And anyhow, she had not yet decided that she would be a singer.

"My child, what on earth could you be expecting to do that...that...would be respectable?" Karen gasped, placing a hand to her throat. "Most decent women are in the home—married and raising children. What kind of a job could you even get?"

At the doubt in Karen's voice, Katie Lee's anger became barely controllable. She wanted to shout that someone had thought she was a wonderful singer. What was so wrong with that sort of employment?

But she could see that she had shocked Karen enough, and thought better of speaking so openly.

"I'm not sure, but I guess I shall be forced to find out, won't I?" Katie Lee said, lifting her chin proudly.

Karen shook her head in despair. "Tsk, tsk," she uttered. "You poor child. You just don't know the ways of the large cities. They can swallow a young thing like you whole. I beg you to change your mind."

"I cannot be a burden on you or anyone," Katie Lee said. "What has been thrust on me is not of your doing. There is no need for you to have another mouth to feed. I shall see to that myself."

Clasping her hands before her, Karen silently studied Katie Lee, then shook her head. "Very well," she murmured. "I see there is no arguing you out of it." She looked at the discarded dress on the bed. "I still want you to have the dress. I would like to know that you look your best when you enter the city. Appearances mean a lot when one is seeking employment."

"If you are sure you wish to part with it, I will gladly take it," Katie Lee said, glancing down at her own soiled and wrinkled dress. "I so appreciate your kindness."

Karen draped the dress over her arm and twined the fingers of her free hand through Katie Lee's as she guided her from the room. "You must set yourself down at the breakfast table and get your fill, and I will iron the dress," she said, breathing heavily as they descended the stairs. "It won't take but a few minutes to heat the iron on the stove. The stagecoach will simply have to wait until you change into it." She smiled at Katie Lee. "But, of course, I don't think the gents traveling aboard the stagecoach will mind the wait at all. You will brighten their journey."

Katie Lee looked at Karen, her lips quivering in a nervous smile as she realized that unpleasantness would accompany the trip to Seattle. Bruce and Leonard Conty did not hide the fact that they had no love for one another.

And then there were the two men who were accompanying Conty—and the bulldog.

The stagecoach would be crowded and hot, a perfect place for tempers to flare....

As Karen quickly set a place for her at the dining-room table, the dress still draped over one arm, Katie Lee felt all eyes turn to her. She gulped hard, feeling as though she had been thrust into a lion's den. Bruce and Leonard Conty were obviously tense. Fire flashed in their eyes as she settled down at the table while Karen piled a generous helping of eggs, bacon and sausage on the platter, then scooted the huge crock of biscuits closer to her.

"There's plenty of butter and jams," Karen said, moving toward the kitchen door. "You eat well, Katie Lee. You've many a mile to go before reaching Seattle. I'll be ironing the dress if you need me for anything."

"Yes, ma'am," Katie Lee murmured as the coffeepot was handed down the line of men. She smiled awkwardly as Leonard Conty took it upon himself to reach across the table and take the coffeepot before it reached her, then lean over the table from where he sat to pour her a cup.

"Thank you," she said, smiling bashfully at him, again reminded of his riches by the diamonds she saw in his cravat and on each hand. But it was his pitiless gray eyes that unnerved her. They appeared bottomless, perhaps mirroring his soul!

"Anytime," Leonard Conty replied, chuckling. He sat down again, reaching for a biscuit and slapping a huge portion of butter and strawberry jam on it. Then he took a bite, his eyes still on Katie Lee, plainly studying her. He wiped his fleshy mouth with a napkin, then let his gaze move over her innocent pink face, her wide blue eyes and sensuous lips. Her hair had a rich, golden sheen, and if brushed and combed, it would be beautiful.

Leonard Conty could hardly contain his glee at his latest find. Not only her singing would draw the crowds. The men would come from miles around to see this woman with the soul and face of an angel!

He must have her for his theater. He must!

"I am sorry to hear about the misfortune of your family," he began smoothly, the weight of his bulldog on one of his feet a reminder that his constant companion was beneath the table. He grabbed a piece of sausage and let the bulldog eat it out of his hand. Then he spread his fingers so that the dog could lick the grease from his palm.

"That is kind of you, sir," Katie Lee replied, suddenly not as hungry as she had thought she was. She picked at her food, made uncomfortable by the watchful eye of Bruce and the attentions of the theater owner.

"And what are your plans now?" Leonard Conty asked, patting his dog and then wiping his hands on his napkin.

"What's it to you?" Bruce interjected. "I would suggest you leave Miss Holden alone and let her eat. Like Mrs. Seymour said—it's a long time between meals here in these parts."

Conty glowered at Bruce, then smiled smugly at Katie Lee. "Miss Holden, it seems Bruce Cabot thinks he owns you and won't let you answer for yourself, so all I can say is that the offer still stands for you to sing at my establishment in Seattle," he said, his voice lower and more serious than usual. "It's hard to find employment in Seattle, especially since you are a lady. I am making it easy on you. I am giving you the chance to begin a career without you even having to search for one." His rings flashed in the light of the morning sunshine filtering through the dining room window. "Like I said, follow me and you'll wear diamonds."

Katie Lee gaped openly at the precious stones, her heart pounding. Never had she seen anything like them. But it was not so much the lure of the gems as the certainty of employment that made her respond without much thought.

She gave Bruce a troubled glance, then looked at Leonard Conty again. She squared her shoulders.

"Sir, I would be glad to accept your invitation," she blurted. "I thank you for the opportunity."

Bruce almost choked. His eyes widened; his throat went dry. Scooting the chair back so quickly that it fell back with a loud thud, he stomped around to where Katie Lee was sitting and grabbed her by one wrist, urging her to her feet.

"We have a few things to discuss, Katie Lee," he said. Then, staring angrily at Conty, "and as for you, you son of a bitch, I've warned you about doing this."

Katie Lee felt her face drain of color as she was half dragged from the room. She had expected Bruce to be angry, but never had she thought that he would go to these lengths.

"Bruce, you're hurting me!" she cried; his grip on her wrist was so firm that the circulation was almost cut off from her fingers. She stumbled into the parlor alongside him, glad there was no one in the room to witness her further humiliation. "Please unhand me, Bruce. Please!"

Stopping, Bruce swung Katie Lee around to face him. He glowered down at her, now holding both her wrists to his chest. "You don't know what you're getting yourself into with Conty," he growled, his golden-brown eyes two points of fire. "God, Katie Lee, I'm trying my damnedest to figure you out. Perhaps you are in a state of shock over your parents' deaths. I don't know. You know you love me but refuse to marry me, and then you decide to perform on the stage of Conty's theater!''

"Bruce, I believe you are overreacting to my wanting to have a measure of independence in my life before . . . before I settle down into marriage," Katie Lee said, her voice trembling. "As for singing in Leonard Conty's theater—if things don't go well for me, I shall stop. But I at least want the chance. I think it could be fun. Lord, Bruce, I haven't had much fun."

Bruce dropped his hands. He raked his fingers nervously through his hair. "Katie Lee, perhaps you need someone to define what fun should be," he said thickly. "Singing in what some consider a whorehouse would end up being way less than fun."

"Whorehouse?" Katie Lee gasped, her eyes wide.

"More than singing goes on in Leonard Conty's theaters," Bruce growled. "In the box seats behind the curtains, other acts you would not want to see are performed. Need I say more?"

"It seems gossip has spread far and wide about what my women do behind the curtains—gossip that is all false," Leonard Conty said, walking into the room, his leashed dog beside him. "Let me clear up the gossip for at least you, Miss Holden. In my establishments there are women who cater to men by entertaining them in the box seats, while encouraging them to buy just a little more of my liquor. This is done all in innocence. The women sit with the gentlemen and look pretty. Now that should come as no shock to you or anyone. It is practiced in some of the fanciest establishments across the country. Why shouldn't I allow it in mine?''

Bruce stepped between Katie Lee and Leonard, blocking her view of the theater owner. He doubled his fists at his sides. ''Katie Lee, I forbid you to accept Conty's offer,'' he said flatly. ''I forbid it!''

A slow rage began to scorch Katie Lee's insides. How dare he! Although they had shared so much in the short time they had known one another, he had no right to behave as . . . as her . . .

''Bruce Cabot, you are sounding just like my father!'' she said, lifting her chin defiantly. ''You don't have the right to tell me what I can or cannot do!''

She took a bold step around Bruce and squarely faced Conty. Breathless, fear gripping her insides, she felt that she had no choice but to prove her independence to herself, and most definitely to Bruce!

''Mr. Conty, as I said a moment ago, I would consider it an honor to be able to perform in your theater,'' she said, her voice quavering. ''That is, if you truly believe my talent is worthy of such a privilege. I have sung only for my own pleasure. It may be difficult for me to sing on the stage in front of so many strangers.''

Conty reached for her hand and held it affectionately. ''Now let us not enter into this agreement so filled with doubts,'' he said, giving Bruce a look of triumph over Katie Lee's shoulder. ''I have faith that you will be the talk of Seattle.''

Bruce clamped his lips shut, now resigned to the fact that no matter what he did, Katie Lee was determined to go through with this farce. All he could do was be close by and keep as good a watch on her as possible. He only hoped that Conty wasn't right. He didn't want Katie Lee to become "the talk of Seattle." If she was ever to become his wife, he wanted her to retain an untarnished reputation.

He had his own plans for her, plans that were righteous.

"Child, here's the dress all ironed and pretty," Karen Seymour said, whisking into the room, holding the dress out before her. "Katie Lee, you'd best hurry and get dressed. They are readying the stagecoach for leaving." She gave Katie Lee a pleading look. "That is, unless you've changed your mind and will stay with us. Seattle is not the place to be without family."

Leonard Conty placed a thick arm around Katie Lee's waist and looked down at her with a possessive air. "Ma'am, she may not have family, but she has me," he said smugly. He looked at Karen. Seeing how his statement had caused her to grow pale, he laughed throatily. "No. It's not what you think. She's not going to be my bride. She's going to become a performer on the stage of my theater in Seattle. She's going to sing her little heart out for all of Seattle." Once more he looked down at Katie Lee, smiling widely. "She has not only the face, but also the voice of an angel."

Katie Lee's eyes met and held Karen's, an unfamiliar shame engulfing her. Quickly she shook off the unwanted feeling. She had made up her mind. No one would dissuade her. No one.

Chapter Eleven

The silent, strained journey was finally coming to an end. Sitting beside a window, Katie Lee peered out at the outskirts of Seattle. Though she had been there countless times before with her parents to gather supplies for their inn, Katie Lee had been no farther than the hotel, her father having always said that he was protecting her from the riffraff that strolled the streets.

A thrill coursed through her to be back in Seattle. But this time she was going to be able to explore it fully, even become a part of it. She let her gaze absorb it all as the stagecoach moved along Front Street. It was high tide. The waters of Elliott Bay lapped against the timber retaining wall that held the street high and dry above the waterfront.

Since Katie Lee's first visit to the city many years before, Front Street had changed from a stump-strewn, ravine-riddled path to a smooth roadway surfaced with wooden planks and bordered by guardrails and an uneven wooden sidewalk.

As she could see, Seattle was a wooden city built from the forest that gave birth to it. Lush greenery surrounded it on three sides, the fourth being the waters of Puget Sound. The wooden streets and sidewalks were shored up by wooden stilts on the downhill side.

Buildings made mostly of wood lined those streets. Seattle was a hubbub of activity—streetcars rattled along their tracks; horse-drawn carriages and buggies crowded the streets.

In Katie Lee's nostrils there were the strange, exciting smell of saltwater and the aromas of cordage and tar.

A flotilla of sailing ships lay alongside the dock. A first mate bawled orders at a group of sailors, and the loading tackle grunted and whined.

On one bay a fleet of Siwash dugout canoes loaded to the gunwales with mixed families of braves, their "klootchman" squaws and papooses, moved into the harbor. The Indians were singing to the rhythmic beat of their paddles.

With an orchestrated splash they grounded the big dugout canoes in the mud flats near the warehouses.

"Katie Lee, it's not too late to change your mind," Bruce said suddenly, drawing her from her reverie. "I implore you to reconsider this decision of yours to sing at Conty Theater. I cannot stress enough to you how unwise this is."

The sound of Bruce's voice stirred Katie Lee with remembrances of how beautiful it was to be held in his arms and to be kissed by him, and she dared not look his way.

"Katie Lee, you can pretend until hell freezes over that you don't hear me," Bruce growled, placing a finger beneath her chin, forcing her face around so that their eyes could meet. "But, by damn, you do hear and you know that I'm right. Forget this foolishness. Now."

Katie Lee swallowed hard, her eyes wide. "Bruce..." she began, but stopped when the stagecoach came to a sudden halt.

Leonard Conty's eyes gleamed as he looked from Bruce to Katie Lee. "Seems we've arrived," he said, patting his bulldog. "Miss Holden, the first thing we should do is tell the authorities about Chief Black Raven. And then I'll get you checked into one of the finest hotels in the city."

Bruce stared into Leonard's face. "Of course she will owe you nothing in return for your kindnesses?" he accused the other man. "Conty, I wasn't born yesterday. Neither was Katie Lee."

"The young lady will owe me nothing until she receives her first wages," Conty said dryly. "Then she can begin repaying me—a little at a time until eventually she will have paid me in full. All I truly want from her are grand performances on the stage. Cabot, I wager to say that what you have asked of her has not been all that decent. If anyone is guilty of taking advantage of..."

Katie Lee blanched at the lewd implication, then gasped and grew weak at the knees when Bruce could no longer hold his temper and slammed a fist into Leonard's mouth. Within an instant blood trickled freely from the corners of those fleshy lips. The bulldog lurched to its feet, barking and baring its teeth. Bruce grabbed Katie Lee by a wrist, swung the stagecoach door open and half dragged her from it.

"Bruce, what do you think you're doing?" Katie Lee cried as she stepped shakily to the wooden sidewalk and made a feeble attempt at yanking her imprisoned wrist from his viselike grip. "Unhand me, Bruce Cabot. Are you no better than a savage?"

Bruce ignored the taunt. Still holding on to her, he caught his valise as the driver tossed it down to him from the top of the stagecoach where all of the passengers' gear had been strapped in place.

Out of the corner of one eye Bruce saw Leonard's bodyguard and brother alight from both sides of the stagecoach, anger flaring in their eyes. He hurriedly led Katie Lee to the rope that secured his horse to the stagecoach and untied his strawberry roan. Lifting her handily, Bruce settled her on the horse and forced his valise into her unwilling arms before swinging himself up and onto his mount.

"By God, you'd best hang on, because if you don't, you're in for a mighty hard fall!" Bruce shouted, lifting his horse's reins and snapping them against his steed's healthy mane. He looked over at the two angry, advancing men. "I do believe I've got a couple of gents hungering for my hide, don't you?"

Then he chuckled and dug his heels into the flanks of his horse, taking off at a fast gallop. "They'll cool down in time," he shouted. "Seems they have no choice!"

Katie Lee clung to Bruce's waist, embarrassed by the spectacle they made in their hasty flight. Everyone along the sidewalks and streets gaped openly at her fluttering skirt and bared legs.

"Oh, Bruce..." Katie Lee groaned, wisps of her golden hair whipping across her face.

Having left Leonard's henchmen far enough behind, Bruce slowed his horse. He glanced over his shoulder at Katie Lee. "Now it will be *I* who will see to your lodging," he said flatly. "And if I have to keep watch on you all night to keep Conty away from you, I shall. My signature on papers that will put me into partnership with my brother, Alex, can wait another day. Darling, you are all that's important for now."

Katie Lee cast Bruce an angry stare. "Don't call me darling," she told him, pouting. "I'm not your darling. I'm not your anything." She paused and lifted her chin defiantly. "You, Bruce Cabot, are nothing to me."

Bruce looked quickly away from her, weaving his horse in and out of the busy thoroughfare, his eyes focused on a hotel ahead. With any luck, Katie Lee wouldn't put up too much of a fuss in the lobby as he registered them.

Her words cut deep into his heart, yet he knew that they shouldn't. She could not have meant what she had said; it was this compulsion of hers to prove her independence that was causing her to behave so irrationally. It was no mystery as to why she felt the need to prove to herself that she could survive on her own. Hadn't he witnessed how overbearing her father had been? Katie Lee had never been given the freedom to think for herself.

Perhaps he should quit fighting her, give her the chance to do as she wished. Once she got a taste of the real world, surely she would want no part of trying to cope alone.

Bruce guided his horse to a stop before a five-story hotel, its wooden exterior weathered by the sea air, its bright red doors with brass handles flanked by potted plants. Suddenly he felt awkward as he took in the fancy buggies and horse carriages reined at the hitching rail. His would be the only lone horse. He and Katie Lee were in stark contrast to the genteel ladies and gents who were coming and going from the fancy establishment. Though Katie Lee's dress was beautifully trimmed with lace, it was not made of silk or satin and she wore no elegant hat. Bruce was dressed in what was considered the fashion of the day for men, except that he had lost his top hat and cane somewhere along the way, and his clothes were wrinkled and dusty.

Setting his jaw firmly, Bruce dismounted and quickly looped the reins around the hitching post.

Katie Lee took the opportunity to slip quickly from the horse, determined to get away. She dropped the valise and turned to run, but her breath was stolen away when she felt two solid hands on her waist.

"Now where do you think you're going?" Bruce growled, spinning her around to face him. "Katie Lee, if you want to make a scene so bad that your name will appear in the Seattle *Times* tomorrow, just go ahead and scream your fool head off. You may become a celebrity without even stepping one foot onto a stage."

Katie Lee choked back the urge to cry, but decided against it when with one sweep of her eyes she saw a crowd assembling, passersby stopping to gawk at Bruce and herself. She felt a blush rise to her cheeks as she lowered her eyes bashfully, then looked slowly up at Bruce.

"You may have your way with me now," she whispered. "But not later."

"We'll see about that," he said dryly, reaching down with one hand to grab his valise. "For now let's at least act a bit civilized. Crowds love spectacles."

Again Katie Lee looked around her. Though the day was pleasantly warm, some of the women wore fur-trimmed stoles over satin dresses that were very full and long in back. Their hair was styled into sleek chignons, and dramatic hats with plumes graced their heads.

Suddenly Katie Lee was quite aware of her plain cotton dress; yet only a while back she had peered into the mirror at Karen Seymour's house, quite proud of how she looked. It was evident that country and city folk dressed quite differently. And the sullen, snobbish stares of the women who looked at her with distaste warned her to expect a difference in personality as well.

She felt a chill course through her, wondering if she could truly be happy here.

Bruce glanced at Katie Lee, seeing how uncomfortable the gawking was making her. He drew her close. "Let's get out of here," he whispered.

"Why did you bring me to this part of the city if everyone is so...so unfriendly?" Katie Lee asked, holding her chin up as she walked toward the door with Bruce. "There are hotels elsewhere. I don't fit in here at all."

"I wasn't about to ride all over town on horseback with you," Bruce said, grasping the brass doorknob. "This was the closest hotel. It will have to do. Besides, it's not so much that these people are unfriendly as our unconventional arrival. The citizens of Seattle are known to be friendly. From the time Chief Sealth and his Suquamish braves frequented the streets of the city, Seattle has opened its arms to strangers."

"Chief Sealth?" Katie Lee said. "The Indian Seattle was named after?"

"The very one. The chief's name was hard to pronounce—so the name ended up as Seattle."

All of a sudden Katie Lee's eyes widened as she stepped into the grand lobby of the hotel. Never had she seen such riches! When her father had brought her to the city, they had not come to such a plush establishment. The hotel's decorations were lavish, with tiled floors and fancy hand-colored plasterwork featuring cupids, baby angels and bouquets.

Glittering crystal chandeliers, dripping with pendants, hung from the ceiling. A wide marble stairway led to the upper floors; ornately framed mirrors big enough to reflect a crowd hung on the walls.

The desk clerk was dressed in a swallowtail coat, ascot and striped trousers. His eyes were cold and questioning as Bruce stepped up to the desk.

Katie Lee clasped her fingers behind her, her eyes wide as she waited for Bruce to get a room. She was beginning to think that she was misplaced in this city of riches, and doubts began to assail her. At that moment she was very glad to have Bruce take charge. Never had she felt so awkward, so out of place.

With a key in hand and his signature on the ledger, Bruce swung around and smiled down at Katie Lee, yet he felt anything but happy. If she were there with him willingly and were soon to be his wife, this time with her could have been wonderful.

But as it was, they were more strangers to each other than if they had never even met.

A bellboy in a bright red outfit stepped briskly up to Bruce and placed his hand on the handle of Bruce's valise. "Sir, I shall show you to your room," he said, giving Katie Lee a quick smile.

Bruce gave up his valise and followed him up the steep stairs. Katie Lee clung to his arm, her face pale. "Everything is going to be all right," he tried to reassure her. "Once we get you settled in the room, I shall order you a bath and leave you long enough for you to freshen up. But, darling, I won't be far away. Don't you even try skipping out on me."

"And how long do you intend to keep up this charade?" she asked softly so that the bellboy wouldn't hear. "Did you even sign the hotel register as though we were man and wife?"

"Would you rather that I hadn't and raise a few more eyebrows around here?" Bruce said, giving her a sour glance. "Katie Lee, why don't you just stop being difficult? Let's make everything legal between us. We could go right this moment and get married. There would be no more cause for arguments . . . for embarrassing situations."

"You never give up, do you?" Katie Lee accused him, sighing heavily. She was glad that the room assigned to them was only on the second floor. She felt too exhausted to climb any more stairs, having just discovered how weary she really was.

She shuffled her feet nervously as Bruce handed the bellboy the key and let him open the door, then take the valise into the spacious room bright with sunshine.

Inside she looked around in awe at the plush furnishings, the red velvet drapes at the windows and the quilted red satin comforter.

The bed was a massive canopied four-poster with plump pillows at the headboard. A highboy dresser, wardrobe and a washstand with a porcelain top, matching pitcher and bowl completed the furniture.

Katie Lee's attention was drawn back to the bellboy when the young man spoke up.

"I hope you will have a comfortable stay," he said, smiling as he accepted a few coins from Bruce. "If you need anything, I'll be happy to oblige."

"We'll need a tub brought up as soon as you can get one here, and lots of hot water," Bruce said, ushering the young man to the door. There he gave him a few more coins. "And bring a bottle of your finest wine and two glasses," he added.

The bellboy dropped his tip into his front trouser pocket and winked at Bruce. "Everything is as good as done, sir," he said, swinging around and walking briskly away.

Bruce went back into the room and closed the door behind him—just in time to see Katie Lee reach inside the pocket of her dress. Moments later Leonard Conty's business card was held within her delicate fingers. Bruce groaned as she turned it over and silently mouthed the address.

No matter what he did, it seemed that Katie Lee was still going to seek out that son of a bitch of a theater owner.

"Katie Lee?" Bruce said, his voice drawn.

Katie Lee started. She slipped the business card back into her pocket and smiled dutifully at Bruce. "Yes?" she inquired, her voice lilting.

"Give me that," Bruce said dryly, his eyes sparking.

"What . . . ?" Katie Lee hedged, smiling crookedly up at him, knowing exactly what he was referring to.

Bruce picked up a match that lay beside a branch of candles. He began moving slowly toward her. "I want that damn business card," he said heavily.

Katie Lee eyed the match in disbelief, then looked up at Bruce. "Do you think burning the card will stop me from going to Conty Theater?" she asked. And with that she yanked the card from her pocket and thrust it toward Bruce. "Just try it and see."

Bruce ignited the match with one flick of his thumbnail. "I know now that nothing I say or do will keep you by my side," Bruce said, watching the flames envelop the card. "But I wouldn't sleep well at night if I didn't try everything to stop you first."

Katie Lee looked up at Bruce then and knew that his motives were good. He did love her; if only she could accept his love. If only he would wait for her....

She watched Bruce drop the half-burned card into an ashtray, then felt relief wash through her when there was a knock on the door. As he went to the door and swung it open wide, she stood back and watched as a copper tub was brought into the room and then buckets and buckets of water.

After the tub was filled and she thought that she and Bruce would be left alone again, the bellboy brought in a bottle of wine and two wineglasses.

Katie Lee set her lips in a stubborn line. So this was what he was up to? Obviously he thought that seduction was more effective than chains. Well, he was wrong about that. Dead wrong.

Chapter Twelve

Refreshed from the bath, Katie Lee could not believe that Bruce had actually left her alone, as he'd promised. She glanced toward the door as she wove her fingers through her hair, straightening its damp tendrils, then looked at the bottle of wine and the two glasses sitting on the nightstand. Surely Bruce did intend to ply her with liquor and then draw her into making love with him. It was man's oldest trick.

"Well, it won't work with me," Katie Lee vowed stubbornly. She went to the table and grabbed the bottle. Groaning, she worked the cork until she finally had removed it, then stomped over to the copper tub and emptied the bottle into the soapy water. "I would say that Bruce is now out of luck," she murmured.

The door opened behind Katie Lee just then. Blushing, feeling guilty, she hid the empty bottle behind her as Bruce came into the room, then closed and locked the door.

Bruce eyed Katie Lee questioningly, "I'm almost afraid to ask what that look is all about," he said, slipping off his coat and removing his ascot. "It surely has nothing to do with your bath."

She giggled softly. "Darling, did you say something about my bath?" she teased, saucily bandying the empty bottle. "Perhaps you wish to take one now? I'm sure you would enjoy the blend of water and wine upon your flesh."

"What?" Bruce gasped, looking at the empty bottle and then at the copper tub.

He glared at Katie Lee. "You didn't," he groaned. "Do you know the price of that wine? I bought the best. God, Katie Lee, I only intended to be sure you drank enough, so that you could get a good night's rest. It was to save you from any more nightmares. I wasn't going to get you drunk, if that's what you thought I was planning."

Katie Lee's smile faded. "Truly? You just wanted me to have a good night's sleep?" she asked weakly, suddenly feeling guilty again. She had to learn to trust. Especially Bruce.

"Exactly," Bruce said, going to her, framing her face between his hands. "Hon, I love you so much. I want to take care of you. If only you'd let me...."

Afraid of the passion his touch ignited, Katie Lee turned away. "I'm so tired," she murmured as she watched the sun fading behind the distant forest. "I don't think I need anything tonight to help me go to sleep. Even now I could go to sleep and not awaken until morning.''

''But aren't you hungry? I was going to have food brought up,'' Bruce said, his eyes searching her face.

Katie Lee freed herself from his embrace and crawled onto the bed, fluffing a pillow beneath her head. ''Why not go and get us something, while I get a few winks of sleep?'' she suggested, her eyelashes fluttering closed. ''The bath has made me so...so...drowsy.''

She forced her breathing to become even, trying to look as though she were drifting into sleep. ''Bring me some seafood, Bruce,'' she said in a faint whisper. ''And if you wish—some more wine....''

Bruce studied her, kneading his chin. She did appear to be listless—as though she *was* going to sleep. Maybe this time he should trust her.

Deciding that she really was too tired to make off for Conty Theater, at least tonight, he bent over her and placed a soft kiss upon her flushed cheek. ''I won't be long,'' he promised tenderly.

Then turning on a heel, his footsteps light, Bruce left the room. He eyed the lock on the door, fingering the key in his pocket.

No. He could not go that far. He would not lock her in like a prisoner. Such an act would spur her to hate him.

Grumbling to himself that she was becoming an obsession, he rushed down the stairs and outside, then went across the street to position himself in the shadows to watch the hotel door. If she tried to escape, he could easily stop her in her tracks. But could he force her back up to their room?

Breathless, Katie Lee rose from the bed and went to the window that overlooked Front Street.

Lifting back a corner of the heavy drape, she scanned the other side of the street, where buildings lined the wooden sidewalk.

The sun was dipping low in the sky, leaving only muted shadows. Squinting against its last rays she looked at each doorway, searching for Bruce. She knew him well enough now to know that he would keep an eye out for her to escape. She had not given him enough reason to trust her.

Katie Lee frowned, and then the gaslights along the street began to flicker on, lifting her spirits. She smiled slowly. There he was—standing in the doorway of the merchant's store exactly opposite the hotel.

"I was right!" Katie Lee half squealed, raking her fingers through her hair. Below her Bruce shuffled his feet impatiently as he watched the hotel door. Occasionally he would look up at the window where Katie Lee was staying hidden from view. She laughed softly, delighted at her cleverness. As soon as Bruce thought she was asleep, he would leave to get their dinner. And then she would finally be free.

Her laughter faded as she watched the sky darken overhead. It had not been in her plans to wander

along the streets of Seattle in the dark. Her father
had warned her of the riffraff, and even now she
could hear boisterous laughter rising from the
saloons. She could hear the squeals of women . . .
someone hammering away on a piano and the splintering of glass.

It seemed that the genteel folk of Seattle came out
during the day, the seamy at night.

Trembling from fear, Katie Lee turned her attention back to Bruce. He hadn't budged.

Suddenly he swung away from the building and
began walking briskly down the block, soon losing
himself in the shadows as he turned a corner.

Katie Lee's heart began to beat wildly; she had just
been given the chance that she had been waiting for.
Yet why wasn't she glad?

She felt herself being torn in two. If she left, perhaps Bruce would hate her forever. If she stayed, she
would lose her identity.

"I must go," she said, hearing the tremor in her
voice.

Searching for the doorknob in the darkness, Katie Lee slowly turned it. Breathless, she stepped out
into the corridor that was softly lighted with candles
flickering in golden sconces along the walls.

She fled down the marble stairs, her pulse racing,
ignored the throng of people in the lobby and hurried on outside.

The damp evening air blowing in from the sound
stung her face and quickly penetrated her cotton

dress, chilling her to the bone. She hugged herself, trying to fend off the cold as she looked first to her left and then to her right. Leonard Conty's theater also was on Front Street, but she had no idea at which end. She would have to study the numbers on each of the buildings.

Her knees weak from fear, her eyes wide, Katie Lee made a wide turn and began walking along the street. A grimace twisted her face when she discovered herself in front of a saloon. Through its windows she could see brightly garbed women, their skirts hiked way above their knees, their faces painted. Some were dancing with men, others were sitting on their laps, kissing and hugging them.

When she saw a man slip a hand up the skirt of one of the women, Katie Lee turned her eyes away, embarrassed, and hurried on. Each footstep became harder. She was having thoughts of returning to the hotel. It would be wonderful to be enclosed in Bruce's arms, to let him protect her....

A hand suddenly circled her wrist, stopping her. Katie Lee's heart skipped a beat and her throat went dry.

Slowly she turned to face her assailant, then sighed with relief when she found that it was Leonard Conty.

Smiling awkwardly, her breasts heaving, Katie Lee eased her wrist from Leonard's thick hand. "My word," she said softly. "Where did you come from? You gave me quite a fright, Mr. Conty."

"I was walking my dog, and who do I see but my abducted promising leading lady," Leonard Conty said, his gray eyes slowly assessing her. "Miss Holden, may I assume you have recently escaped from the rogue who kidnapped you? Surely that is the only reason you are forced to wander the streets of Seattle at this hour. You have to know the dangers in doing so."

Katie Lee looked down at the bulldog, his tongue almost dragging on the ground as he panted, and then past Leonard for any sign of Bruce.

Nervously she looked back at the stocky theater owner. "Sir, it is still my desire to perform on your stage," she said in a rush. "Is the offer still open?"

Leonard smiled smugly. "Always," he said, taking her possessively by the elbow and resuming his walk with her at his side. "But many preparations must be made for your first appearance. Tonight we must get you settled in a comfortable hotel, so that you can get a good night's sleep. Tomorrow I shall take you shopping and show you just how beautiful you really are. And the next day I shall introduce you to the stage. We'll see how many days of practice will be required before you actually make your Seattle debut. But of course, you are willing to do all of these things, aren't you? I *will* make you a star, Miss Holden. You can count on it."

It all sounded thrilling enough, yet a shadow of doubt still lay at the back of Katie Lee's mind. She was hurting Bruce. Oh, how she hated to hurt Bruce!

"Miss Holden, I assume your answer is forth-coming?" Leonard pressed, guiding Katie Lee into the lobby of an even fancier hotel than the one she had left behind. "You are willing to go through all the preliminaries of making you a star?"

Katie Lee swallowed hard; her pulse raced. She looked at Leonard and nodded. "Yes, sir," she murmured. "I truly believe I am."

She looked down at the bulldog as Leonard handed her the diamond-encrusted leash. When the dog looked up at her with dark, bulging eyes, his tongue still hanging from the corner of his mouth, she smiled awkwardly at the animal. Then feeling somehow out of place, she watched Leonard go to the desk clerk and make the necessary arrangements for her to have a room.

A foreboding overcame her as she wondered what Leonard Conty's true intentions would be, once he took her to the room. Briefly she considered whether she should run and never look back.

Then her whole body grew tense when Leonard walked back toward her, a key in hand.

Trembling, Katie Lee followed the short, hefty man up the winding staircase until they reached the fourth floor. Never had she felt so alone, so vulnerable, as when Leonard Conty placed the key in the lock and began turning it.

With the heady aroma of fried shrimp and oysters emanating from a box in his left hand and a bottle of wine tucked beneath his arm, Bruce took the steps two at a time to the second-floor landing of the hotel. Anxious to get back into the room, he quickly opened the door and was immediately engulfed in darkness.

Believing that Katie Lee had fallen into a deep sleep, Bruce walked confidently across the room and felt around on a side table for the matches.

The smell of the fried seafood was making his stomach growl and ache unmercifully. The wine would top it off grandly. He knew all too well how long it had been since they had last eaten. Katie Lee was in need of a good meal, as well.

Unable to find the match immediately, Bruce grumbled and set down the box of food and the bottle of wine, then more determinedly swept his hand over the table.

"Aha," he whispered, finally finding a match. Scraping its head with his thumbnail, he watched the small flame sputter for a moment.

As the light grew stronger, he turned toward the bed, then almost dropped the match. Only an indentation in the comforter revealed that anyone had ever been there at all.

Cursing beneath his breath, Bruce lifted the chimney of the kerosene lamp and placed the match to the wick. He shook the match out as the flame caught, then turned and eyed the bed again.

Slowly he went to the window and drew back the drape, looking down at the spot where he had stood watching for Katie Lee's possible escape. She had probably been watching him from this very window.

"I knew that she was determined, but never would I have guessed this much," he said angrily, doubling his hands into tight fists at his sides. "Katie Lee, what have you done? Where are you?"

Bruce knew of only one place to go. Conty's Theater!

"No. I will not go there and make a fool of myself," he said, flopping into a chair, hanging his head. "If I found her there, I couldn't force her to leave. I have already made an ass of myself over her. Now it's up to her...."

Katie Lee's spine was stiff and her lips were pursed as she stepped farther into the hotel room. It was a room most surely decorated only for a lady; delicate lace seemed to be everywhere—the curtains, the bed's skirt and spread, the pillows... Her trepidation quickly turned to awe.

The carpet was a pale pink cushion beneath her feet. A pink velveteen love seat was graced by sprays of pink roses in tapering vases on side tables.

"I think you will be comfortable enough here," Leonard Conty announced, moving to Katie Lee's side. He cupped her cheek with one gloved hand. "Now you go on to bed and get a good night's sleep. I shall leave you and return tomorrow. Remember? We will have a busy day choosing your wardrobe."

He began leading his bulldog from the room, then turned and eyed her. "Is there anything I can get for you before leaving?" he asked, surprising her with his genuine concern.

Katie Lee's stomach growled loudly. She laughed and placed her hands over it, her face coloring with an embarrassed blush.

"I don't think you have to tell me what you need," Leonard said smoothly. "I'll see to it that some food and drink are brought up to you." He paused, wiping a drop of sweat from his brow. "Is there anything else?"

Katie Lee suddenly recalled that in the confusion of her arrival in Seattle, nothing had yet been done about Chief Black Raven.

She felt herself wavering as she tried not to think of how her family had died. "I would appreciate it if you would send word to the authorities about the massacre," she finally said, her voice breaking. "Chief Black Raven must be found and made to pay." She swallowed hard, clasping her hands in entreaty. "Would you please do this for me, Mr. Conty?"

Leonard squared his shoulders. Already Katie Lee was seeking favors from him. If he played his hand right, she would begin to trust him. How sweet would be the conquest! Soon she would not only sing for him, but be his completely.

"If you want, I shall see to it that you even place the noose around the savage's neck," he said, laughing throatily.

Katie Lee paled, and sickening bile rose into the back of her throat at the thought of what Leonard Conty had suggested. "Lord, no," she said, shaking her head. "That won't be necessary."

"Whatever you say," Leonard said, giving his dog's leash a yank. "Perhaps I will do the honors on your behalf."

His smile faded, and he looked Katie Lee up and down, watching her shiver under his lengthy appraisal. "Katie Lee, though I will be your·employer, I would rather you call me Leonard," he said huskily. "It would be less awkward, don't you think?"

Katie Lee swallowed hard. "Yes, I think that would be just fine," she said, sighing heavily as he turned and went to the door, leaving without another word.

Feeling strangely alone, Katie Lee went to the window and drew back the lacy curtain to peer down at the busy street. "Bruce, I'm going to miss you tonight," she whispered, tears burning her eyes. "I'm going to miss you every night. I'm not even sure if I . . . can . . . bear it."

Chapter Thirteen

The padded black patent leather seats were as soft as air as the fancy carriage rode like a breeze. The sun poured through the window, warming Katie Lee's skin.

Boxes filled with all sorts of feminine attire—corsets, chemises, shawls, silk petticoats and the loveliest dresses she had ever seen in her life—were piled upon the seat beside her, while Leonard smiled at her from the opposite seat, obviously enjoying her pleasure.

Katie Lee looked down at the stack of hatboxes. There was a hat for every formal occasion, and she could not believe that Leonard had insisted that she buy every single one—a morning hat, a toque with a satin bow, an afternoon hat with an egret plume and satin-faced brim, and an evening hat in flowered silk and plaited chiffon.

She gave Leonard a shy glance, uncomfortable that it was he who had encouraged her to buy such a fancy wardrobe. Even though she was determined to pay back every penny, for *now* he was the one who had bought and paid for it all.

Katie Lee's glance fell to the outfit she had worn right out of the shop—an Eton jacket in blue broadcloth trimmed with folds of matching velvet, its lines revealing the curves of her breasts and the smallness of her waist.

She reached her gloved hand to her hat. The "morning hat" on which Leonard had insisted, was one of her favorites.

She felt quite the picture of fashion and revelled in her new appearance. Yet there was one person missing from her newfound world.

Bruce.

As they turned onto Front Street, she craned her neck to try to catch a glimpse of Cabot Sawmill at the far end, but there were too many buildings blocking her view. She had to wonder if Bruce was with his brother, Alex, at this very moment. Was he thinking of her, or engrossed in the business that he was so anxious to be a part of?

"Katie Lee?" Leonard asked a little too loudly, interrupting her thoughts. He bent down to pat his bulldog, who lay panting at his feet, then ran his fingers over the diamond-encrusted collar. "For a moment there you looked quite forlorn. Not at all like the talk of the town."

Katie Lee placed her hands upon her lap, intertwining her fingers. The white gloves still felt strange; after all, she had never before owned a pair in her life. She blanched at what Leonard had said. "Why on earth would I be that? The thought makes me . . . quite uncomfortable."

Leonard readjusted his top hat, then drummed his fingers on his knee contemplatively. "My dear, how many times have I told you that your name will be on everyone's lips?" he said, chuckling softly. "Your voice, ah, it is as sweet as a meadowlark's! It will seduce the city. Just you wait and see."

"Seduce?" Katie Lee said, lowering her eyes bashfully. "What a way to describe how my singing will affect people, Mr. Conty."

Leonard narrowed his eyes and clasped his fingers about his knee. "Do not call me that," he said, giving his voice a threatening note. "You are to call me Leonard. Do . . . you . . . understand?"

Katie Lee felt a chill pass through her when she looked up and saw how ugly Leonard's expression had become. Bruce had warned her about this man, yet she had turned a deaf ear to him. She heaved a lengthy sigh. For now she needed Leonard Conty and what he was so generously offering her. Again she scolded herself, reiterating the lesson that she was lucky to have a chance at the stage.

"I understand that you desire that I call you by your first name," Katie Lee said softly, nervously fluttering her thick lashes. "But, Leonard, sometimes I forget. You must know that I have much to adjust to. Perhaps you could remember this and be patient with me? This is all so new and so very exciting.''

Leonard's gray eyes gleamed, and a slow smile curved his lips. ''I am glad that you are enjoying yourself,'' he said, his voice deep and husky. ''This is just the beginning. You won't regret your decision to become a part of the excitement. I see it every day, Katie Lee. Excitement and glamour. On my stage you will find both, and more. I am glad that you trust me. After Bruce Cabot lectured you, well, I . . .''

When Katie Lee's face paled, Leonard's words faded away. He was annoyed with himself for having even mentioned the man's name. There was no sense in reminding her of him.

Later he hoped that she would turn her eyes and heart toward himself.

He leaned over and placed a gloved finger to Katie Lee's chin, forcing her eyes upward. ''My dear, look from the window as I tell you about this fine city of Seattle.''

''That would be nice,'' Katie Lee said, her smile tight, the thought of Bruce like a fading song within her aching heart.

She looked out the window in an effort to forget him, clasping her hands on her lap.

''I have instructed the driver not to take us to what most call Skid Road,'' Leonard began, looking from the window, watching the frenzied activity on the road. ''It is an area of bawdy houses and low theaters, unlike mine. Skid Road is a place of dead dreams. You will find hardly anything but bums and derelicts looking for a handout so that they can buy themselves another bottle.'' He shuddered visibly. ''They sit on curbs, sleep in doorways. You will see condemned buildings padlocked for nonpayment of rent. There is only one decent place on Skid Road— the mission. Oatmeal can be bought for five cents, with sugar for seven cents and with cream for nine cents. Over the door a sign reads, Be Saved by Sister Faye.''

Leonard cleared his throat. ''But we won't speak of Skid Road any longer,'' he said. ''I just felt it was necessary to warn you of the place. Stay away from it, Katie Lee. It is not for a genuine lady like yourself.''

Katie Lee looked at him and smiled, then turned back to the window. She was shown the eight-story Rhodes Department Store on the corner of First Avenue and Union Street. On Second Avenue stood the Bon Marche dry goods store, the *Times* newspaper office and Sherman Clay and Company, a retailer of musical instruments. Then came the Odron Theater with an admission of five cents, and a photographer's sign: Your Photo on Postcards, Three for Twenty-five Cents.

They passed the Vendome Hotel at 1315 First Avenue, and Katie Lee recalled that she had already visited John Kelly's underwear store on the first floor. There she had bought an assortment of articles for herself.

A horse-drawn ice truck passed the carriage just as they pulled up in front of the Diamond Ice and Storage Company at the corner of Western Avenue and Union Street.

"That establishment is the most successful supplier for owners of iceboxes in Seattle," Leonard was quick to point out. "They have the best ice in town—it has no core."

The carriage made a turn and began traveling along the waterfront. The Ainsworth and Dunn Dock at the foot of Pike Street stood at the northern end of the business district. The piers slanted into the bay, where brigs, clippers and lumber schooners dropped anchor and waited their turn to load.

"And now, my dear, the driver knows to take you to my theater where dreams are alive and real," Leonard declared, reaching to take one of Katie Lee's hands. He frowned when he felt her try to draw away. "Relax, Katie Lee. My intentions toward you are quite honorable. My dear, it is your voice that I am interested in. Now, I would find that hard to seduce, don't you agree?"

A blush rose to Katie Lee's cheeks, and her lips trembled as she attempted to give him a polite smile.

Looking like a logger in his casual jeans and a red plaid shirt, Bruce stood in the ground-floor office of his and his brother's mill, holding the signed agreement in the light as he reread it. His promises to complete his education behind him, his future now to do with as he pleased, he smiled broadly.

"Alex, it's been a long time coming but, by damn, I'm here and we're together. I can't wait to see just what sort of crew we have," he said. "It's so damn exciting, I feel as though I've just made love to a woman."

Alex, thirty-five, was not as refined as Bruce; with his red hair and freckled, rugged face, he was a raffish-looking cuss. He locked a hefty arm around his brother's shoulder. "This business ain't like no woman I've ever bedded," he chuckled, winking at Bruce. "Bruce, this city is filled with more women than you can shake a stick at. I'll be happy to introduce you to a few. I know who's willin', if you know what I mean?"

Bruce frowned. "I appreciate what you're saying," he said blandly, "but, Alex, I don't need any introductions. I think I am capable of taking care of my own carnal needs." His lips curved into a slow smile. "Your interests and mine differ considerably anyway, if you know what *I* mean. And you're going to get into trouble, taking so many women to bed. There are diseases. One woman can give you the same as a dozen, except for what you don't want."

Alex stepped away from his little brother, laughing beneath his breath, his dark eyes dancing. He gnawed a sizable chew from his plug of tobacco and spoke from the corner of his mouth. "Hogwash!" he said, slipping his tobacco pouch back inside his shirt pocket. "I'm enjoyin' being a bachelor. God, Bruce, I like all women—not just one."

Bruce turned away. He placed the contract on his desk and once again looked out the window at the busy thoroughfare. The subject of marriage was reminding him of Katie Lee. And at this very moment she was with that rogue Leonard Conty!

"Bruce, where has your mind wandered to?" Alex said, moving to Bruce's side. He studied his brother's expression and saw pain. "Son of a bitch, I think I touched a nerve. Bruce, who is she?"

Bruce's back stiffened and he tightened his jaw. Though his brother was a shrewd businessman, he was not at all smart where women were concerned, and Bruce did not wish to confide in him that he himself was no smarter.

He concentrated on the whine of the shingle saws down by the river, and the pounding of hammers was exhilarating music to his ears. Mud squirted up through the cracks of the loosely planked roadway as horse-drawn loads of green lumber rattled down the street. The occasional tap of a trowel on scarcely dried brick gave a rare promise of solidity and permanence to this wooden city.

"Alex, let's talk business, not women," Bruce said in a low growl. "That's why I came to Seattle." He gave Alex a slow stare. "Remember?"

Alex spat into a huge brass spittoon at his side, laughing beneath his breath. By damn, his brother had met a special lady. He'd get the name out of him later.

Slinging an arm around Bruce's shoulder, Alex acquiesced. "Little brother, there is still a limitless quantity of timber crowding the mountains," he said confidently. "We have logging camps among trees of unbelievable size in forests of unbelievable depth. We are in a world where the strength of the people equals the riches of the natural resources. And, Bruce, we own a huge part of it."

"It's the best of times, eh, Alex?" Bruce said, still trying to forget Katie Lee's innocent face.

"Lord, I would hope so." Alex chuckled. "The other day our crew cut down a cedar tree whose stump could seat seventy-two persons. Who could resist a country that grows trees like that? That's pure gold in the shape of shingles, shakes and lumber."

Alex swung away from Bruce and took another chew of his tobacco. "Oh, and by the way, before I forget," he said absently. "Knowing you were comin', I bought up two lots on Queen Anne Hill. They are each twenty-five foot wide with houses on both. One is yours, and one is mine. We'll be neighbors as well as partners." He wiped his mouth with the back of his hand, chuckling again. "Little brother, wait until you see my house. It looks like a fancy Mississippi riverboat, long, low and rakish. Yours is a Queen Anne, fittin' the name of the street it is built on. It'll clean take your breath away."

Bruce was only half hearing what Alex was saying. His eyes were following a carriage; then his gut caught fire. Katie Lee—and Leonard Conty! At first he had wondered if it actually was she. He had never seen her dressed in such expensive attire.

Jealousy assailed him; Conty was clearly responsible for this. His heart sank to think that she would very likely be asked to pay back more than money for Conty's generous ways. Somehow Bruce would make sure that she paid back no more than what she owed! Somehow!

"Bruce, you didn't hear a word I said," Alex grumbled. His gaze followed Bruce's, but the carriage was past them now.

Alex knew the carriage well.

"Are you acquainted with Leonard Conty?" he asked, his eyes moving slowly to Bruce. "But, yes, you are. He arrived in Seattle on the same stagecoach with you. Well, I've had some fun in his box houses, but I don't like him—or his attitude. If you and he had words, I can take care of that son of a bitch real quick for you."

"Big brother, you may as well learn now as later, that I am very capable of fighting my own battles," Bruce said dryly. He turned slowly to Alex. "Do you understand?"

Alex nodded, his eyes twinkling. "Yeah, I think I do."

"Be sure of it," Bruce said, doubling a fist at his side as he watched Conty's carriage head toward the theater, which was down the street from the Cabot mill. "And I have one or two battles to fight right now."

Bruce spun around and walked briskly toward the door. "And there's no time like the present," he said, slamming it behind him.

Clenching his fists, he began walking along the planked sidewalk, his eyes still on the carriage. Though he knew that he could not dissuade Katie Lee, at least he could show her that he still cared—just in case she ever needed him.

Chapter Fourteen

Having seen Bruce in the window of his sawmill, Katie Lee halfheartedly stepped from the carriage in front of Leonard Conty's theater. Taking Leonard's proffered hand, she tried to enjoy the thrill of the moment—she would soon see the stage on which she was to perform. But the joy had lessened at the reminder of what she stood to lose in the process.

Bruce!

Oh, could she live without him now that she had traveled to paradise and back in his arms? With each hour away from him, her determination to taste freedom and independence was sorely tested.

"Well? What do you think of my establishment?" Leonard asked, moving his hand to cup her elbow as they walked toward his theater. "Is it grand enough for you? If not, I could make any renovations you demand."

He leaned down and looked into her face. "You see how important you are to me, my dear?" he said smoothly. "I have never offered to renovate my theater for anyone. I always do everything to please only myself."

Hating the blush that heated her face, Katie Lee looked at Leonard's theater, very impressed. It seemed magical, as though she were in a dream.

"Why, it is so grand!" she whispered in awe, looking at the tall building with its fresh coat of white paint. Two large pots, filled to overflowing with bright geraniums, flanked the entrance—double French doors painted a bright red.

A huge black and gold sign hung on the front of the building. It read, Conty's Theater, Leonard Conty, Proprietor.

But it was the chalky scrawl across a blackboard nailed to the side of the door that caught her attention. "See Lady Osmenor change clothes in total darkness in a lion cage. 50 cents for a seat near the stage."

Katie Lee gasped. She placed a hand to her throat. "Will there be a lion present in the cage as she . . . as . . . she changes her clothes?" she asked, her eyes wide and innocent.

Leonard chuckled. "Would you like that?" he asked, stepping aside so that she could enter ahead of him.

"Certainly not," Katie Lee said softly, relieved that the woman at least undressed in the dark. Perhaps Bruce was right about this establishment. . . .

She grew silent as she stepped across the threshold into the lobby. Never had she seen anything quite like it in her entire life.

Leonard clasped his hands behind him and rocked back and forth as he watched Katie Lee. He smiled smugly. She was being drawn into his grasp as would a moth to a flame. Soon she would be too caught up in the glamour and riches ever to want to back away from it.

As each moment passed, she was becoming his, totally his. . . .

Solid oak spiral staircases led to the second floor at each end of the lobby. Glittering crystal chandeliers, dripping with pendants, hung from the ceiling. Red velvet tapestries covered the walls.

But Katie Lee frowned when she saw how soiled the bright red carpet was. All sorts of debris seemed to be mashed into it. This sort of damage was not done by people with breeding. Just what sort of people frequented this theater? What had Bruce called it? A box house?

"My dear, let's go on with the tour," Leonard said, quickly averting Katie Lee's attention. He could not tell her that he had realized long ago how much of a waste of time and money it was to keep the carpet clean or have it replaced. Until he attracted more of the carriage trade, instead of the riffraff who came to his establishment for pleasures of the flesh, rather than the entertainment on the stage, he could expect no more than what he was getting.

"Yes, let's," Katie Lee said, wanting to forget her initial doubts.

She was beginning to see a side of life that she had never known before, and even though she did not want it to affect her, she was becoming drawn into the wonders of it. Except for the soiled carpet, everything was so beautiful.

Her gaze moved slowly around her. The huge cavernous space was empty. The lighting was dim, the wicks in the hanging kerosene lanterns turned low. At the far end of the room was an enormous stage, the drop curtain raised to reveal the gas footlights in green cabbage leaf sconces.

On either side of the stage were double tiers of red velvet boxes elegantly decorated in scarlet brocade, with gilt chairs, velvet railings and red velvet drapes.

Close to the stage, tables were scattered about with a bar at one side. A great display of liquor lining the shelves was reflected in a mirror behind the bar.

But it was the statues of naked women in lewd poses positioned here and there that brought a hot blush to her cheeks.

"Well, what do we have here?"

The husky female voice drew Katie Lee's attention. Her spine stiffened when she found herself face to face with a breathtakingly beautiful woman. Her hair was dark and coarse and hung down her back in heavy waves, way past her waistline. Her fathomless eyes were as dark as midnight, her skin copper, her cheekbones high, giving her the exotic features of an

Indian princess. The dress that she wore left little to the imagination; her bronze breasts were round and full and immodestly displayed.

Yes, she was beautiful, but the coldness in her eyes and the straight, stubborn line of her lips robbed her of femininity.

Katie Lee felt uneasy in her presence, especially since the woman was looking her up and down without bothering to hide the sneer on her face.

"Margo?" Leonard said, his voice flat. "What are you doing here this time of day? You're usually sleeping off the night before." His eyes swept over her. "And you're even dressed for work."

"News travels fast, Leonard," Margo said icily, still looking Katie Lee up and down. "I've got friends, you know. Someone told me about you buying the town out for this...this little girl. It doesn't take much imagination to figure out why." She placed her hands on her hips and glared up at him. "You're plannin' on puttin' her on the stage in my place, aren't you? You threatened me more than once that you would do it, but I never thought you were serious. Leonard, it ain't fair. You know it ain't fair."

Leonard's face flushed and his eyes narrowed. "Margo, you've been warned to leave the bottle alone," he said curtly. "You've been performing half-drunk, and that isn't good for my theater's reputation."

At that the woman threw her head back with a throaty laugh. "Your theater's reputation?" she exclaimed. Composing herself, she glared once more at Leonard. "My God, what do you think this place is? A goddamned palace?"

"Margo, I've heard enough," Leonard said, a muscle in his left cheek twitching. "And I haven't fired you yet. You know I need many performers. If you behave yourself, you'll still be one of them."

"Yeah, with her as the lead," Margo retorted, nodding toward Katie Lee.

"Only the best gets the lead," he said succinctly, then reached for Katie Lee's hand and held it affectionately. "Now let me make the proper introductions." He looked possessively down at Katie Lee, a smug smile on his lips. "Margo, this is Katie Lee Holden, a lady with a voice that will make men melt down into their shoes. I'm counting on her to draw the carriage trade to my theater."

He looked slowly at Margo, his smile fading. "Katie Lee, this is Margo," he said flatly. "She sings and dances. Whenever she is sober, that is."

Katie Lee blinked nervously as she eased her hand from Leonard's. She lifted it toward Margo in a gesture of friendship. "I am proud to make your acquaintance," she said gently. "I look forward to...to seeing your performance. I am sure it will be wonderful."

Margo laughed again, ignoring Katie Lee's hand. "We'll just see who outlasts the boisterous crowds that frequent this dive," she said, flipping her skirt around and walking away. Her teetering and swaying gave evidence of her vice—even in the early afternoon.

"You'll have to overlook her," Leonard said tightly. "She's been getting on my nerves lately. I guess I just might have to let her go."

Behind his pitiless eyes, he could not help but remember that Margo had talents that extended far beyond the stage. And if he fired her, she would never let him touch her again....

"I hope you don't fire her on my account," Katie Lee said, wincing at the thought. "I don't want to cause anyone problems by my being here." She wanted to add that she was having second thoughts and might not stay long herself.

"Come with me," Leonard suggested, taking Katie Lee by the elbow and ushering her around the foot of the stage. "I'll show you which dressing room will be yours. You'll have one all to yourself."

"She's not going anywhere but with *me*," a voice boomed from somewhere behind Katie Lee and Leonard.

Katie Lee's stomach fluttered and her knees grew weak at the sound of Bruce's voice. She turned about to face him, scarcely recognizing him in his jeans and plaid shirt as he stormed around the tables.

Just seeing him made her question all over again her sanity for refusing his proposal of marriage. She ached for his arms, hungered for his kiss, his caresses.

Yet at this moment she felt suddenly terribly afraid of him. His eyes were flashing angrily as he looked from Leonard back to her. His fists were doubled at his sides. His walk was brisk and determined, his jaw tensed.

"Cabot, what the hell do you think you're doing?" Leonard growled, glancing over his shoulder as Doc Porter, his bodyguard, stepped out of the shadows, his hand resting on a pistol.

Bruce ignored Conty and Porter, and grabbed Katie Lee by the wrist. "You're coming with me," he said, half dragging her away from Leonard's side. "We've got something to discuss, Katie Lee. And I aim to do it now."

Stunned, Katie Lee stumbled along beside him. "Bruce, you're humiliating me," she argued, finally getting her breath. As she tried to pull herself free, she caught a glimpse of Leonard Conty's flushed face and his bodyguard's aggressive approach. Fear gripped her heart. Conty looked as though he was out for blood—Bruce's blood. For his sake she quit fighting him and instead drew close to his side.

"All right," she said softly. "I'll go with you. Just please release my wrist."

Bruce glanced down at Katie Lee, then over his shoulder at Doc Porter and Leonard Conty, who were still advancing on him. Damn it, he'd left his holstered pistol draped over a chair in his hotel room. He had not planned to do anything today but sign the contract with Alex and take a turn in the forest.

"I promise to go wherever you take me," Katie Lee said, looking hesitantly up at him. "I don't want to cause you any trouble, Bruce. I never want to cause you any trouble."

Bruce's insides melted at the sweet sincerity in Katie Lee's voice. But for her own good, he forced himself to be firm.

"It's for you that I am doing this," he said thickly, easing his hand from her wrist. "Darling, how can I stand by and watch you being swallowed whole by that . . . that vulture? I can't. I must continue to convince you of what is best for you."

When Leonard saw that Katie Lee was willingly accompanying Bruce, he reached for Doc Porter's arm. "Stop," he ordered his bodyguard. "Let's not do anything hasty. Let her go." A slow, smug smile curved his lips. "She'll be back. She's never seen anything like this place. She is completely captivated by it." He scratched his chin as he watched Katie Lee leave the establishment beside Bruce. "Yes, she'll be back."

The bright sunshine momentarily blinded Katie Lee as she stepped outside with Bruce. Then as he gently placed one arm around her waist and began guiding her away from the theater, her gaze went to the carriage. Her heart skipped a beat.

"Bruce, my things!" she cried. "The gowns...
everything we purchased today is in the carriage."

Bruce glowered down at her. "Darling Katie Lee,
nothing is going to happen to them," he said dryly.
"Don't you know that Leonard Conty won't let
anything happen to his investment?"

Katie Lee felt a blush heat her cheeks, and she
lowered her eyes, unable to fend off the shameful
feeling that was engulfing her.

Chapter Fifteen

Katie Lee walked beside Bruce along the crowded sidewalk, feeling as though she belonged with him, yet strangely uncomfortable. His arm around her waist, so familiar, was stirring feelings inside her that she did not want. She was afraid that she might not be able to turn away from him if he enveloped her within his arms and kissed her. The fear of losing him had made her desire for him even stronger.

"Where are we going?" she blurted, the strong wind off the sound loosing a wisp of hair from beneath the fancy hat.

"All I want is some more time to talk some sense into that pretty head of yours," Bruce said, looking her up and down. "You don't look the same as that first time I saw you. You've lost some of your innocence with those fancy city clothes. You look damn beautiful in them, but it should have been I, Katie Lee, who took you shopping... who helped choose your wardrobe." He looked away from her, his jaw tight. "Not Leonard Conty. How ever did you allow it? How?"

Katie Lee lowered her eyes, stung with shame and guilt, as though her father had just scolded her.

But this was not her father! This was the man she loved! Yet he persisted in treating her like a mindless child.

Jerking away from Bruce, Katie Lee turned and gave him a hurtful stare, then began walking back toward the theater, her chin tilted at a determined angle.

"Katie Lee!" Bruce shouted, uncaring of the stares that people gave him from all sides. He began half running toward her. "Katie Lee, damn it, stop. Wait up!"

Hearing Bruce so close, Katie Lee hurried her steps, but the ruffles of her petticoat impeded her ability to go any faster. Then a hand circled her wrist again, and she was jerked to a stop and spun around to face him.

"Katie Lee, you may as well know I won't give up all that easily," Bruce said, glowering down at her. "If I have to pick you up and throw you over my shoulder, I shall. All I ask is some time with you. How can you deny me that?"

He gazed down into her face; their breathing mingled, their eyes locked. "I love you, Katie Lee," he whispered. "So much that it hurts! Please don't fight your need to be with me. You want it as much. Tell me you don't."

Katie Lee's pulse raced. The open stares of passersby embarrassed her greatly.

"Bruce," she said in a low whisper, looking awkwardly around her. "For heaven's sake, I'll go with you. But let us go quickly. My word, what must people be thinking?"

Bruce chuckled as he swept an arm around her waist and escorted her briskly toward his mill. "My darling, they must be thinking that here are two people very much in love," he said, looking adoringly down at her. "And they are right, aren't they? You do love me. You're just afraid to make a commitment. Tell me I'm right, Katie Lee. Tell me."

Katie Lee gave him a wavering glance. "I do," she murmured. "Oh, Bruce, I do love you. But again I implore you to be patient with me. Give me time."

Bruce frowned. "In truth, time is the true enemy here," he said angrily. "So much can happen to you in just one day. Why can't you listen to me? Why can't you trust what I am saying?"

Katie Lee sighed heavily as she looked up at him. "Bruce, I refuse to say any more about any of this," she said, her voice quavering. "If you can't accept me for what I am, perhaps it is best that we don't see one another again. I grow so weary of battling with you. Surely by now you see that nothing you say will dissuade me from enjoying some measure of independence for a while before...before settling down into marriage. I saw how my mother was imprisoned by her wedding vows. Lord, Bruce, it frightens me to think that I can become trapped in such a way."

Bruce drew back at the desperation he heard in her voice. The scenario she had described helped him to understand so much more about her. And hadn't she as good as told him that in time she would marry him?

A gentle warmth seized his heart. Understanding Katie Lee more now than ever before, he drew her closer. She loved him.

"Darling, I'm sorry," Bruce said, guiding her toward the steps of Cabot Mill. "I'll try to quit forcing so much on you. If you will allow me to, I will just shower you with my love. Surely you can't resent me for wanting to do that. Darling, everyone needs loving. Everyone."

Touched clean to the soul by his sweetness and understanding, Katie Lee gave him an adoring look. "Yes," she murmured, smiling, "everyone needs loving. Especially I, Bruce. Please never stop loving me. I think I would die if you did."

"Then you will live forever," Bruce declared, stepping onto the porch that stretched along the entire front of the mill. He took her hands, squeezing them affectionately. "For you see, Katie Lee, my love for you is forever."

A door opened suddenly at their side, and Alex stepped out, his dark eyes filled with amusement, his right cheek puffed with chewing tobacco. He looked from Bruce to Katie Lee, then swung a sturdy arm around Bruce's shoulder. "Well, so this is the one who has turned your head?" he said, chuckling beneath his breath. He appraised Katie Lee silently. "Little brother, an introduction is in order, wouldn't you say?"

Katie Lee blushed and lowered her eyes, then raised them slowly to meet and hold Alex's. She offered her hand as Bruce made the introductions. "I am very pleased to meet you, sir," she murmured. "Bruce has told me a lot about you. I hope the two of you will have much success together."

Alex shook her hand as though it were a man's. "You're a woman after my heart," he said, smiling down at her. "If Bruce hadn't seen you first, I believe I would willingly leave my bachelor life behind me." He shrugged and eased his hand from hers. "As it is, I guess I'll just have to stay single."

Bruce laughed throatily. "Poor Alex," he said, winking at his brother. "You are forced to keep company with every available female in Seattle. I'm sure your heart is breaking."

Katie Lee looked from Alex to Bruce, then smiled. It was clear that Bruce's brother was a womanizer, and even though he was quite rustic in appearance and reeked of chewing tobacco, there was no denying that he had been born with a good measure of the same charm that made Bruce so special.

"I haven't had a chance to check everything out yet here at the mill," Bruce went on to say, smiling down at her. "It would make me happy if you would come with me. I'd like to show you the second love in my life."

Slipping her arm through Bruce's, she walked between the two brothers as they explained every aspect of running a mill.

She was in awe as she found herself amid brawny men, muscling forty-two-foot logs. Some of the machinery was as large and menacing as the logs, yet with a twist of a wrist and the thrust of a lever, these men were able to maneuver the great ponderosa trunks and position them before the giant saws.

"Speed 'er up!" the foreman shouted, and bang went the giant log onto the pulley, hitting a whirring saw that cut to the very core.

At the far end a conveyor chain, loaded to the frayed edges of the guards, carried a load of perfectly sound lumber to the burner. Katie Lee pulled on Bruce's arm and pointed toward the furnace, which, she had been told, spewed forth heavy smoke from dawn until dusk.

"Vertical stuff is what we want," Bruce said. "The slash grain always goes to the burner. There's plenty more wood where that came from. The best is none too good for our mill."

"It's so interesting," Katie Lee said, very impressed. "I had no idea how a plank of wood was made. When I look at a tree, all I see is a tree."

"When I see a tree, I see money," Alex declared, laughing.

"You would," Bruce said, and smiled at his brother. "But there is no doubt about it, Katie Lee, timber is a clear road to riches." With that he pulled Katie Lee even closer to him and wrapped his arm tightly about her slender frame. Her shining eyes sparkled as she looked up at him.

"Alex, I think I'd like to show Katie Lee that house you were telling me about," he said, squaring his shoulders, hoping his brother wouldn't take this opportunity to joke and tease. Things were strained enough between Katie Lee and himself without Alex making some stupid comment about how many bedrooms the house had.

Alex removed a key from his breeches pocket and slapped it into Bruce's hand. "I hope it will meet with your approval," he said. "And that you don't mind your older brother being your neighbor."

"It's better than sharing a bedroom with you, like we did in the old days," Bruce said, his eyes twinkling. "At least this way I don't have to cope with your dirty socks."

"Nor do I have to cope with your damn stack of books," Alex said, spitting a stream of chewing tobacco out of the corner of his mouth.

"Alex, do you have a buggy handy?" Bruce asked, slipping the key into his pocket. "I don't think Katie Lee is dressed for straddling a horse."

Alex nodded toward the carriage house halfway down the block. "Be my guest."

"Thanks, big brother," Bruce said, slapping Alex fondly on the back as he ushered Katie Lee past him.

"What house are you talking about?" Katie Lee asked. Lifting the hem of her dress, she proceeded down the steps and onto the sidewalk.

"Alex is good at investing our money," Bruce said, taking Katie Lee's elbow and guiding her toward the buggy that was standing on the street in front of the carriage house. "Seems he bought up two prime lots in town with houses already built on them. I'll be seeing all of this for the first time along with you." With that he helped her up into the seat.

Minutes later Bruce was guiding the horse and buggy in and out of the traffic, hustling out of the way when a trolley car passed close behind him. He made a sharp turn, then guided the horse and buggy up a steep incline. Snorting in distress, the animal strained backward against the breeching to keep the buggy from running away.

Katie Lee clung to the seat, afraid even to look back over her shoulder. If the horse and buggy got away from Bruce's steady hand, they would all plunge into the sound.

She sighed with relief when Bruce finally turned into a level street that was lined on each side with beautiful, stately houses. He drew rein in the circular driveway of a house surrounded by a neat, white picket fence.

Katie Lee's eyes widened. It was the house of her dreams with its gingerbread detail and surrounding porch. Flowers bloomed in abundance along the fence and in the window boxes. And behind the house were planted rows of young fruit trees.

"Hmm," Bruce said, snapping his horse's reins as he led it through the opened gate to a stop only a few footsteps away from the porch. "My brother made quite a deal. It's lovely, isn't it, Katie Lee?"

"Yes, very," she responded, believing it was like nothing she had ever seen before. The thought of living here gave her a keen thrill, but she had to dismiss the idea. She couldn't even consider the possibilities. Not yet.

"This is a Queen Anne-style house," Bruce said, admiring it further. "These are dominating American housing all over the country these days."

"Queen Anne seems a curious name for an American style," Katie Lee commented, giving Bruce a quizzical stare.

He laughed throatily. "It is, in fact, a historical accident, darling."

Bruce swung off the buggy and went to help Katie Lee to the ground. "This style was loosely based on medieval buildings constructed long before 1702, the year that marks the beginning of Queen Anne's reign,'' he told her.

Key in hand, he took Katie Lee with him to the front door and slipped the key into the keyhole. Pausing, he turned and eyed her pensively.

''Darling, I feel as though I should lift you in my arms and carry you across the threshold,'' he said tenderly. ''If only you were my wife...''

Katie Lee placed a finger to his lips. ''Please, Bruce,'' she murmured. ''I'm not your wife, and if my being here in any other capacity makes you uncomfortable, well, you can return me to my hotel suite.''

Bruce looked solemnly down at her. Yes, there was a change in her. She was becoming more confident in herself. Maybe someday soon she wouldn't need him anymore....

Chapter Sixteen

With Bruce at her side, Katie Lee stepped into the large center hall that was dominated by an oak staircase. To the left was the dining room, to the right, an enormous parlor. She went with him into the parlor, where bright sunshine poured in through the large windows and was reflected by the highly polished floor. The room was void of furnishings and smelled of fresh wallpaper. A huge stone fireplace dominated one end.

Bruce's eyes narrowed. Sitting on the mantel were a bottle of champagne and two long-stemmed glasses. "It seems my brother thinks of everything," he said, laughing softly as he went to grab the bottle. He held it up to the light, checking the year. "Expensive taste."

"Bruce, be honest with me," Katie Lee said, placing a hand on a hip. "Your brother didn't put the champagne there. You did. You were expecting to bring me here all along."

Bruce lowered the bottle and held it at his side, frowning. "I didn't even know about this house until about an hour ago," he said solemnly. "Alex must have brought the champagne here so that he and I could toast our success. He had no idea there was even a lady in my life until he saw you with me. So you see, Katie Lee, this is all in innocence."

Embarrassed, Katie Lee lowered her lashes. The sun set just then, and the room suddenly became chilly, adding to her forlorn feelings. "I often speak out of turn," she said in barely a whisper. "Of course the champagne wasn't meant for me."

Bruce placed an arm around her shivering frame and drew her close. "But the champagne can be for us," he said hoarsely. "Alex would expect no less, I am sure."

He eyed the logs on the grate and the matches on the mantel. "In fact, we shall sip champagne beside a cozy fire," he announced, seeking her approval as his gaze met and held hers.

"But don't you wish to see the rest of your house first?" Katie Lee asked, desperate to keep her distance.

"Later," Bruce said, walking her to the fireplace. He looked around, frowning. "You have no place to sit. Let me go and see if I can find something. I also need some newspapers to start the fire."

Katie Lee nodded and strolled idly around the room once Bruce left her alone. This would be a golden opportunity to leave, but she didn't want to.

She simply could not step away from these special moments. There was no telling when they would be alone again....

"Seems we're lucky," Bruce said from one doorway. He held up two pillows and a stack of newspapers. "I said that my brother thinks of everything. Well, knowing that I would want to spend my first night in my new home, he had a bed brought in."

He tossed the pillows to the floor. "Make yourself at home in my humble abode, my beautiful lady," he said, then knelt before the fireplace and began arranging wood over twisted newspapers. "I'll have your bones warmed in no time flat. And then we shall sit and watch the flames while we enjoy the champagne."

"I really can't stay all that long," Katie Lee said, straightening her skirt around her as she settled onto one of the plump pillows. "I have my first rehearsal tomorrow. And since I'm new to this, I must have my rest. I don't want to make a fool of myself."

She lowered her eyes, fidgeting with a hat pin as she tried to remove it. "Truly, Bruce, I am not even sure if I have the nerve to walk out on stage," she said, hating to admit her fear. "Who knows? The first time may be the last."

"I only wish," he grumbled beneath his breath, then struck a match. "Damn it, I . . . only . . . wish."

Katie Lee placed her hat on the floor beside her, and her hair spilled over her shoulders in a wondrous golden spray as she leaned toward Bruce.

"You said something?" she murmured.

Bruce looked at her over his shoulder, his frown replaced by a soft smile. "I didn't say anything," he said quietly, suddenly awed by her beauty. "Well, that is, nothing of importance."

The fire quickly took hold, the flames curling around the logs like satin streamers. Bruce settled down on a pillow beside her and popped the cork on the bottle of champagne. Quickly he filled the long-stemmed glasses.

"To us," he said, toasting her. "To us living in this house together as man and wife." Their eyes locked. "Darling, it is going to happen sooner or later. Our love is too strong to deny."

Without having even taken her first sip of champagne, Katie Lee was feeling intoxicated. Being alone with Bruce obliterated the aching loneliness. Since arriving in Seattle, she had been able to partially forget the horrible massacre, yet a nagging pain was always there at the back of her mind.

But at this moment she was forgetting everything. Even her dreams and desires of tasting total freedom.

Sipping champagne, she looked at Bruce over the rim of the glass, and her heart skipped a beat. Then, when he set his glass on the floor and gently cupped her cheek, her heart seemed to stop altogether. His eyes were charged with emotion as he gazed at her. Never had she felt so desired as at that moment.

As he lowered his mouth to her lips, she twined her arms about his neck and with a sob, she welcomed his kiss. Straining toward him, she felt the fire of his passion, his mouth hot and demanding.

And then he withdrew, murmuring her name against her cheek as he drew her to her feet. When he swept her into his arms and began to carry her from the room, she clung to him and closed her eyes, ecstasy having claimed her.

She trembled sensuously as he kissed her on their way up the stairs. She thrilled inside when his hand brushed against the swell of her breast. She parted her lips as his tongue sought entrance, and when he flicked his tongue inside, she felt the now-familiar ache at the juncture of her thighs.

As his lips left her mouth and she felt the softness of the bed against her back, Katie Lee opened her eyes; and with a soft smile gave her approval when Bruce began unbuttoning his shirt.

Under the spell of this man, whom she loved with all of her heart, she watched as the expanse of his tanned, sleekly muscled chest was revealed to her feasting eyes. Slowly her gaze moved lower, following the curling hair that tapered to his waist. When he unfastened his breeches and began inching them down his powerful thighs, Katie Lee sucked in her breath. How he desired her!

Like a puppet on a string, Katie Lee moved from the bed and began undressing herself before Bruce's watchful eyes. She freed her breasts, and he bent his head to draw a nipple between his lips. As his tongue flicked across its hardness she gasped.

"Let me do the rest," Bruce said huskily, eagerly removing the rest of her clothes, unable to stop the pounding of his heart.

As though familiarizing himself with her all over again, he meditatively ran his hands over her exquisite breasts, her slim waist and long, slender legs. His hands began to tremble as his fingers moved over the gentle curve of her stomach and then lower, where the golden triangle between her legs beckoned to him.

Katie Lee's knees grew weak and her breathing came in short gasps. Her golden hair tumbled down her back as she threw up her head in ecstasy and sighed at the feel of his lips along the column of her throat, her breasts, and then down her quivering tummy. When she felt the wetness of his tongue replace his fingers, she became almost mindless; the wondrous pleasure was shooting through her like wildfire.

"Katie Lee, darling..." Bruce whispered, standing to draw her within his embrace. Gently he laid her on the bed. With his loins throbbing, he once again lowered his mouth to her soft, creamy flesh, reveling in the sweet, exotic taste of her.

"Bruce, I want you so badly," Katie Lee whispered, twining her fingers through his hair as his lips moved back to her mouth. "Love me, Bruce. Oh,

Lord, make love to me. My whole body aches with the want of you.''

"Katie Lee, my love," Bruce whispered, spreading himself over her.

As she opened her legs to him, he probed softly with his hardness and then moved gently inside, realizing that this was still something new to her. He framed her face between his hands, lowered his mouth and kissed her hotly, passionately, hoping to stifle that possible moment of pain as he thrust himself fully into her.

Her soft sob against his lips and the momentary lurch of her body were fresh evidence that she had given him her virginity only a few short days before. Bruce was glad when she relaxed against him and arched her hips to meet his strokes with easy movements of her own. His heart thundered inside him and he kissed her wildly. Then his insides melted when she sought his mouth with her lips and kissed him heatedly, her fingers at his buttocks, digging into the hardness of his flesh.

He was trying to hold back that moment of wondrous release, but was finding it hard. It was building inside him, spreading like a fire gone out of control.

And pleasure was spreading its delicious, tingling warmth through Katie Lee, as the slow thrusts of Bruce's pelvis sent her to heights of passion that were even greater than those she'd reached the first time. She swallowed hard when his mouth left her lips and fastened gently on her breast. Her body turned to liquid heat as he flicked his tongue across the nipple, his thrusts inside her quickening.

She could feel the wondrous peak of joy nearing, and as his body tightened against hers and his breath came hard and hot against the flesh in the valley between her breasts, she knew that he was close to ecstasy.

She clung to him, and her heart beat wildly. Her breathing grew short and quick as the effervescence of rapture spilled over and Bruce collapsed above her.

And then they lay within one another's arms, their breaths mingling as they kissed softly, their hands exploring each other's dampened flesh.

"It was so beautiful again, Bruce," Katie Lee murmured, breaking the silence. "These precious moments with you make me forget my sorrows . . . my pain. Thank you, darling. Thank you."

"It could be forever, you know," Bruce said, tracing her breast with a forefinger and smiling as he saw her quiver with pleasure. "It would take only two words."

Katie Lee looked away. "But one must be ready to say 'I do,' Bruce. And I'm not."

Bruce sighed heavily and ran his hand down the curve of her stomach to the juncture of her thighs. "Darling, tonight has proven to you what we could share every night if we were married," he said with feeling. "I shall leave you with that reminder and not propose again. You will now have to be the one who speaks of marriage. Not I."

He placed a forefinger to Katie Lee's chin and turned her face around to him. "And you will, my darling," he said softly. "You will indeed decide that being my wife is better than performing on a god-awful stage before leering, drunken men."

"Bruce, it won't be that way," she argued softly. "Leonard says that my performance will bring in the carriage trade. There will be men and women of class coming to see me."

Bruce's insides became inflamed with anger at the mention of Leonard Conty. How easily Katie Lee mentioned him in their conversation! The son of a bitch was becoming an integral part of her life, and she did not even seem aware of it.

But not wanting to force the issue, he rose to his feet and offered her a hand. He looked toward the window. Darkness was engulfing the city.

"Katie Lee, I best get you back to your hotel suite so that you can get settled in for that beauty sleep you feel is so important," he said, easing her up from the bed. His eyes swept over her. He could not help but take her into his arms and embrace her once more, reveling in the touch of her silken body against his own. He ran his hands over the curves of her buttocks and locked her to himself.

"I so love you," he whispered, his breath hot on her ear. "If anything would happen to you—"

Katie Lee moved her lips to his mouth. "Shh," she urged. "Say no more. Darling, nothing is going to happen to me. Haven't you discovered that I am a survivor?"

Her breath was stolen away as his mouth crushed her lips in a frenzied kiss....

Chapter Seventeen

Bruce leaned on the porch railing outside his mill and looked down the street in the direction of Conty Theater, his brow furrowed. Today was Katie Lee's first stage rehearsal. It turned his stomach to think of the first night she would actually perform in front of an audience. If the audience were of the decent sort, it would not be so hard to accept.

But everyone knew who frequented Leonard Conty's box houses. Everyone, that is, except Katie Lee Holden! he reflected in frustration.

"Your mind has wandered again," Alex said, spitting a brown stream of chewing tobacco into the dirt. He clasped his thick hands on the rail beside Bruce, his gaze following his brother's. He frowned. "You've really got it bad for her, don't you?"

Bruce nodded slowly, his jaw tightening. "Yeah, I guess I do," he said solemnly. "And I know she loves me. She just doesn't know quite how to cope with it. I've got to be patient. If I'm not, I may lose her entirely."

"She's that important to you, huh?"

"Damn important, Alex. Damn important."

"Has she seen the furniture in your house yet?"

"No. Not yet. It's a part of a plan, Alex. First I show her the furniture, and the rest will follow. Slowly I will reveal to her just what she could have if she becomes my wife."

Bruce smiled slowly and looked at Alex. "One way or the other I'm going to have her," he said decisively.

Alex swung an arm around Bruce's shoulders. "I don't think it's going to take long to make her come to her senses," he said, chuckling. "Your house is damn pretty, Bruce. Something no woman would want to turn her back to."

"Perhaps," Bruce said, still peering down the street. "But Katie Lee isn't just any woman. Never in my life have I ever seen anyone so determined to have her way. Mark my word, she will look at the furnished house and adore it, but she will suspect that I have furnished it purely to force the marriage."

Bruce shook his head. "No, I doubt if nice chairs and tables will do it," he said. "But I still want to wait and spring the other surprise on her another day."

"Are you going to tell your big brother about this other surprise?" Alex asked, easing his arm from Bruce's shoulders. He withdrew a plug of tobacco from his front shirt pocket and bit off a chew.

Bruce straightened his back, turning to lean his backside against the rail. "No, if I told anyone what I have planned it would spoil it, Alex," he said, crossing his arms contemplatively. "Hell, I'm not even sure if it will work. But I have to give it a wholehearted try."

"Why wait?" Alex said, his jaw puffed out like a chipmunk's.

"Why?" Bruce repeated, kneading his chin. "Because it wouldn't be as effective if I handed her everything on a silver platter in one evening. Give her time to ponder over the first surprise, and then the second will really catch her attention."

"Yeah, I see what you mean," Alex said, nodding.

Bruce began walking toward the door. "It's time to go back to work," he stated. He wanted to finish soon enough to meet Katie Lee just as she was through rehearsing. He planned to wine and dine her, then take her to his house and show her what could be hers, if she would only say the words.

"I sent a large crew to fell the trees up to four miles back from the Duwamish River," Alex said, his mood all business as he went into his office and sat down at his desk. With large hands he riffled through papers, then handed some over to Bruce as his brother settled down at his own large oak desk. "The logs will be floated through a narrow canal cut through the portage between the river and Puget Sound."

"I know we export much of our wood, but still, we're damn lucky Seattle is booming, with the demand for wood at its peak," Bruce said, glancing over at Alex. "Did you ever think what a fire could do to the city? Do to us?"

Alex frowned. "That thought has crossed my mind," he said hoarsely, shuddering at the thought.

"It's been too damn dry, Alex," Bruce grumbled. "If it doesn't rain soon, the whole damn city could go up in smoke."

Alex gave Bruce a troubled glance, having worried about these dangers for some time now.

Wringing her hands, Katie Lee watched some fascinating Swiss bell ringers perform. When they finished, a woman came onto the stage, carrying a cat. Katie Lee sat on the edge of her seat as the trained cat picked up a soda-water bottle between a paw and its chin and carried it off the stage.

She eased back into the chair when Margo appeared before the footlights, the bodice of her silk dress revealing a good portion of her magnificent breasts, and the full gathered skirt giving her freedom of movement. Within her hands were two massive feathers each large enough to hide behind as she began dancing and weaving around the stage, accompanied by the music of a four-piece orchestra.

In awe of Margo, Katie Lee became breathless; never before had she seen an exotic dancer. Margo knew how to do fascinating things with the large feathers. As they teased and taunted, Margo continued to move across the stage with the grace of a tigress.

Then she began to move more quickly, her long black hair growing wild and tangled, her dress whipping around her legs to reveal a good portion of her thighs. When she gazed down at Katie Lee, her mouth would form a sullen smirk and her dark eyes would fill with fire.

"Bravo!" Leonard suddenly cried from behind Katie Lee. His eyes met and held Margo's as she spun around for one last time, then stopped. She smiled seductively down at him and again gave Katie Lee a look of cold defiance.

"Leonard, did you truly like it?" Margo purred, rushing from the stage. Reeking of alcohol, she pressed her body to Leonard's and clutched at his chest with her manicured fingernails. "I am the best, aren't I? Tell me I'm the best. Tell me." Slowly she slid her hand down his front. "No one is as good as me. Remember that, Leonard."

Katie Lee turned her eyes away, blushing. Margo was not only a wonderful dancer, she was quite bold. It did not seem to matter at all to the woman that others were present while she touched Leonard so familiarly.

Leonard patted Margo on her rounded buttocks and gave her a wet kiss on the cheek. "No, no one is as good as you," he said, his loins aching. "Nor is there anyone who dances as skillfully as you, Margo."

He placed his fingers on Margo's shoulders and eased her away. "But we've yet to see if you have any competition," he said with a low chuckle. "It's time for Katie Lee to show us what she can do and, Margo, honey, you're in for a treat."

"Yeah, I bet I am," Margo said, crumpling into a chair, narrowing her eyes as Leonard went to Katie Lee and offered her his arm.

Margo's gaze traveled over the younger woman, jealousy tearing her heart to shreds; Katie Lee was nothing less than ravishingly beautiful. This afternoon her hair was dressed into a puffed pompadour with soft curls framing her face. The curve of her perfectly rounded breasts was exposed by the low bodice of her ivory silk gown, and ivory silk gloves reached to her elbows. The apple blossoms in her hair made her look as sweet as sugar candy.

Margo smiled smugly as she studied Katie Lee's expression. The girl was pale—obviously frightened. It was going to work out for Margo after all. This country girl could never perform in front of a crowd—especially the sort that frequented Conty Theater.

A low, soft laugh rose from deep inside Margo's throat; she watched Katie Lee clasp her hands before her as Leonard walked away....

Katie Lee's heart was pounding so hard that she felt she might faint dead away. Her fingers and knees were trembling. Her throat was dry. When the orchestra began playing a simple, familiar tune, she tried to open her mouth to sing, but no sound would emerge. It was as though her voice were frozen, way down inside.

She knew that Leonard was watching...waiting....

Closing her eyes, Katie Lee drew a deep breath and let herself be transported back in time. She was back home, doing her daily chores, the songs coming easily, the melodies sweet.

Then a vision of her mother passed before her eyes, and Katie Lee saw the heavy, stooped figure, the careworn face.

Determination flared inside her. She must not let herself become like her mother. She wanted more out of life. She wanted to wake up to mornings filled with promise!

And if she failed now, she just might fail forever!

Margo stood up and went to Leonard. She placed an arm around his waist and pressed her hip against his. "There she is," she taunted him. "Your little songbird. Lord, can she ever sing!" She laughed throatily as Leonard pushed her away and started toward the stage.

But halfway there he had cause to stop. Katie Lee opened her eyes and began to sing so beautifully that it almost caused him to melt into his shoes.

Sighing with relief, Leonard nodded his approval, then sat down and folded his arms across his massive chest.

After Katie Lee had performed several songs, each one lovelier than the last, Leonard rushed onto the stage. He embraced Katie Lee as Margo looked on, her eyes flashing angrily. "My dear, you were stupendous," Leonard said throatily. He patted her back. "You were superb."

Breathless, Katie Lee did not seem to mind Leonard's eager embrace. She laughed and fluttered her lashes nervously. "I truly did sing all right?" she asked hesitantly.

Admiration flashed in Leonard's eyes as he released her and stepped back, holding her hands. "You are exactly what I have been looking for all these months," he said, intense. "Now, my dear, just to be cautious, let us take one more day of practice and then you will make your debut. Tomorrow night will be a night all of Seattle will be talking about. Everyone will want to come and hear my little songbird."

He chuckled when Katie Lee blushed and bashfully lowered her eyes. Placing a finger to her chin, he lifted her face so that her eyes met his. "We're going to have to do something about your being so bashful," he said, smiling smugly. "We can't have you blushing all over the place like a schoolgirl, now can we?"

A familiar voice stilled Leonard's.

"And just how do you plan to change her, Conty?" Bruce inquired, stepping out of the shadows as he walked onto the stage. His neat, fawn breeches fitted him like a glove, and his afternoon coat displayed the white ruffles of his shirt.

Bruce took Katie Lee's hands from Leonard's. "It seems I've arrived just in time. There's no telling what this bastard has on his mind to teach you, Katie Lee." He glowered at Leonard. "Katie Lee, I've told you all along that singing isn't all that he has on his mind. If you wait around long enough, you'll know what I mean."

Katie Lee sighed languidly, shaking her head as she looked from Leonard to Bruce, then back to Leonard. She jerked her hands free and stepped away from Bruce. "I'm sorry, Leonard," she said softly. "But I guess you know that Bruce does not speak for me. I apologize for him."

Frustrated, Bruce raked his fingers through his hair. "Damn it, Katie Lee, there's nothing to apologize for," he said angrily. "In truth, he should be apologizing to you."

Katie Lee placed her hands on her hips. "Whatever for, Bruce?" she demanded. "He is giving me an opportunity I could find nowhere else."

Bruce laughed sarcastically. "Don't be too sure of that," he said, giving Leonard a sour glance. "There are all sorts of dens of iniquity in Seattle that would be glad to have you." He flailed a hand at Leonard. "Ask him. He knows all about the box houses that compete with his. Any of their owners would be glad to pay a year's wages for you. And you wouldn't have to sing a note, Katie Lee. All you would have to do is lift your skirt.''

Leonard doubled a fist and advanced toward Bruce. Doc Porter came into view then at the far end of the stage, his hand resting on a monstrous pistol holstered at his waist.

Katie Lee saw all of this in one blink of her eyes. She glanced from Bruce to Leonard and knew immediately that there was only one way to settle this peacefully.

''Bruce, please let's leave,'' Katie Lee suggested. Taking his hand, she began pulling at him. Then out of the corner of her eye she saw Doc Porter advancing from one end of the stage and Leonard's brother Jacob advancing from the other. As Leonard edged closer to Bruce, it was quite evident that Bruce was outnumbered. She had to convince him to leave— and quickly.

Katie Lee yanked harder. ''Please, Bruce,'' she pleaded.

Never wanting to back away from a fight, Bruce stood his ground a moment longer, glaring at Leonard, then swept an arm around Katie Lee and left the stage with her.

''Let me get my wrap,'' Katie Lee said, rushing into her dressing room and grabbing her embroidered silk shawl.

Then she left the theater with Bruce and walked with him to a fancy carriage. Nodding a silent thank-you to him, she stepped up into the carriage and grew tense when he sat down beside her.

There was a strained silence as the carriage began moving along the crowded waterfront streets. Katie Lee was aware of the steady wash of the surf. Hovering on the edge of the horizon, the afternoon sun was splattering the clouds and water with dark pastels.

Katie Lee's heart began pounding in her throat when Bruce wrapped an arm around her shoulders and drew her close. It was easy to forget that he had humiliated her again in front of Leonard Conty, and this time not only in front of Leonard, but also Margo! The jealous woman had surely enjoyed Katie Lee's discomfort.

"Bruce, please don't give me any more lectures this evening," she asked softly. "I don't think I could bear it!"

"No. No more lectures," Bruce said, smoothing his fingertips over her shoulders as he inched her shawl aside. He bent his lips to her perfumed flesh and kissed her soft breasts. "I have other, more pleasant things planned for us this evening, darling. Are you game?"

A rush of sensual pleasure swept through Katie Lee as he cupped her breast through the silken fabric of her dress. "Should I say yes without even asking what you're up to?" she murmured, the ache between her thighs evidence of her wondrous need of him.

"Say yes," Bruce whispered, his tongue tracing the outline of her lips. "You won't be sorry, darling."

"Yes . . . yes . . ." Katie Lee murmured, breathless with ecstasy.

"First I shall take you for lobster caviar and champagne, and then we shall let the rest of the evening take care of itself," Bruce said, tilting her chin.

He kissed her hotly, passionately. The horse's bridle jingled as it drew the carriage along the waterfront between Main and Jackson, and the driver drew rein beside a restaurant built on a pier.

"I think we've arrived," Bruce whispered, trailing his hands down Katie Lee's back as she strained toward him.

"Where?"

"Captain Jonathan's."

"I hear it's wonderful," Katie Lee whispered, heady with passion.

"Yes, my darling," Bruce said, smoothing her mussed hair. "That's exactly why I brought you here. And then later I plan to take you somewhere else."

Katie Lee drew away from him, her eyes wide. "Where, Bruce?" she asked, anxious.

"My home," he said nonchalantly. "Where else?"

Katie Lee lowered her eyes, a hot blush scorching her cheeks. How hard it was to turn him down when she longed for him as much as he did for her. She wished to end this affair, but the finality of marriage held so many risks.

"Katie Lee?"

Katie Lee turned her eyes to Bruce. She smiled and offered him her hand as he helped her from the carriage. She felt as though she were walking on air; at this moment in her life she was so very happy.

Chapter Eighteen

Bruce led Katie Lee into a dark restaurant that was lighted by kerosene lamps hanging from the ceiling, their wicks turned low. Candles flickered on each of the tables covered with red-checked tablecloths. Fishnets were draped from the ceiling at the four corners of the room, and a large Suquamish Indian canoe with its carved sides stood at the far end.

Large windows overlooked the waters of Puget Sound, and a pianist played soft tunes on a piano beside the bar.

Waitresses dressed in colorful peasant dresses rushed from table to table in the crowded restaurant. Bruce spied an empty table beside one of the windows and ushered Katie Lee over to it. He took her wrap, then pulled out the chair for her to sit down.

"Do you like it?" he asked once they were seated. "Doesn't it smell heavenly? This restaurant prepares the best seafood in Seattle."

"Yes, I like the restaurant," she said softly, reveling in the feel of Bruce's hands as he entwined his fingers with hers. She inhaled deeply. "And, yes, it smells divine, Bruce. I didn't realize how hungry I was until now."

"We shall begin with lobster caviar and French champagne," Bruce said, raising a hand to beckon a waitress. "And then we shall have prime rib or anything your heart desires, darling. It's yours for the having."

"Everything sounds delicious," she said, smiling at the waitress as she arrived with a flip of her skirt. "Bruce, you order for me. I know I shall be happy with anything you choose."

Bruce placed the order, and champagne was quickly brought to their table. As one waitress set long-stemmed glasses before them, another popped the cork and poured, then left them to themselves.

"Bruce Cabot, you're spoiling me," Katie Lee declared, giggling as she sipped the champagne. "Please don't feel that you always have to ply me with champagne. Why, I never so much as had a drink of wine before I met you."

"You never experienced much in your life before at all," Bruce grumbled.

Katie Lee looked away, fearing a lecture was near, although he had promised not to preach.

The sun had all but disappeared beneath the horizon. But enough of the fading orange light remained for Katie Lee to see a ripple in the surface of the water below. She strained closer to the window, then emitted a deep sigh.

"Bruce, look down there," she said. "It's a little animal looking straight up at us! It is so cute!"

Bruce glanced from the window, then back at Katie Lee, whose eyes were sparkling vivaciously, he noted. "That's a sea lion," he explained. "Some have become tame in these waters. They like to hang around to feed on the smaller fish that are thrown back when the fishing vessels dock here.

"Sea lions breed in large herds, and the males establish harems—so perhaps the male is more intelligent than man," he teased. "How would you like to be part of a harem, darling? Most women in harems are treated like queens and never want for anything."

Afraid that they would once again get into the debate over marriage, Katie Lee was glad when the waitress brought the lobster caviar with small, tempting crackers and fancy breads. The main course followed shortly afterward, juices running from the prime rib onto the plate alongside buttered carrots cut into long strips.

"Eat to your heart's content," Bruce said, slicing his meat as he watched Katie Lee marvel at her plate. "It will taste as good as it looks, darling."

Picking up the knife and fork, Katie Lee put the first bite into her mouth, and it seemed to melt right onto her tongue. After that she could not help herself. She ate ravenously until every morsel was cleaned from her plate. She had even consumed the caviar as though it were dessert.

Laughing softly, Katie Lee reached a hand to Bruce, who was about to order dessert and shook her head. "Darling, no more," she said, feeling light-headed from the champagne. "I think I've had enough of everything. Please, no dessert."

"Are you positive that you don't want a piece of apple pie?" Bruce asked persuasively. "The apples are grown right here in Seattle."

"No. No pie," Katie Lee insisted, then her eyes grew wide as she heard a sudden racket out in the street. She watched as several people rose from their tables to rush outside.

"What the hell . . . ?" Bruce exclaimed, looking toward the door. He pushed himself from the chair and grabbed Katie Lee's shawl. "Let's see what all the commotion is about."

Feeling slightly tipsy Katie Lee was aware that she giggled and swayed as she rose from the chair. She leaned toward Bruce as he wrapped the shawl around her shoulders and led her to the door. The night was now dark, and people were standing along the side-walks to watch a large brass band that was marching along the thoroughfare. Others were running along beside it.

As soon as the band had passed by, Bruce helped Katie Lee up into the carriage and instructed the driver to follow the band. Slowly they rode behind it until it stopped in the street near Conty Theater, where another crowd was gathered. On the corner of Second and Washington a barker shouted out the theater's attractions, boasting loudly of the new lady who sang like a songbird and who would appear the following night.

Katie Lee leaned closer to the window, her eyes wide. "Why, that man is speaking of me," she said in surprise, placing one hand to her throat. "My word, Bruce, I do believe I will be one of the theater's main attractions."

Bruce folded his arms across his chest, wishing now that he had not been so inquisitive. All of this excitement would only add to the allure of the stage.

"Bruce!" Katie Lee exclaimed, straining to see from the window. "Would you look? The musicians from Leonard's theater are climbing onto some sort of platform on the roof."

Bruce studied the brass band that was positioned in front of a box house across the street from Leonard's. Then he regarded the musicians on the platform of Conty Theater. Now he knew what was happening. The band was from a rival establishment. There was going to be a duel in music. While an admiring crowd quickly gathered, the rival band was nearing the end of another song.

The selection ended, and the leader of the band bowed low to the surrounding crowd and to his brave supporters. In the meantime, the Conty Theater's musicians were ready to begin their own loud show. There were four of them. The leader was armed with a violin, which he handled with the daredevil grace and ease of a plowman handling a six-shooter. Another dark-faced young man with a melancholy cast of countenance strummed a huge harp. The third defiantly played a husky clarinet, and the fourth strummed a banjo.

When they struck up a lugubrious melody, a stalwart young man with lungs of leather added his voice to their efforts.

"She stole nine thousand and six hundred," he bellowed in the deepest of baritones. "Say, babe, I know we will be happy after a while...."

The band across the street hesitated to return the fire as the crowd looked toward them for an answer. Suddenly around the block was heard the discordant blare of an obviously untutored brass band, accompanied by the voices of men and women upraised in a popular street ditty.

But the words were different—they seemed to have been adapted from a hymn book. It was the Salvation Army!

"My goodness!" Katie Lee exclaimed. "Another band! How exciting!"

Fifty strong, the uniformed soldiers of the Lord swung into the street, flags flying, torches smoking and musicians playing like mad.

The approach of the Army caused pandemonium to break out between the two dueling factions of theater musicians. The crowd cheered as the brass band and Leonard's orchestra quickly teamed up to outplay the Salvation Army.

Giving up, the Salvationists marched on. The brass band became winded, leaving Leonard's orchestra to finish the lively melody, "There'll Be a Hot Time in the Old Town Tonight."

On both sides of the street lusty-lunged spielers shouted the advantage of their respective shows. Katie Lee's insides grew cold when she heard Leonard's barker shouting out the girls' names. He was inviting all men to come and enjoy the wine, women and faro. And whoever wished could even watch the stage shows!

As the musicians filed into the theaters, the crowd divided and followed them.

"Did you hear what that man said?" Katie Lee gasped, settling back inside the carriage. "Surely Leonard did not wish for him to place the stage show second to... to the women in the box seats. That is so... degrading."

The streets quiet once again, the carriage rolled on through the city toward Bruce's house. Bruce studied Katie Lee in the flashes of lamplight as they left behind one gaslight and approached another. He slipped an arm around her shoulder and breathed much more easily when she cuddled close to him and placed her cheek upon his chest.

"Katie Lee, places such as Leonard Conty's make their profits from liquor and card tables," he said hoarsely. "The girls who do not perform spend their time circulating among the customers, escorting them to the bar. For every drink they cozen a customer into taking, the girls receive a metal tag, which the management redeems in cash. If the girls peddle more personal wares, the management does not object. I have heard that some box house owners have cribs along Skid Road, where the women take their gents for what money they can get from them. But the box seats at Leonard's theater are deep and the waiters are discreet, giving the women no incentive to lift their skirts elsewhere.''

Disillusioned, Katie Lee clung to Bruce. "Are you saying the women entertain men on the premises of Leonard's theater?'' she inquired in barely a whisper. "That while I am singing, they. . . ?''

"Exactly," Bruce said dryly. "Need I say more?''

Katie Lee did not answer him. She was glad that he had had his say and did not pursue it any further. Though she was still giddy from the champagne and fine food, she was sufficiently aware to realize that life at Leonard's theater was not going to be a bed of roses.

"Enough talk of theaters," Bruce said as the carriage drew to a halt in front of his house. "Darling, let's forget everything tonight except for being together." He hurried from the carriage and went around to help Katie Lee down. He swung her to his side and began walking her up the steps. "Darling, I have quite a surprise for you tonight.''

Katie Lee looked up at him, seeing that his eyes were twinkling. "Surprise?" she repeated, arching a carefully plucked eyebrow. "What sort?"

She looked toward the front windows of the house. "Is someone here?" she asked in a whisper, tensing. "Your house is flooded with light."

"I lighted the lamps before I came and got you at the theater," Bruce said, slipping a hand inside his front breeches pocket and circling a key with his fingers. "It was my intention to bring you here before the night was out. I have something to show you."

Katie Lee did not have time to say anything else, for Bruce had unlocked and opened the door. Walking beside him, she passed through the foyer and went into the parlor, where a pair of velvet-covered wing chairs was drawn invitingly to the fireplace. Various other gilt and satin furnishings were placed around the room.

Breathless, Katie Lee went with Bruce into the dining room, where expensive china and crystal were on display on a dining-room table crafted from solid maple. A blazing chandelier was reflected in the polished wood.

"It's all so lovely!" Katie Lee exclaimed, placing both hands to her throat. She turned to Bruce, questioning him with her eyes. "My word, this house was furnished so quickly. And it's all just perfect for the house." She fumbled with the gathers of her skirt. "Did some lady help you?"

Bruce drew her to his side and guided her into the foyer and up the oak staircase. "No, no lady has been inside this house since I purchased it but you," he said, chuckling. "I did a damn good job, didn't I?"

"It's wonderful," Katie Lee said, reaching the second-floor landing. Flooded with remembrances, her face grew hot as Bruce led her to the bedroom where they had made maddening love.

But this was momentarily blotted from her memory when she saw the loveliness of the decor. A massive oak four-poster bed with a lovely gathered eyelet skirt and a quilted coverlet of a soft rose hue stood between two windows. The brocade drapes were of the same color as the coverlet.

"So you like this room also?" Bruce inquired, swinging her around so that their gazes could meet and hold. "It is a room you are comfortable in?"

"Very," Katie Lee answered, her pulse racing when she recognized the look of passion in his eyes.

"Comfortable enough to make love in?" Bruce asked, his voice suddenly turned husky. He began removing the combs in her hair until the tresses streamed down her back. "I love you, Katie Lee. So very much."

Caught up in a spell of delicious feelings, Katie Lee let Bruce remove her gloves, and her body began to grow hot and seemed to swell as he kissed her fingers, sucked her thumb and moved his tongue around her palm in slow revolutions.

Needing him so badly that she ached, Katie Lee reached back with trembling fingers to unfasten her dress, then moved away from Bruce so that he could watch her undress. Her clothes lying in a heap on the floor, she trembled as she waited for Bruce to pull off his shirt and breeches.

Going to Katie Lee, Bruce twined his fingers through her hair and sought her mouth, and when he did he tasted champagne. His tongue crept through her parted lips. He teased, probed and tantalized. Heady, she melted into his arms as he carried her to the bed.

"You are so good for me," Bruce whispered, holding her gently for a moment, his chest rising and falling as he breathed deeply. He cupped her breasts, tracing the outline of the hard pink nipples. "I must have you now. I can wait no longer, Katie Lee."

"Bruce, I need you as much," she whispered as he lowered himself to lie full length upon her. He wedged one leg between her thighs, letting his pelvis sink toward her. "When I'm with you, nothing else is important. You become my breath...my heart-beat. Oh, yes, do make love to me. Now...now...."

Bruce lowered his mouth to her lips and kissed her wildly. Giving in to the heat of her body, he thrust his hardness deep within her.

She felt herself opening to him, wanting him still closer, and joined his movements, matching his hungry thrusts.

As powerful as an ocean wave, the pleasure was mounting and spreading within her as his hips moved against her own. And she met him movement for movement. She rode the waves of pleasure, swimming closer to that peak of ecstasy.

Yet she did not want to experience it quite yet. She wanted to hold onto the feelings and capture them in the deepest recesses of her heart as something to turn to when she was lonely...when she wasn't with Bruce.

But it was impossible. His lips had moved to her breast. Taking the nipple in his mouth, he aroused it gently with his tongue.

"Oh, Bruce, it is so wonderful," Katie Lee sighed, closing her eyes to the dense golden light in which she felt herself suspended.

When Bruce's body stiffened and he groaned against her breast, she clung to him until he finally lay still, content.

Bruce rolled to his side next to Katie Lee and traced the sensual swell of her breasts, then moved lower to cup the soft mound of golden hair between her thighs. It did not seem right that she would leave him tonight to go and sleep elsewhere.

Yet he would not beg her to stay. She would have to decide to stay on her own.

By now Katie Lee was feeling the sweet euphoria that was always there after making love with Bruce, and looked slowly around the room. She suddenly felt as though she didn't belong. Though Bruce had proudly shown her the new furnishings for his house, he had not once asked her to marry him again, to live in this lovely home. When she first saw the furnishings, she had thought he had bought them to persuade her to marry him.

Now *her* pride would not let her be the one to bring it up. She had already said no too many times.

"I really must go," she murmured, fluttering her eyelashes at Bruce, as if suddenly nervous. "I must have my rest—tomorrow night I make my debut." She waited breathlessly for Bruce to argue with her about her decision to perform, waited anxiously for him to mention marriage.

But he did neither. Now she was sure that a part of her had lost him.

Shame and disappointment filling her, Katie Lee crept from the bed and began dressing. Bruce watched her, aching to ask her to stay, to be his wife. But pride would not allow him to do this, only to have her say no to him again.

No. He would have to try again after her first performance. He knew enough about her now to understand just why she hesitated to become a wife. She did not want to follow in her mother's footsteps.

"I'll dress and get you safely to your hotel," Bruce said, puzzling over the hurt look in her eyes. He shook his head. He might never understand her.

Chapter Nineteen

Katie Lee marveled at the many bouquets that had been brought to her dressing room. As she checked each card to see who had sent them, her heart ached; none was from Bruce. Every single one was from Leonard Conty.

Behind her the door opened, and Katie Lee heard the froth of petticoats at her ankles rustle as she turned around. Again she was disappointed; it was only Leonard.

But of course she could not have expected it to be Bruce. He did not approve of her being there in the first place.

The evening was quickly losing much of its excitement.

Dressed for the occasion in an expensive dark suit that displayed a red satin embroidered vest, wearing a diamond stickpin in his ascot, Leonard stepped into Katie Lee's dressing room. His chest swelled with pride as he looked her up and down. Her cheeks were flushed pink with excitement, he could see; her eyes were innocently wide.

His gaze swept lower, and he felt his loins ache as he saw the swell of her breasts. Until now he had controlled his urges by thinking only of the money she was going to make for him. But tonight . . .

Leonard held himself in check a moment longer, afraid of frightening her if he became so bold as to actually try to kiss her. "My dear, you look absolutely ravishing," he said huskily, narrowing his eyes as he took a step toward her. "Tonight the men in the audience will get a rare treat."

Katie Lee was becoming uncomfortable, knowing the look of lust in a man's eyes when she saw it.

"I hope it is my voice they find captivating," she said, hearing the drawn note in her voice. "Not me."

"Dear, don't you know that it all comes in one lovely package?" Leonard said, his pulse racing. He reached a trembling hand to her face. "You . . . your voice . . . your lovely innocence? It is a combination that can very rarely be found in a woman."

Tense, scarcely breathing, Katie Lee slowly removed his hand. But that did not deter him from further action. Soon he was framing her face between both his hands and drawing her to himself.

"Katie Lee, I cannot help myself," he said throatily, his breath hot on her face as his lips drew close to hers. "I must kiss you. Allow it, my dear. You may find that you enjoy it. Together we could have the world. I shall shower you with diamonds. I shall give you anything, if you will just let me.''

Panic rose inside Katie Lee. She pushed at Leonard's chest, but could not free herself. As his mouth bore down upon her lips in a wet, almost slobbering kiss, she recoiled. She thought she was going to retch.

She groaned and pushed, but that only seemed to spur him onward. One hand held her in place, while the other sought her breast and cupped it through the silken fabric of her dress.

A sudden knock on the door drew Leonard quickly away from her. A voice from the hallway called, ''Five minutes!'' Leonard ran one finger nervously around his shirt collar; he felt himself wavering as he looked at Katie Lee and saw how pale she had become.

''Katie Lee, that was damn foolish of me,'' he said thickly. ''I shouldn't have.''

Katie Lee's heart was racing. Mortified, she inched away from him. Had he not been interrupted, he most surely would have taken total advantage of her.

''No, you shouldn't have,'' she said, knowing that her voice quavered. She spun around, searching for her shawl. She could not stay in this place for another minute. Had she listened to Bruce, she wouldn't have been there at all.

''I will take my leave, sir,'' she said icily, pulling her wrap about her shoulders. ''You can find yourself another performer who does not mind being manhandled by you!''

Panic rose inside Leonard. He looked wildly at Katie Lee as she jerked the door open. Horrified at the thought of losing her, he rushed to her and blocked her exit. "Let's not be hasty," he said, trying to laugh. "You can't walk out on me. I've told everyone about you. You would make me the laughingstock of Seattle."

"I am sure you already are," Katie Lee retorted. She looked him up and down with loathing. "You are nothing but a very repugnant man."

Leonard glared at her, and he tightened his hands into fists. "My dear, I am sorry you feel that way," he said through clenched teeth. "But aside from such feelings, I implore you to reconsider leaving. You have much talent as a singer. Do not cast aside the opportunity to show everyone just how much. Stay, Katie Lee. Perform. If you will, I promise never to lay a hand on you again."

Hearing the orchestra playing made Katie Lee's heart hammer anew within her chest. She was torn by so many emotions that her head was spinning.

"Katie Lee?" Leonard asked, relaxing his hands at his sides. "You will perform, won't you? If you don't, you will always wonder what you missed."

"I shall sing if you are serious in your promise," Katie Lee responded, her chin held high. "Otherwise, I must leave. I don't want ever to be touched by you again. Do you understand?"

Leonard cleared his throat. "Yes, I understand," he said heartily. He dared then to reach for the shawl and remove it from her shoulders, wincing when she slapped his hand.

"Never touch me at all!" she cried, taking off her shawl herself.

"Never again," Leonard stated, his mood darkening. No woman had ever humiliated him so. Most were eager for his attention, knowing they would be paid well for it.

But this little miss was different—in every way. Her morals were quite intact!

"Then I shall perform tonight," Katie Lee said. Suddenly she felt her stomach turn. She was soon to walk onto the stage. The very thought terrified her.

"But what if I can't?" she asked, her throat constricting at the idea. "I am suddenly so...so afraid."

Leonard refrained from comforting her by placing his arm around her waist, and instead gestured with a hand toward the door. "My dear, let's go behind the scenes," he suggested. "Watch Margo perform and see how confident she is. There was a time when even she was terrified. But once before the audience, she became oblivious of everything but her love for what she does. So shall it be the same for you, Katie Lee. You'll see."

Nodding silently to him, Katie Lee stepped out of her room. She blushed when several scantily attired women rushed by her, then winced as she heard the sounds of drunken men shouting in the audience. She inched close to the curtain and watched Margo finish her feather dance, twisting and twirling. Katie Lee wondered at the pinched expression on Margo's face; clearly the woman was not enjoying herself.

In the crowded room a hundred or more men sat smoking and chewing tobacco. Boys ate peanuts, throwing the shells onto the red plush carpeting.

"Damn those drunken bastards," Leonard swore, narrowing his eyes to follow Katie Lee's gaze. "This place is a gold mine, but Margo's having trouble, getting them to pay attention to her." He turned to Katie Lee. "My dear, that's where you come in. You shall turn all of their heads. After tonight everyone will come to my establishment."

Katie Lee only half heard what Leonard was saying. She was trying to control her heartbeat by taking in several deep breaths. Perhaps the men would settle down when she got onto the stage. And once the carriage trade began coming to the theater, the audience would be refined . . . appreciative. . . .

Margo rushed from the stage, her eyes reflecting her rage. "Damn them all to hell," she stormed, tossing her feathers aside. "Those sons of bitches don't know talent when they see it. It's wasted on them, Leonard. Wasted!"

Katie Lee grew cold inside when Margo turned to her, a sneer now marring her striking features. She could feel the woman's hate like a knife in the heart.

"And you, little girl, you won't get any better reception," Margo said, laughing boisterously. "You'll be laughed right off the stage. Nobody wants a prim and proper act in here. They want to see flesh, honey." Margo familiarly placed a hand upon Katie Lee's shoulder. "Have you got any to show?"

Katie Lee shuddered and drew away. Just then Leonard nodded toward the stage, and without actually being told, she knew that it was time for her to make her appearance. With rubbery knees and a racing pulse, she turned and moved before the footlights. The brightness of the lamps momentarily blinded her, causing her to stumble. But she soon regained her footing and found herself standing in the middle of the stage. The orchestra was already playing a familiar song, one meant just for her to sing.

Her eyes adjusted to the light, and Katie Lee was able to see into the crowd of rowdy men and lewd women, their faces laughing up at her. The place was full. The bar, which stretched along one wall, was crowded enough to keep three bartenders busy, and nearly every table was occupied. Women with painted cheeks and skirts almost up to their knees roamed the room, smiling at the patrons. And from the curtained box seats in the low balcony came laughter and shouts and giggles and a steady ringing of bells, as Conty's women summoned waiters.

Katie Lee glanced again around the room. The noise in the theater temporarily distracted her.

"Katie Lee! You must sing," she heard Leonard from the sidelines. "Damn it, sing!"

She gave him a fleeting glance, smiled briefly, then focused her eyes above the crowd. As she began to sing, she was soon able to ignore the click of dice, the chink of coins, the shuffling of cards and the stench of tobacco fumes.

She did not even see Bruce as he paid fifty cents for a seat near the stage. She did not see his look of anger change to one of adoration when she continued to sing softly, sweetly enough to turn heads and silence whole tables full of men.

And she did not see the hatred intensify on Margo's face behind the scenes.

All that Katie Lee was aware of was the pleasure that singing was giving her. Tonight it was special, because she was being accompanied by an orchestra. She felt as though she was a star, and it was wonderful.

The song finished, Katie Lee rushed from the stage. The applause and the request for an encore made a hot flush rush to her cheeks.

"No, don't go back out," Leonard said, smiling from ear to ear. "Let them hunger for more. They will pay double tomorrow night."

Breathing hard, Katie Lee nodded. "I don't think I could sing another song, anyhow," she said, and laughed softly. A sensual shudder coursed through her. "Oh, but it was so exciting."

Leonard smiled smugly. "Which proves that you were born a performer!" he said, walking with her to her dressing room. Recalling their last confrontation, he did not accompany her inside. "My dear, congratulations. You did not let me or yourself down. After tonight, everything will be even easier for you." He performed a half bow, then turned and walked away.

Walking as though on clouds, she went into her dressing room and closed her door. But her euphoria was short-lived. Margo was there waiting for her, her face a grotesque mask of hatred.

"What are you doing here?" Katie Lee gasped. She took a step back as Margo moved boldly toward her.

"Did you know that Leonard threatened to give me my walking papers tonight?" Margo cried, digging her fingernails into the palms of each of her hands. "All so he can give the lead to a nobody from nowhere!"

Katie Lee jumped with alarm and emitted a cry when Margo slapped her hard across the face. She did not have time to regain her composure before the crazed woman coiled her fingers through her thick hair and with a jerk threw her upon the floor to straddle her.

"You little bitch, I'm going to show you a thing or two about life here in Leonard's box house," Margo threatened, removing a penknife from her pocket and holding it to Katie Lee's throat. "There isn't anything nice or sweet about this whorehouse. You don't belong here, sweetheart. To make everyone agree with me, I plan to mess up that pretty face of yours."

Katie Lee was frozen in fear. She could feel the cold tip of the blade at her throat and cried out when the razor-sharp edge cut painfully into her flesh. Blood began to trickle in a slow stream down her neck.

She closed her eyes, waiting for death. Never had she known anyone who could hate as deeply as Margo. She had never given anyone cause to hate her before. Even now she was innocent. It was because of Leonard Conty that Margo was doing this!

Her eyes flew open when Margo suddenly screamed; she was no longer pinning Katie Lee down.

Bruce was there and had wrestled Margo to the floor. "You damn bitch," Bruce growled. "I ought to strangle you, but you're getting off easy." He released her and jerked her to her feet. "You get the hell out of here, and if you ever go near Katie Lee again, you'll have me to answer to."

Shaking, Katie Lee looked away as Margo staggered from the room. Bruce helped her up from the floor and placed a handkerchief over her wound. Sobbing, she moved into his embrace.

"Surely you have had enough of this place," Bruce murmured, caressing her back. "My God, Katie Lee, do you know how close you came to...to—?"

"Please don't say it, Bruce," Katie Lee pleaded. "Just take me from this place."

"I hope you don't plan to return," he said, and guided her toward the door.

"I don't want to talk about it," she insisted, shuddering. "Please don't say any more about it, Bruce. It was a most frightening and embarrassing experience."

"I understand," Bruce said, then ushered her outside, where his carriage awaited them. "Well, I shall see that all of this is forgotten, Katie Lee. You come with me and see what real dreams are made of."

Chapter Twenty

Bruce had not given Katie Lee even the slightest hint as to what he had to show her as he walked her toward his well-lighted house, but, she reflected, anything would be wonderful after Margo's degrading attack.

She recoiled at the idea of ever returning to Leonard's theater; she had not survived an Indian attack to be slain by another woman!

Yet deep inside she knew that she must return, if only to show Margo that she would not be frightened away so easily.

Her thoughts were brought back to the present when Bruce did not open the door himself, but instead raised the large brass knocker as though he were a visitor.

Katie Lee looked up at him, and her puzzlement increased when she saw his mischievous smile.

Unable to stand the suspense any longer, Katie Lee started to question him, but words failed her when the door suddenly opened, and, silhouetted in the light from the foyer, a tall, lean man dressed in butler's attire bowed to them.

"Good evening, Mr. Cabot. Good evening, ma'am," the man said in a distinct English accent. He gestured with one hand for Bruce and Katie Lee to enter as he moved aside.

"Good evening, Lawrence," Bruce said, his eyes twinkling as he led Katie Lee into the foyer.

"Your wrap, ma'am?" Lawrence asked with a tilt of his chin.

Swinging around, Bruce removed Katie Lee's shawl and draped it over the butler's outstretched arm. "That will be all for now, Lawrence," he said. "Thank you."

"It is always my pleasure to serve you, sir, ma'am," Lawrence said, closing the door behind them.

Bruce led Katie Lee into the parlor, where a fire burned brightly in the fireplace. He leaned down and whispered into her ear. "Did you like him?" he inquired. "If not, I can replace him."

Katie Lee was stunned speechless by having been met by a butler at all; now Bruce was willing to dismiss the man, if she so desired? That a butler was now a part of Bruce's household came as a total shock.

"Well? Should I?" Bruce asked again, taking Katie Lee's hands and turning her to face him.

"Should you dismiss the man?" Katie repeated. "I would think not—at least not on my account."

She swallowed hard, scrutinizing Bruce. "Bruce, I did not expect you to have a butler," she whispered. "You so surprise me at times."

"So you don't approve of having a butler?" Bruce said in a teasing fashion. "Or perhaps even a maid?"

"A maid?" Katie Lee felt her astonishment growing as footsteps sounded on the threshold.

Katie Lee turned—to find a maid—a pretty woman with a friendly smile and dark, laughing eyes. Her hair was flecked with gray and drawn back from her round face with combs, and she wore a floor-length, crisp black cotton dress with a high white collar and white cuffs.

Katie Lee took a deep breath—the house was full of the same smells she remembered from her mother's kitchen.

"Katie Lee, let me introduce Catherine to you," Bruce said, watching Katie Lee's eyes light up when Catherine curtsied politely. "Catherine, this is Miss Holden. Whenever she is here, you are to treat her as though she is a member of the household. It is my hope that one day she will be."

"Yes, sir," Catherine said, cupping her hands politely before her. "I shall be delighted to do so." She smiled softly at Katie Lee. "Is there anything I can get for you now, ma'am?"

Katie Lee quickly shook her head. "No, thank you, nothing," she said softly. She was beginning to understand everything. First the lovely house...then the furniture...and now maids and butlers....

It was all for her! It was all a way to prove to her that life with him would be nothing like the sort of existence she was used to. He was proving to her that the one thing she feared most in marriage was no longer a concern. She would not become old before her time. She would not have to spend her entire day seeing to burdensome chores.

She was overwhelmed by these signs of his devotion, but was she worthy of such treatment?

She didn't think so, for she had fought him tooth and nail ever since they had met one another. She had fought for her freedom, while all along he had offered her a liberty she had never thought possible, and heaven was to be found within his arms every night for the rest of her life.

Still, she felt obliged to return to Leonard's theater for just one more night, if only to show Margo a thing or two.

"There's one other person I would like you to meet tonight," Bruce said, guiding her past Catherine and out into the long corridor that led to the kitchen at the back of the house. "Do you smell the wonderful fragrances? Breads and pies are being prepared for tomorrow's meals. I hope that you will be here to share them with me."

Upon entering the kitchen, Katie Lee was introduced to a cook, a small Chinese man who smiled more than he talked as he continued to knead and pound the dough against the large kitchen table.

"So there you have it, darling," Bruce said, ushering Katie Lee toward the staircase. Slowly they began to ascend the stairs, their arms wrapped around each other. "I know I don't have to explain all of this. I can tell by your expression that you understand exactly what it is all about. As I said earlier, you would never want for another thing if you became my wife. It is up to you now to decide."

"How can you be so generous, when I have been nothing but a big bother to you?" Katie Lee asked, contrite. "In truth, you should hate me. Instead, you offer me so much because of your love. I am so moved by all of this, Bruce. So very, very moved."

"All I want is to shower you with my love forever, darling," Bruce said with feeling, leading her to the master bedroom that was bathed in soft candlelight. "I want to protect you. If only you will let me."

He closed the door behind them. He turned to her and ran his fingers through her long, golden hair, spreading it across her shoulders. "Stay with me tonight, Katie Lee," he asked huskily. "Don't return to that dreaded hotel room ever again. Let's find a preacher and arrange for a wedding tomorrow. Tomorrow night you could be staying here as my wife."

Katie Lee felt herself melting beneath the passion in his eyes, and her skin was on fire where his fingers lowered her dress. It was hard to keep her sanity when he was stirring so much rapture within her, his tongue now stirring her nipples to hardened peaks, his fingers caressing the soft mound at the juncture of her thighs as her clothes fell to lie in a heap around her ankles.

Yet she had to keep reminding herself that she could not marry him tomorrow; she had one more task to perform before turning her back on Leonard Conty and his stage.

If only Bruce would understand and be patient with her for just one more day.

"Don't give me an answer right away," Bruce said, seeing her hesitate. "I won't badger you, darling. Stay the night with me and then give me an answer. I hope that it will be the one I have sought since the first time I saw you, for even then I wanted you to be my wife."

His fingers trembled as he placed his arms beneath her and lifted her to carry her across the room. After placing her gently upon the bed, he stood back and looked at her, then slowly began undressing as she watched him adoringly.

"Yes, darling," Katie Lee blurted. "I shall stay the night. I think it would be wonderful to awaken in your arms. So very, very wonderful."

Bruce stepped out of the rest of his clothes. He had wanted more of a commitment, but there would be tomorrow.

Climbing onto the bed, he slid to her side and savored the feel of her silken flesh against his own. Cupping her breasts with his hands, he pressed his hardened manhood against her pulsing womanhood, drawing soft gasps of pleasure from her.

Their lips met in a frenzy. Bruce lifted his hips, then lowered his hardness deep into her and began his rhythmic strokes. They made love as never before. As the sun and rain create flowers, they were breathing life into something between them that was beautiful. One minute Katie Lee felt as though she were the center of the universe, and the next she felt as though cool waters were flowing through her veins.

Bruce slid his hardness in and out of her softness. His body jolted and quivered with the burning current of desire. He plunged deeper and deeper, trying to reach the point of ultimate pleasure. With his tongue he parted her lips and delved into the sweet recesses of her mouth.

Their bodies suddenly arched tightly together and exploded, and each experienced a strange incandescent blaze of brightness.

And then there was calm.

Katie Lee twined her arms around Bruce's neck and clung to him, not wanting him to leave her. Slowly she closed her eyes and felt a wonderful peace that transcended time. She fell asleep with Bruce's lips on her breast....

The rays of the morning sun spilled through the windows, awakening Katie Lee. Rubbing her eyes, she opened them slowly and found Bruce at her side, watching her.

"You slept as though you've not slept in ages," Bruce said, smoothing back fallen locks of hair from her eyes as she smiled up at him. "Was it the bed or your sleeping companion, darling?"

"Perhaps both," Katie Lee answered, and snuggled into his arms as he drew her close. Her breasts were pressed against his chest, causing the nipples to harden with desire. He moved his hand along her thighs and then around to touch the core of her womanhood. Katie Lee moaned throatily. She closed her eyes, enjoying this new way of awakening to a new day. She welcomed Bruce as he straddled her anew and thrust his hardness inside her to begin his deep, even strokes once more. Her heartbeat went wild with building passion as she locked her ankles around his waist.

"My darling, I am ravenous for you this morning," Bruce whispered, running his tongue over her lips, then down her throat and to her breast. "I need you, Katie Lee. Oh, God, how I need you. Say that you need me as much."

The liquid fire of ecstasy spreading through her, Katie Lee breathed her answer against his cheek. "Yes, oh, yes, I do need you as much," she declared. "Love me, Bruce. Now."

Katie Lee moved her hands over his body, savoring the tautness of his muscles. She sank her fingernails into the flesh of his hips and urged him onward, feeling her breath coming in short, pleasurable gasps. When his body stiffened and then lunged wildly into her, she opened herself to him and enjoyed the same release....

Exhausted, Bruce set Katie Lee away from him and slipped from the bed. Drawing on a pair of breeches, he went to the window and looked out. "It is the best of all seasons here in Seattle," he murmured. "The salmon are striking out in the bay, and in the valleys the vegetables have matured early." Already farmers were making their way along the planked streets, hauling wagon loads of lettuce, peas and rhubarb to the markets.

He looked toward the forest where the firs were fringed with new green growth.

Katie Lee pulled up a blanket to cover her nudity. "Then why do you sound so melancholy, when you say it is the best of all seasons here in Seattle? I would think that you would be glad. Surely your business is prospering."

Bruce kneaded his brow, then turned and went back to the bed to sit down beside Katie Lee. "Darling, no rain has fallen during this entire first week of June. There was no rain in the last half of May. Day after day the weather is clear and warm, and Seattle's wooden empire has become tinder dry. It worries me, because I know there are many firetraps in this city. One fire could destroy so much. It is a worry, Katie Lee. I can't help it."

"I'm sure you are worrying about nothing," Katie Lee said, trying to reassure him, touching him gently on the cheek. "But I am beginning to see that it is part of your nature. You have worried about me since the moment we met.''

"And I shouldn't have?'' Bruce asked, glowering. Then he took her hands and held them tightly. "Are we going to go and visit that preacher today, Katie Lee?''

Katie Lee lowered her eyes and felt her face grow hot with a blush. "Oh, Bruce, it would be so easy to say yes,'' she murmured, then gasped when he jerked his hands away.

"You say that as though you are not going to say yes,'' Bruce declared angrily and rose quickly to his feet. He glowered down at her. "Katie Lee, for God's sake, what is it now? Why are you hesitating still?''

Hearing the frustration in his voice, Katie Lee rose quickly from the bed and snuggled into his embrace. "Darling, I shall marry you tomorrow,'' she said, looking slowly up at him. "Just one more day, Bruce. Surely you can agree to that. I will become your wife. Tomorrow.''

Bruce framed her face between his hands and forced her to meet his eyes. "Tomorrow?'' he said dryly. "What's so damn special about tomorrow?''

"Because I have plans for today...and tonight,'' she said, wincing beneath his angry glare.

"It's that damn theater, isn't it?'' he growled. He looked at her. "Why Katie Lee? After what happened, I would think you would never want to go there again.''

"Margo is my reason for returning," Katie Lee said stubbornly, ignoring the eyes dark with hurt before her. "I can't let her think that she bested me. Please understand. It's a matter of pride, Bruce. I have no other choice."

Bruce wavered. She was so courageous, so proud. He shook his head, then went to her and drew her into his arms. "This is going to be a hell of a long day," he said thickly. "I'm not sure I can stand you going there."

"I must be at the theater for both the practice and the performance," Katie Lee said softly. "But that will be the last, Bruce. My darling, I love you so much. I have wanted to be with you all along, but feared so much what marriage had to offer. My mother—"

Bruce placed a hand to her mouth. "I know," he replied. "But never again do you have to worry about that. And, darling, didn't you know that I have known all along how you felt about me?"

"You are the first—and you are the last," Katie Lee whispered, tears streaming from her eyes. She couldn't wait for tomorrow.

Chapter Twenty-One

June 6, 1889
Thursday... 2:40 p.m.

Madame Feitsworth-Ewens, who specialized in reading the future by means of colored clam shells, was giving a customer some advice in the flimsy, wooden Pontius Building on Front Street. In the office next to hers Dr. Sturgens, a dentist from Boston, was peering into the mouth of a logger. On the ground floor, J. P. Madigan was showing some boots to a housewife. And in the basement James McGough, who ran a paint store and woodworking shop, was finishing a cabinet. His assistant was heating glue over a gasoline stove. The glue boiled over, and some of it fell onto the stove and caught fire. Flaming gobs of glue splashed onto the floor, which was littered with wood shavings and soaked with turpentine. The flames spread quickly over the boards. McGough tried to douse the blaze with water from his fire bucket, but the fire continued to spread. McGough and his assistant fled.

Even before the cabinetmakers rushed from the building, someone on the street had seen the smoke and run for the fire department. By this time the flames had burst through the wooden ceiling, driving Madigan and the housewife from the shoe store, Dr. Sturgens and the patient from the dentist's office, and Madame Feitsworth-Ewens and her client from the farsighted clam shells.

A hose cart pulled from the station at Second and Columbia reached the scene first. Close behind the cart came the town's first steam fire engine. The hose company tied up to the hydrant at Madison and the steam engine took the next hydrant south, two blocks away.

The burning glue and leather threw off so much smoke that the firemen had trouble finding the source of the blaze. They shot water onto the outer walls of the two-story building and onto the roof, until someone pried off the clapboard siding at street level. By now the basement was a furnace. The firemen poured water into the cellar, but it was too late. The fire was out of control.

The first shop engulfed by the fire was the Dietz and Mayer liquor store. Whisky barrels in the basement exploded and showered the walls with flaming alcohol. When the Crystal Palace saloon caught fire a moment later, more high-proof fuel was added to the flames.

Twenty minutes after the glue pot tipped over, the entire block from Madison to Marion was ablaze....

Katie Lee was brushing her hair in her dressing room at Conty Theater, relieved that thus far she had not seen Margo. She could not hope that the woman was gone for good; Margo did not seem the sort to give up all that easily.

As the minutes passed, Katie Lee just wanted to put this day behind her. Though the stage had been exciting, performing had too many drawbacks. Now that she had proven that she could do it, she could start her new life with Bruce with a contented heart.

"So you've returned, have you?"

Katie Lee's heart stopped. She had not heard the door open, but she heard it close, the lock clicking into place. Scarcely breathing, she turned to face Margo.

"I see that you carry no knife today," Katie Lee greeted the other woman stiffly. "Surely you feel naked without it."

Margo flipped her midnight-black hair back from her shoulders and stretched her fingers before her; her long fingernails looked like the claws of a cat. "Little girl, today I finish you with my bare hands," she said, laughing throatily. "You haven't got a chance."

Katie Lee went numb with fear, but she would not allow herself to show it. "If you think your words frighten me, you're wrong," she said dryly, raising her hands to show that her own fingernails were just as lethal. "I am surely much stronger than you are. I was raised in the country, where I had to help with the chores like a son helps a father. I have muscles where you're not even aware they exist."

Katie Lee leaned forward and motioned with one hand. "Come on, Margo. Let me prove to you just how strong I am," she dared her enemy, feeling braver by the minute.

"You little bitch!" Margo cried, prancing slowly around Katie Lee. "I'm going to show you just how wrong you are. After today you'll run back to the farm to let Daddy coddle you. Or perhaps you will suckle on your mama's breasts?"

Katie Lee winced at the mention of her parents. "My parents are dead," she said, hearing her voice crack. "Don't you dare breathe their names again."

For a moment Katie Lee thought she saw a tinge of regret in Margo's eyes, but then the silent rage again seethed in their depths.

Suddenly Margo pounced. Katie Lee found herself grabbed by the hair and dragged to the floor. She screamed with pain, then gathered all the strength that she could and shoved Margo aside, quickly straddling her and holding down her wrists against the floor.

"Now who is the strongest?" Katie Lee demanded, breathing hard. "You can't get up, Margo. Not unless you beg. That is all I need in order to feel that I can walk out of this place and never look back."

"I thought you loved the excitement," Margo taunted her, straining against Katie Lee's firm grip. "I heard you tell Leonard that was how you felt."

"Yes, it was exciting, and I shall never forget the experience, but I've proven many things to myself these past days," Katie Lee replied, her heart warming as she thought of Bruce. "My needs haven't changed. It's just that I have been given the opportunity to find them in a much safer, more respectable place."

"So if you aren't going to be performing here, what the hell are we fighting for?" Margo asked, again trying to get her wrists free.

"It's not that simple, Margo," Katie Lee said, and tightened her grip. "You have attacked me twice now. I even have a scar because of it. I guess you might say I need revenge and I am getting it." She leaned down and stared into Margo's face. "Beg, Margo. Beg and I will let you up."

"I have never begged for anything in my entire life," Margo blurted, her eyes narrowing. "I won't now."

Katie Lee smiled mischievously. "Then I guess we shall stay here forever. That suits me just fine, and you aren't able to perform, anyhow. Didn't Leonard fire you?"

"That was all forgotten after last night," Margo bragged. "I showed Leonard a few new tricks and persuaded him that he couldn't do without me. If he wouldn't agree to let me go back on his stage, I would deny him what he likes most.''

Both women became aware at the same time of the commotion outside. In the distance Katie Lee could hear fire bells…and the steam whistles from the mills and ships shrieked steadily. Church bells tolled, and scores of people screamed and shouted in the streets. Katie Lee felt a nervous chill deep in her bones.

Bruce and Alex shouted orders to the bucket brigade that was wetting down the roof and sides of their mill, but Bruce already knew that it was only a matter of time before their mill would go up in smoke. Henry Yesler's mill was already a blazing ruin.

His face blackened by the smoke, Bruce groaned as he saw the pilings under the piers flame like the interior of a furnace. Even the streets were burning, the flames coming up through the cracks between the boards like yellow grass.

Volunteers were carrying goods from stores and furniture from houses into the dry planked streets, where sparks and firebrands showered over them. Firemen dragged their equipment, most of it useless in a relentless heat that melted even the hoses. Other firemen retreated with their engines to Second Street.

Alex rushed toward Bruce, his eyebrows and hair singed. ''Bruce, the whole goddamn town is burning up!'' he shouted. ''It's no use. We've got to get the hell outta here!''

''I hate to give up!'' Bruce shouted back, trying to make himself heard above the roar of the advancing flames. ''Alex, this is our life!''

''Wrong, brother, our life ain't worth a plugged nickel if we stick around here any longer,'' Alex declared, pulling his younger brother away from the mill. He looked toward the inferno along Front Street and could not help but think of the stolen nights of pleasure some of the establishments had provided. All of that was gone now as storefronts collapsed into the streets, engulfing the discarded furniture and dry goods that fifteen minutes before citizens had thought to save.

''Goddamn it all to hell,'' he growled. ''I just may have to get married, after all. There ain't goin' to be no place left for me to go.''

Bruce stopped dead in his tracks. Katie Lee! Here he had been worrying about losing a mill that could be rebuilt, but he had not thought at all of Katie Lee!

Jerking away from Alex, he looked wildly at his brother. ''My God!'' he gasped. ''Katie Lee! She's supposed to be rehearsing at Conty Theater this afternoon!'' He tried to see through the heavy pall of smoke that hung between him and Conty's box house, but everything visible seemed to be in flames, or near to it.

Alex grabbed at Bruce as he whirled and began to run down Front Street. ''Bruce!'' he shouted.

"Damn it, Bruce, Mayor Moran has given orders to set off dynamite to cause a fire gap. You may get caught in the explosion!"

Bruce turned and shouted over his shoulder, "Alex, you take care of things here as best you can! I've got to go and see about Katie Lee."

Alex nervously raked his fingers through his hair, then noticed that the wind had changed. Now even the wharves were on fire as the flames were blown offshore. Slowly the bucket brigade dwindled. The stragglers who had been coming and going from the wharves with supplies of water appeared through the smoke like shadows in a black rain of cinders. Flames flared in the gloom behind them.

Alex turned again and looked at their mill. His heart ached as he witnessed the wooden building first smoke, then burst up into flame....

Smoke billowed into Katie Lee's dressing room from beneath her door. Her pulse raced as the commotion grew louder and louder. Fire bells rang out incessantly.

She released Margo and rose quickly to her feet. "I think we'd best get out of here," she said, unlocking the door. "Perhaps the theater is even on fire."

Margo rose slowly, her eyes on Katie Lee's back. Now was the time. Moving past the dressing table, she inched toward Katie Lee. In her hand she now clasped a heavy ceramic vase. Slowly, her breathing labored and her eyes narrowed, she raised the object and brought it down on Katie Lee's head with one hard blow.

Katie Lee's head spun, and blood ran down her forehead. Slowly she turned and looked Margo straight in the eye, then crumpled to the floor.

Laughing throatily, Margo finished unlocking the door, then fled into the smoke-filled corridor. Within seconds her lungs were filled with the stinging soot and her eyes with tears. Fire seemed to be everywhere.

"I must get away," she sobbed, nearly choking on her next breath. Blindly she turned, searching for the rear exit. Instead her foot became caught in a coil of heavy rope. Panic seized her as she twisted hard, suddenly losing her balance. Her forehead slammed with a sickening thud against the steel girder that supported the catwalk.

Ignoring the biting sting of falling cinders, Bruce ran into the burning Conty Theater. Feeling his way, he stumbled around the tables. Finally he made out the stage just as the curtains caught fire. In vain he tried to move faster. Soon the whole place would be an inferno.

Tears streaming from his eyes, he pulled himself up over the footlights and onto the smooth surface of the stage. Nothing moved. With relief he realized that no rehearsal had been held today. That left only one other place to look—Katie Lee's dressing room.

Bruce struggled to move faster, knowing that each moment longer that he spent in this place was tempting death. Kicking down the dressing-room door, he staggered from the shock of seeing Katie Lee lying in a small pool of blood.

She was slowly regaining consciousness. Upon opening her eyes she found another pair looking down at her—golden-brown eyes, framed by a blackened face.

"Bruce!" she gasped, and almost lost consciousness again as he gathered her to his chest. "Margo?" she asked, not seeing her would-be murderer. "Bruce, she tried to kill me again," Katie Lee blurted, and winced as a flash of pain seemed to pierce her skull. "She left me here to die . . . to burn alive."

She coughed and grabbed at her chest, the smoke now so thick that she was hardly able to breathe, and felt herself sinking again into the advancing darkness.

Fear twisted Bruce's gut. The cracking of flames drew closer; the heat was oppressive, unbearable. He looked down at Katie Lee. Chances were that they would never see another lovely sunrise or sunset. Could it all be over so quickly?

Gritting his teeth, he lifted Katie Lee into his arms. "I shall try, darling," he whispered, coughing as his lungs continued to ache and fill with smoke. He bent briefly to place a kiss upon her cheek. "Just remember that I love you. Forever, darling. Forever."

Bracing himself for what lay ahead, Bruce headed into the flame-filled corridor.

Chapter Twenty-Two

Katie Lee regained consciousness once again as Bruce carried her toward the one rear exit. Coughing, she clung fiercely to him and hid her face against his heaving chest.

Bruce glanced down at her with a sense of relief. Now if he could only carry her to safety....

He pushed onward through the smoke, wincing when flames seared his face and arms. His shirt sleeves were already scorched; in places the cinders had burned all the way through. Breathing heavily, fighting for air, he lunged against the door and was silently relieved when it swung open.

"Air at last!" he exclaimed, inhaling deeply. He smiled down at Katie Lee as she took deep, shuddering gasps. "Darling, how are you?"

"I'll be fine," she said, trying to encourage him, though her head ached from the blow and her lungs burned. She looked around her at the devastation, appalled. "Thus far, that is. Lord, Bruce, it looks like the end of the world."

"No—just downtown Seattle," he answered lightly, then flinched when the glass in the theater's windows began to pop, splintering into the air. He ducked his head and huddled over Katie Lee. "We've got to get out of here."

"But which way?" she asked, seeing smoke and fire in every direction.

"I've got to get you to higher ground," Bruce said, rushing down the steps. "That's the only place you will be safe. I'll take you to my house."

Katie Lee was suddenly aware of Bruce's heavy, harsh breathing, and realized that every step was a struggle for him with her in his arms. "Bruce, let me walk," she said, pushing at his chest. "I am well enough to move on my own now. Truly I am. The blow to my head only momentarily stunned me."

Bruce looked down at the caked blood in her golden hair, and then into her liquid blue eyes. "Darling, you're hurt," he insisted, stubbornly moving on through the smoke. "Let me carry you. I don't want you to faint again on my account."

"I won't," she reassured him. "Bruce, please let me down. We will be able to move much more quickly."

Bruce raised his eyebrows, then eased her to the ground. He took her hand then, and together they began to run.

A pall of smoke hung over the city, giving it a doomsday air; church bells tolled steadily. There was an ominous, continuing rumble of drays on the planked streets, and the hurricane roar of the fire continued.

A heavy explosion echoed across the sound as dynamite was set off to help contain the fire. The impact knocked Bruce and Katie Lee from their feet. Side by side they lay stunned, then Bruce shook his head clear and reached for her prone form.

"Darling?"

Katie Lee wiped tears from her eyes. "Yes, I'm still alive," she said, laughing awkwardly. She looked over at Bruce as he pushed himself into a sitting position. "How about you?"

"Yeah, just fine," he growled. "I guess it was the mayor's idea to set off the explosive to make a fire gap. He and everyone else should know that it's virtually impossible to do that at this point. The fire is too out of control."

Scrambling to their feet, they continued up the hill. The fire was now consuming the wooden shacks of Skid Road. Prostitutes in negligees, bartenders with black cash boxes under their arms and dirty white aprons whipping about their knees, and pimps in top hats were scurrying along the road, adding to the pandemonium with their screaming and yelling. Some brave firemen were tearing down a group of smoldering shanties in the advance of the fire, dumping them over the hill into the bay. The burning sidewalks and street planking were torn up and thrown after them.

Yet still the fire burned on, leaving a graveyard of smoking ash in its wake.

Breathless from the exertion, Katie Lee was glad to see a break in the smoke just ahead. She climbed the steep street, struggling with every sore, strained fiber of her being to reach green trees and green grass.

And then she fell to the ground, exhausted, the grass acting like a restorative as she buried her nose in its cool blades. She closed her eyes and took deep gulps of the fresh air, oblivious of the other people struggling up the hill around her. She was almost too tired to think. Every bone in her body ached, and she wondered if her lungs would ever recover.

Bruce sat down beside Katie Lee and held his head in his hands, near to complete exhaustion, realizing how lucky he and Katie Lee were to be alive. One more minute in the theater and they would have died.

Now, sitting on his front lawn, he brushed his hands through his singed hair and looked at Alex's house.

Panic suddenly seized him. "Alex!" he whispered harshly.

Katie Lee sat up quickly as he bolted to his feet. "Bruce, what is it?" she asked, hearing the scratchiness in her own voice. Bruce didn't respond. Consumed with anxiety and worry, he took off toward Alex's house.

Somehow Katie Lee found the strength to run after him. A sick feeling consumed her at the thought that something might have happened to Alex, the kind and gentle man who was soon to be kin.

Stumbling behind Bruce into the spacious, well-furnished home, Katie Lee stood trembling, as Bruce rushed through the house. His shouts echoed through the quiet rooms. When he came back, his eyes dull, his shoulders slouched in defeat, her hands went to her throat.

"He isn't here," he said dully, then shook his head as if to clear it. "But he wouldn't be! He's most likely down on the waterfront, helping with the fire. How could I have expected him to be here?"

Katie Lee slipped into Bruce's arms and hugged him. "Darling, how could you be expected to think clearly at such a time as this?" she murmured.

Bruce framed Katie Lee's face between his hands and looked down at her sternly. "Darling, I must return," he said firmly. "You go to my house and let Catherine prepare you a bath. You rest until I return."

Katie Lee squared her shoulders. "No, I can't do that," she said matter-of-factly.

"Why on earth not?" Bruce gasped.

"Because there are many who could use my help, also," she said softly, seeing his astonishment. "I could comfort those who are injured."

Bruce gently touched Katie Lee's head wound. "But, darling, you too are among the wounded," he said softly. Then, suddenly angered, "That bitch could have killed you. If I hadn't come along—"

Katie Lee placed a hand to his lips. "Shh," she said. "Let's not talk about it any longer. We have too many things to do."

Together they rushed onto the front porch, where the panorama of the smoking city stopped Katie Lee in her tracks. "Oh, Bruce, your beloved sawmill," she murmured. "It must be gone by now, and with it all of your dreams."

Bruce smoothed a lock of blood-dried hair from Katie Lee's forehead. "We'll rebuild," he declared. "After today I hope we learn to build more than a wooden city. Brick and stone don't burn. So maybe business for us won't be so great, but we can always export the lumber. And all the ships were saved."

Suddenly they heard a familiar greeting, and turned to find Alex rushing toward them, his face as black as his clothes. Katie Lee clasped her hands and smiled as Bruce rushed to meet Alex, embracing him wildly.

Arm in arm they made their way back to the house. "The fire's all but put out, Bruce," Alex said, his voice hoarse. "Elliott Bay stopped the fire to the west. The farthest north it got was a water lot at the foot of University Avenue, and the eastward spread was checked at Yesler Way."

"How about fatalities?" Bruce asked, frowning.

"As far as anyone can tell no one was killed or severely hurt," Alex said, sighing heavily. "But it's still a nightmare, Bruce. A damn nightmare."

It was shortly before eight in the evening. The blood-red sun was dropping behind the mountains across the bay. As darkness settled, the glow of the burning city was reflected on the scattered clouds.

The fire burned on until three in the morning, when finally there was nothing left to burn. The fire had swept through a hundred and twenty acres. Twenty-five blocks, the heart of the city, were burned to the ground. Every wharf, every mill from Union to Jackson Streets was gone.

Chapter Twenty-Three

Awakening from a deep sleep, Katie Lee looked at Bruce. His eyebrows and hair were severely singed, and traces of ash remained around his eyes and mouth.

She cuddled close to him, listening to his peaceful breathing. She had tried to help the throng of people who had found escape in the trees and sweet-smelling high grass on the hill. They huddled together, sleeping through the warm June night under the stars. After a few hours she had returned to Bruce's house and had heartily welcomed a bath, yet had felt guilty that so many others had much less.

Bruce stirred suddenly. He yawned and stretched his arms above his head, licking his parched lips. One at a time he opened his eyes, and when he saw Katie Lee smiling at him, everything in the world seemed right again.

Sweeping his arms around her, Bruce pulled her to lie on top of him, pressing her breasts into his chest. "Good morning," he said and smiled broadly. He reached a hand to her head wound, now cleansed of its dried blood. "It is a good morning, isn't it?"

Katie Lee combed her fingers through his hair. "After almost burning to death, I feel as though perhaps I have nine lives!"

"A cat ready for a little loving, huh?" Bruce teased back.

A sensual shiver raced across Katie Lee's flesh at the sight of those eyes dark with passion; she could feel his hot desire against her belly. "But, darling, surely you have better things to do this morning?" she said, tracing the outline of his lips with her tongue. "Alex said for you to meet him at the crack of dawn. There's supposed to be a meeting of businessmen at the armory."

"Katie Lee, once I get involved in plans for rebuilding Seattle, our future will be of secondary importance," he said heavily. "We'd best get in a little loving while we can." He lifted her hair and kissed the column of her throat. "And I need it, darling. After loving you, I'll be ready to tackle the devil, if need be."

"I think the devil has already attacked," Katie Lee said pensively. "Poor Seattle. It did not have a chance."

Bruce cupped her breasts, circling the nipples with his thumbs, causing them to harden into the palms of his hands. "Soon Seattle will rise like a phoenix from its ashes. The citizens will be so proud, nothing will be allowed to happen to the city again."

"If everyone is as determined as you, it will happen," Katie Lee added, tears of pride in her eyes. "Before this time next year your sawmill will even be a reality again."

"By this time next year many things will have happened," Bruce said, placing his hands at her waist and moving over her. "We will be married. Perhaps we will even be expecting a child."

"Oh, if that were only so," Katie Lee murmured.

She became lost to all thought when he entered her. She shuddered and gripped him tightly as he began his smooth and easy strokes. His mouth sought her lips and kissed her heatedly. His fingers ran down her body, drawing her still closer.

She arched willingly, savoring the sensations that seared her insides. Now his tongue lightly brushed her lips, and his hands moved to her breasts.

The slow thrusting of his pelvis teased and tormented her, and she heard herself moan in response. Her tongue met his with a fury; she raked her fingers lightly down his spine, then rested them against his firm buttocks. She kneaded his flesh, and the intensity of her feelings for him soared.

Bruce's blood was quickening with passion, the enticing feel of her fingers driving him wild. He emitted a thick, husky groan, and felt a wild tremor tear through his body as it exploded in spasms of desire. He laid his lips against her cheek and whispered her name, hearing her soft moans as ecstasy claimed her also.

At a soft knock on the door, they quickly separated. A voice soon came from the hallway.

"Sir," Catherine said, "you gave me orders to awaken you at dawn. I have brought you and Miss Holden coffee." She paused for a moment. "I even have a morning paper for you, sir. One was brought to the house while it was still dark."

Bruce raised himself on an elbow. "A newspaper?" he exclaimed, taken aback. "It must be the *Daily Press*. The *Times* was burned to the ground."

"It seems the publisher is quite an ambitious man," Katie Lee said, drawing up a blanket to hide her nudity as Bruce climbed from the bed and pulled on a pair of breeches.

"We will soon see a whole ambitious city, darling," he said, squaring his shoulders proudly. "No damn fire is going to stop us."

Opening the door, Bruce took a tray with coffee and cups and sweet breads from Catherine, and tucked the newspaper beneath his arm. "Thank you, Catherine," he said, smiling at her as she curtsied before turning to leave.

He took the tray to the bed, where Katie Lee poured two cups of coffee and reached for a piece of sweet bread. Starved, she began eating while Bruce read aloud.

"Oh, lighthearted, industrious Seattle, pushing rapidly to industrial and commercial greatness, with hearts full of cheer and hands so willing to work, to be reduced to ashes in a single afternoon, and to have the sun of prosperity darkened by a cloud of mocking smoke..."

Her wardrobe having burned along with the hotel, Katie Lee was wearing a dress that she had borrowed from Catherine. A few tucks at the waist and it fitted her well enough. Her hair drawn back and braided so as not to get in her way on this windy June day, Katie Lee walked along the streets to see for herself the devastation wrought by the fire.

The morning sun slanted down on a gutted city, and ash still filled the air. Exhausted women slept on the street corners beside their household goods. Many had set up tents, Katie Lee observed. Others had bedded down in lean-tos of boards ripped from buildings that had not been completely destroyed.

Lifting the skirt of her dress to keep it from dragging in the rubble, Katie Lee felt a pang of remorse for a mother who was nursing her child in a shelter made from two lace shawls.

Then she looked toward the militia who marched the dead streets. And some toughs on the waterfront had found a fifty-gallon barrel of whiskey and were enjoying a riotous wake for the city. On Cherry Street Mr. McConnell's grocery store had been miraculously spared, and he stood out front serving coffee and crackers to the hungry.

Then Katie Lee watched as the stern-wheeler Quickstep pulled in and unloaded emergency provisions. There was the revenue cutter Wolcott, from which food and blankets were being landed. And a train had just pulled into the station. What could it have brought? she wondered.

Soon she knew the answer; Katie Lee was helping serve three thousand free meals in a big tent at Third and University. Down the road tents with beds were being set up for the homeless.

Smoothing back a perspiration-soaked lock of hair from her brow, Katie Lee continued to pour soup into bowls as people quietly moved along in line. Then a familiar voice caught her attention, and she found herself staring into the gray eyes of Leonard Conty, who did not seem to have been at all affected by the fire. His clothes were immaculate, his diamonds still on his fingers, and his top hat was perfectly in place.

The only thing missing was his bulldog....

"I see you made it through the fire no worse for wear," Katie Lee said icily, perceiving that he must have deserted the theater at the first sign of fire. "But of course you saw to yourself first, didn't you, Leonard?"

"I'll be the first to admit that I ran scared," Leonard confessed. "But I returned. You had apparently left, but I was able to save Margo. She's at my house now."

Katie Lee felt herself grow pale. "Margo was still in the theater?" she gasped. "All along I thought that . . . she had left me alone to die."

Leonard gave her a puzzled look, obviously ignorant of Margo's wicked intentions. "No, dear, I found Margo unconscious on stage left—she must have taken a nasty fall. She's got quite a gash in her forehead."

"She is all right then?" Katie Lee asked, hearing her voice waver. As long as Margo remained in Seattle, Katie Lee knew that she would never be safe.

"She's got a skull fracture and some bad burns, but in time she'll be as good as new," Leonard stated, then chuckled. "She'll be able to ruffle her feathers in no time flat."

He leaned closer to Katie Lee just then. "Katie Lee, I plan to begin my business again real soon," he said. "I've already got a tent set up. All I need now is someone pretty to draw the crowd in. That someone should be you."

Katie Lee looked at him, stunned that nothing seemed to stop him.

"Leonard, I'm not interested now, nor shall I be later," she said dryly, looking at the hungry people lined up behind him. "Please move on. I must give these people some soup."

"Katie Lee, please reconsider," Leonard persisted, refusing to budge. "I've lost a lot in the fire. You could help me regain some of it." He looked at the floor. "I lost my dog, Katie Lee. I feel lost without him." Slowly he moved his gaze back to meet hers. "Can't you sympathize with such a loss? Katie Lee, I need you. Do me this last favor, and I'll pay you fabulously well."

Katie Lee fluttered her lashes nervously. "I do sympathize with you over your dog," she said softly. "I know what he meant to you. But my sympathy can go only so far. I do not want to sing for you. I will not sing for you. Now will you please move on? Others are not as fortunate as you, Leonard. Let them get their soup."

Leonard's eyes narrowed. He stepped out of line, making room for the man behind him to step up for his soup. "I won't give up on you, Katie Lee," he said darkly. "You owe me, and I always collect my debts."

"Is he giving you trouble, Katie Lee?"

With quick strides Bruce was beside her, and she saw his eyes flash angrily as he looked from her to Leonard. She squared her shoulders and lifted her chin, giving the theater owner an icy stare. "No, none at all," she said firmly. "He was just leaving."

"I won't let this alone," Leonard insisted, glowering first at Bruce, then at Katie Lee. "One way or the other, Katie Lee, you will make this up to me."

At that he saw Bruce double his hands into tight fists and take a bold step toward him. But without his bulldog by his side and Doc Porter in the wings, Leonard had no interest in taking on the younger man. Raising his hands, he turned and left the makeshift tent.

"I truly doubt if he'll cause you any more problems," Bruce said, handing soup bowls to Katie Lee. "He looked like a scared rooster to me."

Katie Lee laughed softly and looked shyly toward Bruce, loving him so much. Then her smile faded as she realized that now Margo was not the only one to hold a grudge. Leonard was out to get back at her, too. These next few months would not be easy.

Katie Lee opened her mouth to confide in Bruce, then thought better of it. Bruce already had the weight of the world on his shoulders with his business destroyed in the fire. He didn't need anything else to burden him.

"So? How was the meeting, Bruce?" she asked, forcing a lighthearted softness into her voice.

"It was great," Bruce said, smiling at a young boy who reached for a soup bowl. "Over six hundred businessmen showed up."

"And?" Katie Lee prodded.

"Just as I thought," Bruce said. "The business district is to be rebuilt entirely of fireproof materials. We voted against temporary wooden buildings. Everyone will work from tents until the construction is complete."

Katie Lee glanced at Bruce; even his smile could not hide the anxiety in his eyes. "Darling, if everything is going to be built of brick and stone, what of your lumber business?"

"Of course, there is the export trade," he said slowly. "But our business thrived on the boom time right here in Seattle." He cleared his throat nervously. "Alex and I will think of something, Katie Lee. We don't give up all that easily."

Her attention was diverted when Alex, thumbing through a booklet, lumbered into the large tent. When he sidled up to Bruce, his eyes shone with excitement.

"Bruce," Alex said, clasping a firm hand on Bruce's shoulder, "spindles! We're going to manufacture wooden spindles!"

Katie Lee and Bruce glanced at one another. "Spindles?" they repeated uncertainly.

Chapter Twenty-Four

As soon as the rubbish could be cleared away, the business district blossomed with lily-white tents pitched on the charcoal-black ground. Familiar names were quickly reappearing on signs, and business was being carried on under canvas while work was started on new buildings of brick and stone.

Bruce sat at his desk in his own sprawling tent, studying the plans of his and Alex's new sawmill. Katie Lee poured him a cup of coffee, then sat down and sipped from her own cup, happy even though no time had yet been taken to set the wedding date. Business had to come first. It was important for Cabot Sawmill to be rebuilt so that Bruce and Alex could begin making their fancy spindles for the buildings and houses that were being constructed.

"I'm so happy for you, Bruce," Katie Lee said, placing her coffee cup on his desk. She scooted to the edge of the chair to peer down at his complicated floor plans. "It's wonderful that you and Alex know in which direction the future is going for you."

Bruce tapped the unsharpened end of a pencil against his lip, deep in thought, having only barely heard Katie Lee. Then he looked up at her and laid the pencil aside. He knew that of late he had been neglecting her. If he wasn't careful, he would give her reason to look elsewhere for excitement. If Leonard Conty drew her back into his clutches, it might not be possible to get her back a second time.

Rising from the chair, Bruce went to Katie Lee and drew her into his arms. He kissed her gently on the lips and wove his fingers through her thick, golden hair. "Darling, thank you for being patient with me," he said hoarsely. "I'm glad you know how important this project is. Haste makes waste in this industry."

Katie Lee gently placed a hand to his cheek. "Bruce, my patience was learned from you," she said. "You were so very, very patient with me. Now I am repaying you in kind. I can wait forever for you, if need be."

Bruce laughed throatily. His eyes gleamed. "Darling, it won't be that long," he said. "Once the building begins to take shape, we can make plans for a fancy wedding—the fanciest Seattle has ever seen. You will look like an angel in your wedding gown."

His eyes feasted on her, now dressed in a new outfit that he'd had shipped from Tacoma. The pale yellow silk matched her hair. The dress was flared at the waist with a gathering of eyelet at the bodice and waistline. She wore a yellow satin bow in her hair, its ends dangling down her back.

Bruce wrapped an arm around Katie Lee's waist and guided her around the desk. He nodded toward his plans. "I'll try to explain a little about what Alex and I are hoping to do for the city," he said. He led her out to the side of the street, where they could get a good view of the activity along the busy thoroughfare. "Confidence in the future is going to find expression in architecture—the more confidence, the more spindles, jigsawed brackets and band-sawed cresting. The more humble requirements will be met by Gothic windows, cut glass transoms and fancy butted shingles. And the bastions of the mighty will be marked by round towers at the corners."

"And you and Alex are going to be the ones who make and supply these fancy trimmings to the builders," Katie Lee said matter-of-factly. "How grand."

"And that is only half of what we plan to do," Bruce said, smiling down at her. "Refinements of ornamentation won't stop with the outsides of the buildings. Heavily carved newel posts will greet the eye through the beveled glass of the front door. Columns will be as profuse inside the house as outside. The fancier the column, the more impressive the house."

Katie Lee looked up at him with wonder. "My word, but you do have it all figured out," she said. "You can't help but be successful."

Loud clapping and boisterous laughter drew their attention to the other end of the street. The crowd was gathered around a large tent where a band was playing louder and louder.

"Conty's place," Bruce growled. "I heard that a burlesque queen was to arrive today. She's supposed to be from Turkey."

"She's from Turkey? How intriguing!" Katie Lee gasped, a sudden ache inside telling her that she did miss the thrill of performing. "Do you think she knows how to speak English?"

Bruce looked again at Katie Lee, fear gripping his heart. A haunting hunger showed in her eyes, and he realized that she had not yet gotten performing out of her system. How could he have been so stupid as to expect she would? She hadn't been given a chance to really see the degrading side of Leonard Conty's existence.

Bruce suddenly realized that now was the time. Grabbing her by the hand, he began half dragging her toward Leonard's tent.

"My word, Bruce, what are you doing?" Katie Lee gasped.

Her surprise grew when he began shoving his way through the crowd under Leonard's tent, pulling her along after him. "Whatever are we doing here?" she asked, then started when she saw a small stage at the far end, where a scantily attired, dark-skinned lady beat her hips in time with the pianist's music. The dancer's breasts were barely covered, the cleavage deep. Her hips were grinding with the music now, causing her naked navel to become more prominent for the gawking men who rooted and shouted lewd comments.

Embarrassed, Katie Lee felt herself blush and looked away, finding herself now eye to eye with Leonard Conty as Bruce led her to stand directly before him. Her gaze wavered beneath Leonard's questioning stare.

"Well, what have we here?" Leonard said, chuckling. He clasped thick hands before him as he slowly rocked back and forth. "Has my little songbird come home?"

Bruce's gut twisted as he reached into his front breeches pocket and pulled out a thick roll of money. He held it out before him. "You wish," he growled, motioning with the money. "We've come to repay her debts to you. Take the money. Count it. You will find that it is enough to replace that which you spent for her wardrobe. She owes you for nothing more, and you damn well know it."

Katie Lee was stunned, speechless. She had never seen so much money in her life, and was sure it was meant to have been spent on supplies for Bruce's new sawmill. She began to object, but Bruce gave her a stern look.

Grabbing the money from Bruce's hand, Leonard unrolled it. He knew immediately that here was even more than was due to him. Bruce was in a sense making payment for way more than any clothes were worth....

"Now hear me well, Conty," Bruce said, leaning toward him. "Never approach Katie Lee again. She is now my wife, and I will kill you if you come near her."

Katie Lee saw Leonard's head jerk up, his gray eyes grow wide. She looked quickly at Bruce. She had never heard him lie before, and could hardly believe that she had heard right. But she knew not to question him just now.

Leonard's eyes narrowed. He rolled up the money, then smiled crookedly. "There was no gossip of a marriage," he said, laughing cynically. "Tell me another big one, Cabot."

"I owe you no explanations, Conty," Bruce growled, taking a firm hold on Katie Lee's waist and swinging her around.

Bruce led Katie Lee out of Leonard's tent. Once outside, she pulled away to look up at him questioningly. "Bruce, you lied to Leonard," she accused him hoarsely.

Bruce reached out to clasp her by the shoulders. "Katie Lee, only through marriage—or the threat of it—can I protect you from that man. He can give you something that I never can. The lure of the stage—the excitement. Darling, it is not so much that I don't want you to have these things. Just not in a box house. Choose a first-class theater, and I will never argue with you about it. I would say the world is yours to do with as you see fit! But, darling, never could I bear to see men grovel over you as we just saw them grovel in Leonard's tent.''

"Are you saying that if I choose to, I can still sing?" Katie Lee gasped. "If I was offered an engagement on a legitimate stage, I could accept?"

"Exactly," Bruce said. "If you would like, I could talk around and find out if anyone is interested in an audition."

Katie Lee beamed with joy. She threw herself into Bruce's arms and hugged him hard. "How was I so lucky to have met you?" she murmured, tears stealing a path down her cheeks. "You have been so good to me from the start."

"Well, not exactly," Bruce said, framing her face between his hands. "Darling, there should have been a wedding long ago. And there is going to be. What I told Leonard? It's going to be a reality before the hour's gone."

Katie Lee's cheeks flamed; her eyes danced. "We're not waiting for a fancy wedding?" she asked softly. "We're going to get married now?"

"As soon as we can find a minister," Bruce said, placing a firm arm around her waist as he walked her away from the throngs outside Leonard's tent. "Darling, you may as well begin practicing your new name, for it is going to be yours very soon and forever."

"Mrs. Bruce Cabot," Katie Lee said, almost drunk with happiness. She looked up at the sky.

"Katie Lee Cabot!" She shouted loud and clear. "Oh, Mama and Papa, I wish you were here to see my dreams coming true!"

"I wanted to do this the first night I brought you to my house," Bruce said, carrying Katie Lee over the threshold. "Now that I can, it makes everything official."

Katie Lee clung to Bruce's neck, her cheek on his chest, and laughed softly as she saw Lawrence and Catherine standing just inside the door, their eyes wide with wonder.

"Don't just stand there, Catherine," Bruce said, smiling. "Please go and fetch my wife and me a bottle of champagne. Bring it up to our room with two glasses. We have some celebrating to do."

Catherine placed her hands to her cheeks. "Your wife?" she asked breathlessly. She clasped her hands before her, smiling radiantly. "Oh, I am so glad. So very glad." The petticoats beneath her long black dress rustled as she hurried away. "I shall get the champagne immediately!"

Lawrence took a step forward and held out a stiff hand. "Congratulations, sir," he said, a smile hovering at the corners of his tight lips. "Marvelous, sir. Marvelous."

Bruce eased Katie Lee to her feet and accepted the handshake. "Lawrence, see that no one disturbs us," he said seriously. "Unless, of course, it is Mr. Alex."

"I understand, sir," Lawrence replied. "No one but Mr. Alex will disturb you and your wife."

"Wife," Katie Lee murmured, clinging to Bruce as they began ascending the stairs. "That sounds so beautiful, Bruce."

"I know of a time when that word was a dreaded one to you," Bruce said, squeezing her tight as they reached the second-floor landing. "I honestly didn't believe you would ever get over your misconceptions of marriage." He nuzzled her neck. "Darling, I'm so glad you did."

He guided her into their bedroom and drew her into his arms to kiss her hungrily. At the sound of footsteps and the clinking of glasses, they drew apart, and Katie Lee blushed as Catherine entered the room and deposited the bottle of champagne and the glasses on a table, then with a shy smile hurriedly left.

"I would say that we are being taken care of grandly enough," Bruce said, laughing softly. He went to the door and closed it, then turned and eyed Katie Lee hungrily. "Darling, it is real, isn't it? You are my wife?"

"Until death us do part," Katie Lee said, tears filming her eyes. She rushed to Bruce, then clung to him. "I so love you, darling. I have from that first moment I saw you. I shall love you forever."

Bruce twined his fingers into Katie Lee's hair and lifted it from her neck to kiss the column of her throat. With his other hand he unfastened the hooks of her dress. "Darling, do you want champagne now, or later?" he asked huskily.

"Need you ask?" Katie Lee whispered, breathless with desire. "I want you, darling. You."

"Your wish is my command," Bruce said, then eased her dress from her shoulders. He knelt before her to pull her clothes away. Splaying his fingers over her abdomen, he began kissing her lightly where the feathering of golden hair at the juncture of her thighs hid so much promise of heaven.

Katie Lee wove her fingers through his hair and held him closer to her as he slowly, lightly, began to caress her breasts. She let her head fall back as she closed her eyes to enjoy the ecstasy that was building within her. She trembled, shook, and finally cried out with pleasure before melting into Bruce's arms.

"My beautiful wife," Bruce murmured as he carried her to the bed. He hurried out of his own clothes and joined her on the bed, molding himself perfectly to the curved hollow of her hips.

"I didn't know that I could ever be as happy," Katie Lee said, stifling a sob of contentment against his shoulder.

"Nor I," Bruce said, quivering as Katie Lee ran her fingers along his pulsing hardness and began drawing him into herself. He pressed gently into her yielding folds...deeper...deeper....

Katie Lee felt as though they were the only two people in the universe. There were no more worries, no more cares. There was only happiness—their happiness!

A coil of heated energy flooded Bruce's body with flaming passion, and he groaned against her lips; the sweet warmth of her body was driving him wild. He kissed her still more hungrily. Their bodies jolted and quivered, and then it was over. Slowly Bruce's breathing steadied and he relaxed against her, raising his hand to gently caress her breasts.

"My wife," he whispered as he rolled over to draw her on top of himself. He smoothed her hair from her face and gazed up at her. "Until you, life was only to be lived. Now I live only for you. The mysteries of life unfolded the night I held you that first time. When your lips came to mine so timidly, I knew that fate had drawn me to you. My wife, how do you feel about me, your husband?"

Katie Lee leaned down to kiss his eyes closed, one by one.

"My husband, until you I was only half alive," she murmured, tears shining bright in her eyes. "I knew not what life could or should be, only that something within me was missing. The first time I saw you I felt as though you had touched my soul, when in truth you had only glanced my way for a second. That night, when you drew me within your arms and kissed me, it was as though something beautiful had been awakened in me. I had never felt as alive . . . as needed, as then. You, my husband, are a special man. You give so much without taking. I hope that

I can repay you somehow for all that you have done for me. Since my parents' deaths you have become not only my lover, but also my family."

She lowered her eyes and swallowed hard. "Though my papa failed to see the side of you that he should have, he would have if he had lived, and he would love you just as much as I. My mama would absolutely idolize you, darling."

Bruce had tears in his eyes as he kissed her gently on the lips. "Darling, I want you to have everything," he said with feeling. "A home, children, and even the stage, if it is something so important to you."

Katie Lee laughed softly. "Perhaps it is time for me to settle down. I am a wife now, you know."

"Are you saying that wives aren't supposed to sing?"

"No, not exactly, Bruce."

"Then, darling, don't toss aside the idea as though it were only a burned-up matchstick. We will give it a chance. If you still have a desire to sing on the stage, once the respectable theaters are rebuilt, well, I say go at it. Give it a wholehearted try. I shall be the one who cheers you on from the wings. I shall be the one who comes out onstage to present you with a dozen red roses."

Katie Lee's eyes were bright as she listened and envisaged what Bruce was so vividly describing. The more she thought about it, the more her heart throbbed with excitement. "Do you truly think it is possible?" she asked. "I was on the stage only that one time. Perhaps even then I made a fool of myself and was too caught up in the thrill of it all even to realize it."

Bruce shook his head, laughing softly. "Katie Lee Cabot, I hate to be the one to admit that Leonard Conty could ever be right about anything," he said hoarsely. "But when it came to you, he knew talent when he saw it. My darling, you do sing as sweetly as a songbird. I've never heard anyone sing as beautifully."

Katie Lee sighed and cuddled close to him. "I'm so happy," she whispered. "So very, very happy."

Bruce looked at the unopened bottle of champagne, then down at his wife. "Darling, can we drink the champagne a little bit later?" Bruce asked, leaning away from her.

"Oh, Bruce, I absolutely forgot about Alex," Katie Lee said quickly, sitting up. "Of course you need to check in and make sure that everything is all right with your new building. And, darling, you must tell him about our wedding." She felt her gaze waver. "He'll probably hate us for not allowing him to be present."

Bruce moved to his feet and drew on his breeches. "I doubt it," he said. "Alex doesn't like to say the word 'marriage,' much less go to a wedding. Even his brother's."

Katie Lee lay down again, reveling in her happiness. "Give him my regards anyway," she said, watching Bruce hurry into his clothes.

"I won't be long," he said, and slipped into his shoes. He gave Katie Lee a quick kiss, then fled from the room, his thoughts tumbling one over the other. If Alex agreed, they would build a theater and let someone else manage it. Katie Lee would never know that it was theirs. She would be the star attraction. And Leonard Conty's mouth would water with envy!

Chapter Twenty-Five

Two Years Later

A city had been reborn. After the fire, Seattle's population continued to grow and the business district expanded rapidly northward. The streets were paved with brick. Streetcars clanged along tracks. The volunteer fire department had given way to paid fire fighters, and several new stations had been built.

Bruce and Alex were in the office of their new brick and stone sawmill. Looking from the window onto the waterfront, Bruce smiled at the sight of fully loaded ships preparing to depart. He clasped one arm around Alex's shoulder.

"You know, even after we are long dead, a part of us will live on in almost every single building here," he said proudly.

"Yes, all things good happen to those who wait," Alex said, moving away from Bruce. He picked up a copy of the morning's *Times*. "And evil befalls those who tempt fate one time too many."

Bruce looked down at the headlines as Alex spread out the paper across his oak desk. "So Leonard Conty got shot last night," he said, furrowing his brow.

"Yeah. Margo did it," Alex said, chuckling beneath his breath. "Conty messed with her just one time too many. He apparently had been too afraid to fire her, so he was trying to keep both her and the Turkish wench bedded and happy. Margo found out that he had her and the belly dancer quartered in different apartments on separate sides of the city. Well . . . that Leonard Conty sure did lead the good life. I'd have switched places with him anytime."

Bruce gave Alex a sideways glance. "Sure, and get your head blown off in the process," he said dryly. "Alex, whenever are you going to find a woman and settle down? Don't you want to be a father—hold your son instead of mine?"

"It's not in the cards for me," Alex said, shrugging. He locked his fingers around his suspenders and glanced back at the newspaper article. A shudder coursed through him. "It took a lot of guts for Margo to turn the gun on herself like that."

"I'd say she was one stupid lady to kill herself over a man like Leonard Conty," Bruce said in a low growl, recalling Margo's viciousness. Thank God the woman had forgotten her vendetta against Katie Lee. These past two years had been peaceful. Only a few weeks had passed after their wedding when Katie Lee had discovered that she was pregnant. Since then she had been content being a wife and mother. Only recently had she become restless....

"Are things set tonight for Katie Lee's debut?" Bruce asked, settling into his chair behind his desk. He placed his fingertips together and looked up at Alex with a slow smile. "The theater sure has been a money-maker, and Katie Lee has no idea that it's ours. She would not take kindly to that fact."

Alex sat down at his desk and smiled mischievously. "Little brother, she was accepted for the engagement as an unknown. The day she went for tryouts, the manager was ill. Someone else was conducting the auditions. Katie Lee was chosen as the best that tried out that same day. It is legitimate, Bruce. You have yourself quite a songbird on your hands."

Bruce laughed softly and ran his fingers through his hair. "Well, I'll be damned," he said. "That's a great relief. Now I don't feel as though I'm duping my wife."

"The fact that Katie Lee doesn't know that we are the majority stockholders in the theater is not all that honest, Bruce," Alex said.

"Yes, I know." Bruce sighed, seeing his brother's thick, dark brows furrow into a frown. "But as it was from the beginning, Alex, I am willing to do anything to make Katie Lee happy. If it requires a measure of dishonesty, then so be it. Have you ever seen her look so radiant as lately? She can't wait for the performance tonight.''

"The shy side of her just may surface again when she steps out on the stage, Bruce," Alex said, eyeing Bruce warily. "What then, little brother?"

Bruce sucked in a deep breath. It had not been that long ago when Katie Lee was so innocent and shy. And she had only performed on a stage one time.

Bruce rose from his chair and went to glance at the newspaper again. Another headline caught his eye. "Damn it!" he gasped. "Did you see this about Chief Black Raven? The army finally caught up with him, but he plunged to his death in Puget Sound before they could lay a hand on him."

"Katie Lee will be glad to hear that," Alex said, biting into a plug of tobacco.

Bruce folded the newspaper and dropped it into a wastebasket beside his desk. "I'm not going to tell her," he said flatly.

"Why the hell not?" Alex asked, clearly surprised.

"Because she's been able to put the past behind her," Bruce said, folding his arms across his chest. "Why bring back memories?"

"Yeah, I see your logic." Alex nodded. "I think you're right."

The door opened at the far end of the room, and Bruce's face lighted up when Katie Lee appeared, wearing a pale blue velveteen suit with a matching hat. Clasping her hand was a little boy dressed in a short-legged velveteen suit that matched Katie Lee's.

Bruce went and kissed Katie Lee softly, then lifted his son into his arms. He looked into golden-brown eyes that mirrored his own, but his son's round, pink face was framed with curly, golden locks.

"So, Katie Lee, what have you and our son been doing today?" Bruce asked, weaving his fingers through his son's cotton-soft hair. "I see that the slow drizzle hasn't dissuaded you from getting some fresh air."

"I needed to walk off an attack of nerves," Katie Lee said, clasping her hands behind her. "This is my big night. I can hardly believe it's truly here. My knees are already trembling."

Bruce lifted Tony into the air over his head, laughing as his son broke into a fit of loud giggles. "Think of something else for the rest of the day." He winked at Katie Lee. "Darling, think of me."

Katie Lee nestled close to him, placing an arm about his waist. "Darling, I always think of you," she said in a soft purr. "Always."

"Then think of Tony," Bruce said as he set the boy on the floor. Tony then toddled over to Alex and held up his arms to his uncle. A deep feeling of satisfaction at seeing his brother and son together swelled Bruce's chest. He was not wrong in thinking that Alex would be a wonderful father. Perhaps one day the right woman would come along.

Bruce leaned close to Katie Lee. "Let's leave the two of them together for a few minutes."

Katie Lee smiled as she left the room with Bruce. Although she had been shown the mill countless times now, she went with Bruce again and let him show it off to her.

They walked from the office to the factory and plunged into the maelstrom of whirring machinery. A band saw twanged harshly on fancy brackets and roof cresting. A jigsaw provided a rapid staccato. And a row of lathes hummed like cellos as fancy spindles and porch columns emerged from the sharp gouges.

Otto the carver was at work on a monstrous oak newel post for a grand staircase. Cupids, seashells and garlands rioted over the fancy work.

"You have so much to be proud of," Katie Lee said, leaning against the rail of the gallery that overlooked all of the activity.

Alex came to stand beside them, carrying Tony. He smiled at Bruce, then at Katie Lee. "One day this young rascal will follow in our footsteps," he said, snuggling Tony closer to his chest. "He'll carry on the Cabot name when we are long gone."

Katie Lee snaked one arm around Alex's, the other around Bruce's waist, and stood between them. Her smile was radiant.

Her aria over, Katie Lee smiled at the large orchestra seated in the pit at the foot of the stage. She knew she looked good in her fully gathered white organdy gown, and relished the fact that diamonds sparkled at her throat and ears. She felt her face grow warm with excitement as the crowd gave her a thundering applause.

After bowing low, she glanced back as Bruce stepped up to the edge of the curtain. He was attired in white tie and tails, Tony and a huge bouquet of roses filling his arms.

Smiling broadly, she bowed again, then her knees grew weak as Bruce came onto the stage and laid the bouquet of roses upon her left arm, placing her son's hand in her right. Tears ran down her cheeks. Never had she been so happy.

Tonight she had succeeded as a singer and as a devoted wife. She understood everything—she even knew that Bruce and Alex owned this theater. Realizing that Bruce had done this for her from the goodness of his heart, she had pretended not to know. If giving her such an anonymous gift was so important to him, then she was not the one to make light of it.

"Bravo!" the crowd cheered. "Encore! Encore!"

No, it did not take anything away from the wondrous feelings of the moment to know that her husband had made even this possible for her, for the applause was sincere. No amount of money could pay this many people to pretend that they'd enjoyed her performance.

Smiling at Bruce, Katie Lee edged closer to him. "Thank you, darling," she said softly. "You always have ways of making me feel special."

Bruce gave her a puzzled look, then shrugged and placed an arm around her waist. Together they bowed to the crowd.

*   *   *   *   *

COMING NEXT MONTH

#43 THE GENTLEMAN—Kristin James

In the eyes of St. Louis society, Stephen Ferguson was the
picture of gentility and elegance. But when he arrived in
Nora Springs, Montana, valet in tow, Jessie Randall
thought him a rarefied fop. She soon found out just how
much of a man Stephen was....

#44 SUMMER'S PROMISE—Lucy Elliot

Everyone whispered about Caroline Fielding, the sadder-
but-wiser girl who'd sailed to the Colonies to avoid
scandal. Her only dream was for a life of peaceful
seclusion in the New England wilderness. French trapper
Daniel Ledet shared the same need for solitude—until he
met Caroline.

AVAILALBLE NOW:

#41 HIGHLAND
BARBARIAN
Ruth Langan

#42 PASSION'S EMBRACE
Cassie Edwards

**In April, Harlequin brings you the
world's most popular romance author**

JANET DAILEY

No Quarter Asked

Out of print since 1974!

After the tragic death of her father, Stacy's world is shattered. She
needs to get away by herself to sort things out. She leaves behind
her boyfriend, Carter Price, who wants to marry her. However, as
soon as she arrives at her rented cabin in Texas, Cord Harris, owner
of a large ranch, seems determined to get her to leave. When Stacy
has a fall and is injured, Cord reluctantly takes her to his own ranch.
Unknown to Stacy, Carter's father has written to Cord and asked
him to keep an eye on Stacy and try to convince her to return home.
After a few weeks there, in spite of Cord's hateful treatment that
involves her working as a ranch hand and the return of Lydia, his ex-
fiancée, by the time Carter comes to escort her back, Stacy knows
that she is in love with Cord and doesn't want to go.

**Watch for *Fiesta San Antonio* in July and
For Bitter or Worse in September.**